GIORGIO SCERBANENCO

"A gem ... A vivid portrait of Milan's seamy underbelly ... Scerbanenco reveals Duca Lamberti to us; in doing so, he also unveils the Italian hardboiled hero." **—CRIME FICTION LOVER**

"Scerbanenco's dark, moody novels have much in common with the darkest of Scandinavian crime fiction ... This forgotten noir classic from 1966 is finally available in translation. That's good news!" **—LIBRARY JOURNAL**

"There is courage in his books, the courage to call things by their name ... No filters shield you from the reality, which is as desperate, fierce, and stark as in the best novels of James Ellroy or Jim Thompson." **—CARLO LUCARELLI**

"[Scerbanenco can be] as dark as Leonardo Sciascia, as deadpan realistic as Maj Sjöwall and Per Wahlöö, as probing in his observation of people as Simenon, as humane as Camilleri, as noir as Manchette ... but with a dark, dark humor all his own." **—DETECTIVES BEYOND BORDERS**

"The Duca Lamberti novels are world-class noir, and their publication in English is long, long overdue." **—THE COMPLETE REVIEW**

GIORGIO SCERBANENCO was born in Kiev in 1911 to a Ukrainian father and an Italian mother, grew up in Rome, and moved to Milan at the age of eighteen. In the 1930s, he worked as a journalist and attempted some early forays into fiction. In 1943, as German forces advanced on the city, Scerbanenco escaped over the Alps to Switzerland, carrying nothing but a hundred pages of a new novel he was working on. He returned to Milan in 1945 and resumed his prolific career, writing for women's magazines, including a very popular advice-for-the-lovelorn column, and publishing dozens of novels and short stories. But he is best known for the four books he wrote at the end of his life that make up the Milano Quartet, *A Private Venus*, *Traitors to All*, *The Boys of the Massacre*, and *The Milanese Kill on Saturdays*. Scerbanenco drew on his experiences as an orderly for the Milan Red Cross in the 1930s to create his protagonist Duca Lamberti, a disbarred doctor; it was during this period that he came to know another, more desperate side of his adopted city. The quartet of novels was immediately hailed as noir classics, and on its publication in 1966, *Traitors to All* received the most prestigious European crime prize, the Grand Prix de Littérature Policière. The annual prize for the best Italian crime novel, the Premio Scerbanenco, is named after him. He died in 1969 in Milan.

HOWARD CURTIS translates books from French, Italian, and Spanish, and was awarded the John Florio Prize (2004) as well as the Europa Campiello Literary Prize (2010).

TRAITORS TO ALL

TRAITORS TO ALL

GIORGIO SCERBANENCO

TRANSLATED BY HOWARD CURTIS

 MELVILLE HOUSE
BROOKLYN · LONDON

 MELVILLE
INTERNATIONAL
CRIME

MELVILLE INTERNATIONAL CRIME

TRAITORS TO ALL

First published in Italy in 1966 as *Traditori di tutti* by
Edizioni Garzanti S.p.A., Milano
Copyright © 1966 Giorgio Scerbanenco Estate
Published in agreement with Agenzia Letteraria Internazionale
First published in the United Kingdom by Hersilia Press
Translation copyright © 2013 Hersilia Press

First Melville House printing: June 2014

Melville House Publishing   8 Blackstock Mews
    145 Plymouth Street   and   Islington
    Brooklyn, NY 11201   London N4 2BT

mhpbooks.com   facebook.com/mhpbooks   @melvillehouse

ISBN: 978-1-61219-366-3

Manufactured in the United States of America

1   3   5   7   9   10   8   6   4   2

A catalog record for this book is
available from the Library of Congress.

TRAITORS TO ALL

PART ONE

When television came the first person to install it was my fiancé, the butcher. The whole of Ca' Tarino would go to his house to watch it, but he'd pick and choose, he'd invite my parents, so I'd go too, and that's how we ended up engaged. In the dark, he'd put his hand on my knee, then move it up, and as soon as he could he asked me if I was a virgin, and with that hand on my leg and my mother close by I was a bit annoyed so to make fun of him I said, yes, I'd been keeping myself specially for him.

1

It isn't easy to kill two people simultaneously, but she stopped the car at the exact point she had studied many times and knew almost to the centimetre, even at night, and could recognise because of the curious, gothic, Eiffelesque little iron bridge that spanned the canal, and, as she stopped the car in the exact square centimetre she wanted, like an arrow hitting the dead centre of a target, she said to the two people sitting inside, the two people she intended to kill, 'I'm getting out to smoke a cigarette, I don't like smoking in the car,' and got out without waiting for a reply, although the two people, made sluggish by their big dinner and also by their age, did grunt, yes, she could get out, and once free of her presence they arranged themselves as if to sleep better, old and fat as they were, both of them in white raincoats, the woman with her woollen scarf around her neck, the scarf a similar liverish Havana brown colour to her neck, which made her look even fatter, her face resembling that of a big frog, even though, millions of years earlier, when the war wasn't over yet, the Second World War, she had been very beautiful, so they said, this woman the girl was about to kill, together with her companion: this woman officially known as Adele Terrini, although in Buccinasco and in Ca' Tarino, where she was born and where they knew a lot about her, they called her Adele the whore, whereas the girl's father, who was American and stupid, had called her Adele la Speranza: Adele Hope.

The girl was American, too, but she wasn't stupid and, as soon as she got out, she closed the car door behind her, locking it, just as all the other doors were locked, and then she lit her cigarette and looked across at the other side of the canal, the main road to Pavia, where, given the hour, there weren't many cars passing, which was another thing she had calculated, and then, as if strolling, she came up behind the car, a modest, lightweight Fiat four-seater: she didn't know what model it was, but she had sized it up and knew it was ideal for her purposes.

Anyway, there in the middle was the canal, called the Alzaia Naviglio Pavese: it was quite a difficult, incomprehensible name for her, as she was an American and her Italian teacher in San Francisco, Arizona – nothing to do with the other San Francisco – hadn't stooped to explaining such niceties as the fact that *alzaia* was the name of the rope used for towing boats and barges against the current of a river or a canal and referred to the fact that they rose slightly as they were towed, *alzaia* deriving from *alzarsi*, to rise. It wasn't the etymology or philology of the name that interested her, though, but the fact that the canal was perfectly situated between two roads, and the fact that in that season the waters of the canal were high, and the bigger of the two roads, the tarred one, was an A-road – she had carefully noted the official name, it was State Highway 35, Strada dei Giovi – while the other, the untarred one, still touchingly rustic, was the old canal road. And between them was the canal.

And canals contain water, if they haven't been drained, and this one hadn't, and what's more, this one didn't have railings or ropes or posts of any kind: on a dark night, a car could fall in without anything to stop it. And so all she had to do was push it slightly, this Fiat of which she didn't even know the model, and everything was straightforward and easy, everything happened easily in a few seconds, as she had predicted – she had set it all up, the position of the front wheels, which she had left turned slightly to the right, towards the canal, and the engine idling, so that it was like pushing a cart down a slope – and the car, with those two people inside it, made sluggish by the chicken with mushrooms and the gorgonzola and the baked apples topped with zabaglione and the dark Sambuca, all paid for by the American girl they probably thought was as stupid as her father, who had been a past master at stupidity, the car with Adele the whore or Adele Hope and her companion inside it slipped with wonderful ease into the canal, into the high waters of the canal, and that fall into the water happened exactly when she had planned it to happen, in other words, when there were no cars passing on the main road on the other side of the canal – State Highway 35, the Strada dei Giovi – and it was almost completely dark, and all you could see was the lights of cars approaching in the distance.

Water splashed up and hit her, even wetting her face, although it didn't extinguish her cigarette, then another, almost sibilant splash hit her on the chest like a jet from a pump – she had never imagined that a car, in falling into the water, would provoke such a fountain – and she felt her cigarette go limp between her lips, it was definitely extinguished now, and she peeled it from her lips and spat it out, that mess of wet paper and tobacco, her face and hair also wet with the foul-smelling water of the canal – the Alzaia Naviglio Pavese – and then stood waiting for bubbles to appear on the surface.

She waited in the darkness. The road on this side of the canal, where she was standing, was completely dark; the road on the other side of the canal, the tarred road, was also in darkness, but arrows of light broke through the soft fabric of the night, the lights of cars, the cars of Milanese coming back – not from the river, because it was a weekday and you can't go to Santa Margherita on a Wednesday, can you, because on Wednesday you have to be in the office, or even if you don't have any commitments in the office, you have to track down people in other offices – but during these mild spring days some Milanese went in the evening, after the office, to out-of-town trattorias, the least adventurous stopping at those along the Via Chiesa Rossa, or going further, but no further than Ronchetto delle Rame, and the bold ones going past Binasco and even Pavia, all the way to high-class taverns that weren't really taverns, where they ate and drank vaguely genuine food and wine in a vaguely rustic atmosphere, and now, at this hour, they were returning home, to Milan, driving slowly on that beautiful spring night, until there were other cars in front or behind and they surged forward, flashing their lights, and these were the lights she could see as she waited for the bubbles to come.

But the bubbles didn't come. Through the lowered windows, at least those in front, the car had immediately filled with water, and immediately there was complete silence, and it was just a question of watching and waiting, hoping nobody came along the road: a penniless couple on a Vespa looking for shelter on the rustic canal bank, a drunk cyclist on his way home, a cart filled to the brim with young men from the nearby hamlets and farms on the lookout for girls from other nearby hamlets and farms, provoking long but not bloody feuds between one farm and the next in the area between Asago, Rozzano, Binasco and Casarile. And still she waited, she waited for at least five minutes: if the windows are open, it's possible to get out of a car even if it's underwater, and so she waited, looking at the water, overcome with fear that one of the two, or even both, might emerge all at once from the water, still alive and screaming.

For a moment, she was lit by the headlights of a car on the other road beyond the canal, just as if she was on stage, and if they did come up out of the water, she thought, as she stood in that ray of light, she would be able to hold her hand out to them and pull them out, and say she didn't know what had happened, because of course the two people hadn't realised that she was the one who had pushed the car – but what if they *had realised*?

She waited, and only when she was sure that five minutes had passed, or perhaps twice five minutes, perhaps three times, when she was sure that the stinking souls and stinking bodies of those two would never again foul the streets of the world, only then did she move away from the edge of the canal and head towards the little iron bridge, opening her handbag as she did so and taking out a few little squares of soft paper and wiping the rest of the canal water, now almost dry, from her face. The front of her overcoat was wet, though she couldn't do anything about that, and there was water in her shoes, so when she reached the bridge she sat down on one of the steps, took off her low-heeled shoes, shook the water from them, let them dry a little in the air, then put them back on, even though her stockings were also wet, but she couldn't do anything about that either: how strange, she had never imagined she would get so wet.

She climbed the steps onto the little bridge that crossed the canal – it was like a toy rather than a bridge, but she wasn't a child and she couldn't enjoy herself on the bridge – and she was shivering, but not from cold – oh, if only! – but no, she couldn't turn the clock back, once you've killed two people there's no point wanting to turn the clock back, you can't bring them to life again, and when she was at the top of that schizophrenic bridge which was like a mixture of a Venetian bridge and something out of Jules Verne she swallowed several times to fight her impending nausea at the image of the two people trapped in the car, in the water, struggling, and she started to descend the steps on the other side. After all she wasn't a professional killer, although theoretically she was an expert, she knew everything, the ways to kill are infinite but she knew almost all of them, she knew that a hot knitting needle, inserted into the skin so that it goes through the liver – you only need a basic knowledge of anatomy – causes a slow, agonising death. Tony Paganica, an American citizen whose parents had come from the Abruzzi, and whose surname the Americans found a bit hard to pronounce, abbreviating it to Pani, had died that way, with a knitting needle in his liver. The thought stopped her from vomiting, stiffened her resolve, and she descended the last three steps from the bridge. The second part was beginning.

Now she was on the tarred road, and the cars were passing in a steady stream, although well spaced out because it was getting late. They passed almost within a few centimetres of her, catching her in their headlights, but they did not stop even though she raised her hand to ask for a lift: a female vagrant on her own in the middle of the countryside, what have we come to? They flashed their lights, but did not stop. Eventually, though, a car did stop: good, kind Lombards from good, kind Lombardy, a husband and wife and a little boy, who either had a taste for adventure or a compassionate urge to help a fellow human being, a poor young girl in the middle of the road at this hour, anything might have happened to her, let her get in, Piero, look, her coat's all wet, let's hope she's all right.

And so Piero pulled up and the girl got in, and as she got in she summoned all her years of studying Italian, because she didn't want it to appear in any way that she was from San Francisco, Arizona, and said, 'Thank you, you're very kind, are you going to Milan?' And down there, under the water, in that canal beside which the car was travelling, the two of them were still there, and she had put them there.

'Yes, Signorina, where do you want to go?' Signor Piero's wife said, turning to her as she sat in the back seat next to the boy and laughing, she was good-natured, communicative, sociable, charitable in her way.

'Daddy, she's American,' the boy said, as the car neared the tollgate and slowed down. 'I heard someone talking like that once before. Is it true you're American?' the nine-year-old or eight-year-old or even less asked her directly, and there was a risk if anyone found out that they had given a lift to an American girl, picking her up at the exact spot where a car was found in the canal, maybe as the result of an accident or maybe not, she had to disappear, leave not a trace behind. But this eight-year-old, nine-year-old, whichever he was, had recognised her accent, and she couldn't get out of it now, the whole mechanism she had created could fall apart thanks to the boy's pedantry and good hearing.

'Yes, I'm American,' she said: you can deceive an adult, but not a child.

'You speak very good Italian, I would never have guessed,' the extrovert Lombard woman said.

'I learnt it in six months, from records,' she said: it was a rule taught in all the schools – the schools of crime, that is – to draw people's attention to some harmless subject in order to step them concentrating on another, more dangerous subject.

Signor Piero, who up until a moment earlier had been suspicious – he didn't like having a stranger in his car, her overcoat was wet, God alone knew from what, she was getting his car dirty, and with all the riffraff you saw these days, only a baby like his wife would have let her get in – all at once became interested. 'In six months? Really? Did you hear that, Ester? So what they say about learning languages from records is true.'

'Oh, yes, it's true,' the girl said: suddenly she was a saleswoman for language records. 'Six months ago, all I could say in Italian was *O sole mio*.'

'You know, Ester, we should find out about these records, for Roberto, Malsughi could get me a discount,' Signor Piero said – they had passed the tollgate and now were driving along the Conca Fallata, where the Lambro Meridionale splits into two then joins together again beyond the Naviglio Pavese – and as he spoke the girl looked at her watch: it wasn't even five to eleven, she had followed her timetable precisely. For a few more minutes, as they drove along the almost deserted avenues, purplish in the purple light of the fluorescent street lamps, the couple giving her a lift conversed among themselves about language records, until she said, 'Here, please, I'd like to get out here, in this square.'

'It's up to you,' Signor Piero said: he could have joined a theatre company as an actor, so well did he pretend to be sorry that she was going and that he wouldn't have the pleasure of driving her wherever she wanted, for as long as she wanted.

'Thank you very much,' she said, opening the door as the car pulled up and immediately getting out, before they could see her face properly, 'thank you, thank you.' She waved her hand and immediately plunged into the shadows of the big tree, hiding from the cadaverous light of the streetlamp beneath which the Lombard had parked.

It had been a dangerous ride to take, but she couldn't do

anything about that now. Alone in the huge square on the very edge of Milan, in the mild but slightly cool late April wind, she was afraid, but fear serves no purpose and she dismissed it. She knew there was a taxi stand in this square, she had studied the place carefully, and now she headed straight for it, having already seen the two green taxis drowsing under the big trees.

'Palace Hotel.'

The taxi driver nodded: he was pleased, this was a decent run, the kind he liked, all the way across the city to the area near the station, where it was easy to get another fare at any hour, and the girl too must be a decent sort if she was going to the Palace. In the darkness of the cab, she again looked at her watch by the light of a street lamp: seven minutes past eleven, she was seven minutes ahead of schedule.

'Could you please stop at that bar?'

They were in the Via Torino, calm in this slack hour when people haven't yet come out of the cinema, there was almost nobody around, and no cars, but even at this hour you couldn't park in the Via Torino, except that the driver acted as if he was in the driveway of his own house, driving his cab up onto the pavement and stopping just in front of the bar.

'A gin,' she ordered: it was an odd bar, long and narrow, like a corridor, into which a miniaturist rather than an interior decorator had somehow fitted everything, from a juke-box to a telephone and even a pinball machine. Even ordering a gin had been a mistake – a girl alone at that hour drinking such an exotic liquor – and the four men who were in the place, apart from the owner, looked at her more closely, it was obvious she was the Anglo-Saxon type, and with her stockings and shoes still damp, she was leaving quite a trail behind her, or maybe not: the city was full of foreigners because of the Fair, and by the evening most of them had been drinking and were rather eccentric. Back in the taxi, she lit a cigarette, which, coming on top of the gin, gave her strength. It was over, she had done it. She did not even spend three minutes in her room in the Palace Hotel, it only took her two to change her shoes and stockings and put on her raincoat, and one to close the suitcases, which she had prepared earlier. The bill was ready, and she had her money ready, she spent another minute distributing tips and waiting for the taxi she had called. Two minutes later, the taxi had dropped her at the station.

She was already familiar with that Babylonian temple, and she knew everything. 'To the Settebello,' she said to the porter who picked up her two suitcases and leather shoulder bag. As she followed the porter, a Southerner offered her his company, smiling at her with a frighteningly horse-like set of teeth, his upper lip adorned with a moustache he must have thought irresistible to women, but two Carabinieri were coming along the platform where the Settebello stood waiting and just the sight of them must have put this ladies' man off because he abruptly left her alone.

She already had her ticket, and a reserved seat. Four minutes after she got on, the Settebello set off. At eight in the morning, she would take a plane for New York from Fiumicino. She had studied the schedules, they were engraved in her memory: at three in the afternoon, local time, she would land in Phoenix, one among the hundred and ninety-five million American citizens, a very, very long way from the Alzaia Naviglio Pavese.

2

The doorbell rang, too politely, but however a bell rings, there are times when it isn't a good thing for it to ring, when it's better for nobody to turn up, because everyone is obnoxious. But the man to whom he was forced to open the door, given how politely the bell had rung, was even more obnoxious than predicted.

'Dr Duca Lamberti?'

Even his voice was loathsome, in its perfect Italian, its perfect courtesy, its perfect clarity, he could have taught an elocution course, and Duca hated anything that was too perfect.

'Yes, that's me.' He stood there in the doorway, without letting him in. Even the way he was dressed was obnoxious: it was spring, certainly, but this man was already going around in a cardigan, without a jacket, a light grey cardigan, with dark grey suede at the wrists, and so that nobody should think that he didn't have the money to buy himself a jacket, he was wearing a pair of light grey driving gloves – not those vulgar ones that left the back of the hand uncovered, but whole gloves, with the back and fingers complete and the palms interlaced – and they were clearly visible, because he displayed them ostentatiously, in order to make it clear from the start that he owned a car appropriate to these gloves.

'May I come in?' He was full of cordiality and false spontaneity.

Duca wasn't pleased, and made no attempt to conceal it, but let him in anyway, because the ways of life are infinite and mysterious. He opened the door to his defunct surgery, or rather his abortive surgery, and let him in. 'Go ahead,' he said, not even inviting him to sit down, he even turned his back on him and went and sat down on the window sill: when you have a window that looks out on the Piazza Leonardo da Vinci, with the trees all newly green for spring, you have everything you need.

'May I sit down?' Ignoring the way he was being treated, the man – he couldn't have been more than thirty – continued to give off an obnoxious air of sociability and cordiality.

Duca did not reply. At eleven in the morning, the Piazza Leonardo da Vinci is a placid desert on the edge of town, which even prams with innocent children in them can cross easily and where the occasional almost empty tram passes, and at that hour, in that season, on that mild, cloudy April day, you could still love Milan.

'Maybe I should have phoned first,' the unknown man said, completely impervious to any show of hostility, 'but there are things that can't be said by phone.' He was still smiling, still trying to establish some kind of complicity with him.

'Why?' Duca said, from the window sill, watching an honest housewife on her way home with a shopping bag on wheels.

'I'm sorry, I haven't introduced myself. You don't know me, I'm Silvano Solvere, but you certainly know a friend of mine, in fact, he's the one who sent me.'

'And who is this friend?' He wasn't at all curious, except, perhaps, about one thing: what filthy genie this man was about to let out of the bottle. With his elegance, his good manners, the cleanliness of his body – but only his body – he really did seem a merchant of filth, and it was only a matter of knowing exactly what kind of filth he was going to try and sell him.

'Attorney Sompani, you remember him, don't you?' He did not wink, he was too well brought up to wink, but in a subtle way he made his voice wink, if a voice can wink, still with the intention of creating between him and Duca a current of familiarity, almost of complicity. In cunning people, obtuseness is congenital and incurable.

'Yes, I remember him.' Oh, yes, he certainly did. The worst punishment had not been to spend three years in prison, but to be in prison with Turiddu Sompani. His other cellmates were bearable, they were just ordinary villains, thieves, would-be murderers, but not Turiddu Sompani, no, he was repellent, partly because he was so fat and flabby, and partly because he was really a lawyer and there's something both ridiculous and frightening about a lawyer in prison. He had got two years, instead of the twenty he probably deserved, because he had let a friend of his, who couldn't drive and was also blind drunk, get into his car and drive it, and this friend had driven with his girlfriend straight into the Lambro, near the Conca Fallata, while he, Turiddu, stood on the bank and called for help: a story so murky that not even the meanest public prosecutor could do anything with it, even though everyone – judges, jurors, the public – was of the opinion that Turiddu Sompani's friend could not have driven into the Lambro by chance.

'Well, Attorney Sompani told me that you could do me a favour,' said the perfect Silvano. He pretended to be embarrassed, but it was only pretence, he seemed like the kind of person who wouldn't be embarrassed sitting naked astride Garibaldi's horse in the Largo Cairoli at the aperitif hour.

'What favour?' Duca asked patiently – you had to be

patient or you'd kill yourself – getting off the windowsill and going and sitting down on a little stool in front of the merchant of filth, and it was almost as if he could see him with his bottles of filth in his hand, about to open one. A doctor struck off the register, as Duca was, is an interesting specimen to some people. Since he had left prison, he'd had plenty of opportunities for work. All the pregnant girls in the neighbourhood, all the girls who were afraid they were pregnant, had turned to him, crying, threatening suicide, but in vain, and there had been so many that he had finally taken the nameplate saying *Dr Duca Lamberti* off the door, all that was left was the two little holes where the screws had been, but it had been no use. And after the pregnant girls, there were the drug addicts, they'd also offered him a lot of work: as far as the addicts were concerned a doctor struck off the register would be more willing to issue the right prescriptions, he still had the prescription books, and as his career was in ruins they could do business together, without any risk, said the drug addicts with their pale nails, the backs of their hands mottled with what looked like pink bruises, making him truly sick of life. And after the drug addicts came the prostitutes who'd got diseases, 'I daren't go to my usual doctor, he'd only inform on me to the police, and they'd just lock me up,' because of course he wasn't the usual doctor, he was an exceptional doctor, a doctor who had done three years in prison for euthanasia, so obviously he knew how to cure syphilis, he must have been a specialist in that when he was in San Vittore, musn't he?

At last the visitor took out his bottle and uncorked it. 'It's a rather delicate favour, doctor. Attorney Sompani told me you're very strict and will probably say no, but it's a special case, a very human case, a girl who is supposed to be getting married and ...' – and at last the revolting filth came out, flowing from the bottle, in the perfect voice of this perfect bearer of filth. What it amounted to was a hymenoplasty: the special case, the very human case, was a girl who was supposed to be getting married, and her bridegroom wanted her to be a virgin, and in fact was convinced that she was. In reality the girl, and this was very human, had not had the courage to confess to her fiancé that she had lost her virginity in a blind fit of passion, long past, because she knew that if he discovered the truth he might even be capable of killing her. A hymenoplasty would resolve the matter in an elegant, undramatic fashion, the fiancé would be happy that his bride was a virgin, the bride would be happy that she had married well, while he, the doctor, Duca Lamberti, would get, for performing the hymenoplasty, one million three hundred thousand lire now and seven hundred thousand once the operation had been performed. In cash, of course.

'I'm giving you ten seconds to get out of here before I smash your head in,' Duca said, getting lazily but resolutely to his feet and theatrically picking up the stool on which he had been sitting: he had learned to act, too, and had no intention of forgetting it.

'Let me say one more thing,' the other man went on, unfazed, because the more cunning they are, the more obtuse. 'You might like to get back on the register, I have a contact who ...'

3

He walked from his apartment to Police Headquarters. Superintendent Carrua was eating, on the desk there was a plate with a roll, just a roll with nothing in it, plus a few black olives and a glass of white wine. Duca talked to him as he was eating the olives, peeling them carefully with his teeth, then put down on the desk the thirty ten-thousand-lire notes that had been given him by the merchant of filth, and in the darkest corner of the office – because here in Headquarters, as his father had once explained, the sunnier it is outside, the darker inside – in that dark corner sat Mascaranti, who had written everything down: he couldn't help himself.

'He told you he could get you put back on the register?' Carrua said, working conscientiously on an olive.

'Yes, he even told me how he'd go about it, it was obvious he's familiar with that world.'

'Do you think he could do it?'

'I think he could, if he wanted. He even knows an influential politician, someone we both know well, who could be of great help.' He told him the name.

'And do you think he really wants to get you back on the register?'

'I don't think so at all.' It had been a nasty encounter, which smelt to high heaven, but he was in it now, in this kind of work, and he couldn't hope to go back to the respectable world.

'Mascaranti, tell the bar not to send me old olives.'

'I already told them.'

'They're shameless, they sell rotten produce even to the police,' Carrua said. Having finished the olives he started to nibble at the bread, and as he did so looked at the little heap of ten-thousand-lire notes. 'Are you really determined to go down this road?'

'I need the money,' Duca said.

'And you think you can make money by playing the policeman? You have some strange ideas.' He drank a little white wine. 'Mascaranti, get me the Sompani file.' Another sip of wine as Mascaranti left the room. 'You see, there's something odd about this young man coming and offering you a pre-nuptial patch-up job, which is that he told you he'd been sent by Turiddu Sompani, because Turiddu Sompani died a few days ago, together with a lady friend of his. They were found in a Fiat 1003 in the Naviglio Pavese. Now I find it hard to believe that this young man of yours with the patch-up job didn't know that Turiddu was dead, and I don't understand why he introduced himself to you using the name of a dead man, especially as you might also have known that Turiddu was dead.'

'Actually, I did.' Duca got up and took the last battered olive that Carrua had left on the plate. He was hungry, he was alone in Milan, nobody was cooking for him, the restaurants were expensive. It didn't taste too bad after all. 'And I know something else, even without looking at Sompani's file, which is that three and a half years ago, Turiddu leaves his car to a friend and this friend's girlfriend, the friend can't drive, he's drunk, and he ends up in the Lambro, at the Conca Fallata. Repetitions bother me. Sompani's friend and the friend's girlfriend drown pathetically, if we can put it that way, at the Conca Fallata, inside a car, and a few years later, Sompani and a lady friend of his also drown pathetically inside a car, in the Naviglio Pavese. Don't they bother you too?' He meant repetitions.

Carrua took another sip. 'I think I'm starting to understand,' he said, putting down his glass. 'A doctor is the policeman of the body, a disease is almost like a criminal who has to be tracked down, you were a good doctor because you're a policeman, like your father.' A final sip of the wine. 'Yes, repetitions bother me too, but if we're right, then this could turn out to be something big, maybe even dangerous.'

Then Duca got up. 'All right, if you don't want to give me a job, it's up to you, I'm going.'

At last the true Carrua, who up until now had spoken in an improbably normal voice, revealed himself by shouting, 'No, I don't even want to see you! You're too highly-strung, you do even this kind of job with too much anger, too much hate. You want to eat up the criminals, you don't want to arrest them, or defer to the authorities, or defend society. You have a sister and your sister has a child and you ought to think about them, instead of which you come here asking to put your hands on these unexploded bombs, "I'm here," you say, "I'll defuse the detonator, I don't mind getting blown up."' Angrily, he picked up the ten-thousand-lire notes and waved them in front of Duca. 'Do you think I don't know why you accepted this money from that piece of dirt? To join in the game. And if I find you in some ditch, with your throat cut, what do I tell your sister? And you know the State won't pay even ten lire if you die, because all you are is an informer, that's the highest rank I can give you, and do informers get a choice how they die? Why don't you travel around Italy as a pharmaceuticals salesman, and earn some decent money?'

Duca wasn't really listening to him: he liked Carrua

when he shouted, but the spring weather was making him impatient with everything. 'Maybe you're right, I'm too highly-strung to be a policeman. Not you, you're calm.' And he walked towards the door.

'No, Duca, come here.' Carrua's voice was suddenly low, it almost moved him. He went back to the desk.

'Sit down.'

Duca sat down.

'I'm sorry if I shouted.'

Duca didn't say anything.

'How did things end up with that piece of filth? I don't remember if you told me what his name was.'

Mascaranti, who had come back in a minute earlier with Turiddu Sompani's file, had heard this. 'His name is Silvano Solvere. I already looked for him in records, there's nothing on him. We could check the fingerprints, because the name's a bit strange. But I did find the woman's file, an interesting file: *verbal assault on a police officer, verbal assault, verbal assault, verbal assault, drunk and disorderly, drunk, drunk*, she was admitted to an asylum that time, then there's *attack, with strikers, on the headquarters of a political party*, you remember the time they set fire to that place?' He paused for breath. 'Plus prostitution and vagrancy.'

'What's the name of this shrinking violet?'

'Adele Terrini.'

'Let's go back to before. How did you leave things with Silvano Solvere? Strange name, it reminds me of Solvay soda.' He was becoming an idiot too, Carrua thought, after spending so much time shut up in this office.

'That he'll come and pick me up and take me to see the young lady.' Simple.

'In other words, you have to go where he takes you.' Obvious. 'And when you're with the young lady you have to operate on her? By the way, is it a dangerous operation, does it take long?'

Duca explained the operation, using technical terms, nothing vulgar: both he and Carrua hated gratuitous vulgarity. 'Of course, as a doctor who's been struck off the register, I can't even apply a sticking plaster, but I could perform this operation with police consent.'

'What if the girl gets an infection and dies, what do we do then?' Carrua asked.

'You know there's an answer to that question,' Duca said irritably. 'Either you make contact with these people and take the chance of discovering something crucial, or else you leave the files on Turiddu and his lady friend in records, pretend you've never heard the name Silvano Solvere, and I go home.'

'I was thinking of you,' Carrua said very softly, 'if the girl dies, or is seriously ill and the thing comes out, even if you did it for the police, it's all up with you.'

'Why, hasn't it been all up with me for a long time now?'

Carrua stared at the sun outside the window. When he spoke again, he actually sounded sad. 'So you've made up your mind.'

'I thought I'd already said I had.' Even the most intelligent people, like Carrua, could be obtuse sometimes.

'All right.' He hated and admired Duca, just as he had hated and admired Duca's father, for his doggedness and inflexibility. With no money, no career, with a sister and a little child to support, instead of minding his own business and sorting himself out, he was throwing himself into the most hopeless kind of work there was, the work of a policeman, an Italian policeman at that, an English or American policeman would have been another matter, but an Italian policeman gets it from everyone: stones from strikers, bullets or stab wounds from criminals, insults behind his back from the general public, reprimands from his superiors and not much money from the State. 'All right, but do things the way I say. Mascaranti is coming with you.'

He liked that idea.

'And the car will have a radio.'

He wasn't too keen on that. 'A car with a radio is too conspicuous,' he said. 'They gave me the money, so it's quite likely they're keeping their eyes on me, that's why I came here on foot today. If they notice the radio in the car, that'll be the end of it.'

'Mascaranti will have to make sure you're not spotted. But that's not all, I'm also going to have our special team, the S. squad, tailing you.' He started shouting. 'And don't tell me that's too many people. If you know anything at all about this profession, you must already have realised what could happen to you.'

No, he didn't tell him it was too many people: Carrua was absolutely right.

'And Mascaranti will also let you have a gun,' he said it harshly, but without hope. 'With a special temporary permit, of course, because you aren't allowed to carry a weapon.'

'No, no guns, I don't like being armed.'

'These people are often armed.'

He refused categorically, vaingloriously. 'Don't give me a gun, I'm already dangerous enough without one.' He wanted to say more – that if he had a gun he wouldn't hesitate to fire it, he wouldn't hesitate at all – but he didn't say it, because Carrua knew.

'All right, forget it,' Carrua said, yielding. 'That means Mascaranti will have to take care of both of you. Another thing is, these people will phone you at home, so we'll put a tap on your phone and record all the calls you make or receive.'

That was fine with him.

'And one more thing: I have to inform the Commissioner of the investigation.' He stood up. 'If anything happened to you, I'd be fired, they'd send me back to Sardinia to eat bread and olives.'

'You seem to be eating plenty of olives here.'

'Don't try and be clever,' Carrua said. 'Just tell yourself I have no desire to be fired, so I don't want anything to happen to you. It doesn't matter to me if we discover anything or not, because we're not going to eradicate these people all by ourselves. But I want you in one piece, and I don't want us all to end up in the newspapers.'

Duca also stood up, a little less irritable now. 'Let's go, Mascaranti.'

'Yes, doctor,' Mascaranti said.

Carrua also stood up. 'He doesn't like to be called doctor,' he said to Mascaranti: he was the one who was irritable now. He picked up the pile of ten-thousand-lire notes. 'And you have to keep this and spend it was as if it was yours. These people may search you and they need to find their money on you.'

Of course. Below, in the courtyard of Headquarters, a pigeon, a single pigeon, stood motionless in the sun, as if it was asleep, or as if it was a fake bird made of stone, and the car with the radio, which Mascaranti had gone to fetch, passed within one metre of the pigeon, but the bird did not move.

4

The bell rang, very, very politely. Mascaranti shut himself up in the kitchen and moved his gun from his holster to his jacket pocket. Duca went and opened the door. They didn't do this every time the bell rang, but since nobody ever rang that bell now that his sister and niece were in the Brianza, and in fact nobody had rung it for four days now, especially not in that polite – too polite – way, they knew this was the moment they had been waiting for. And as soon as he opened the door, Duca saw the case, it really was a case, not a big bag, and he saw the woman's beautiful long legs, such young legs, and such a young face, and her body encased in a bright red dress coat.

'Dr Lamberti?' The voice was less young, and much less polite than the way the bell had rung: although she spoke Italian, there was a strong tinge of Milanese dialect, that heavy, vulgar Milanese from the far edge of the city, from Corsico or Cologno Monzese, where Milanese, unrefined but pleasant, merges with more rural and alien-sounding dialects.

He nodded, yes, he was Dr Lamberti, Duca Lamberti, and he let her in, because he had already understood.

'Silvano sent me,' she said in the hall. She wasn't wearing make-up, apart from lipstick and false eyebrows drawn with a pencil, with blank spaces beneath where the real ones should have been, an effect he found clownish and repulsive. He motioned her towards the surgery. The case must be a little heavy, to judge both by the look of it – it was rather like an instrument case, with metal straps – and by the way she was holding it. 'Take a seat.' They were clever: they had sent the girl here instead of coming to fetch him, as he had been told they would. Had he been told the truth about anything?

Before sitting, she put the case down in a corner, then took off her dress coat. Under it she was wearing a red slip and sheer black stockings. She picked up her handbag, sat down, looked in her handbag for her cigarettes and lit one. They were Parisiennes. 'Would you like one?' She held out the packet.

'Thanks,' he said, taking one: he liked Parisiennes, and it might mean that the girl spent time in Switzerland or France.

'Is there anyone else here?' she asked.

'Yes, a friend of mine.' You had to be open with these people, he couldn't exactly hide Mascaranti in a wardrobe as if this was a bedroom farce. 'Why?'

'Don't lose your temper, I was only asking.' She was sitting back, comfortable and composed, in the little armchair. 'It's quite hot, isn't it, even with the windows open?'

From the extremely modest glass cabinet he took the instruments he needed, in order to sterilise them. He wasn't wearing a jacket, and his shirt sleeves were rolled up, but he didn't feel the heat the way she did. But heat is a subjective sensation. 'Yes, it's starting to get hot.'

'Sometimes, though, I feel cold, even in July.'

'I'll be right back.' Carrying the instruments in a glass bowl, he went into the kitchen, and without looking at Mascaranti, found a cooking pot in the dresser, filled it with water, threw the instruments into it and switched on the gas.

This was his first return to the sacred mission of medicine. The last act he had performed as a doctor had been to kill an old woman who was sick with cancer – you call it euthanasia but you end up in prison all the same – and now once again he was doing a bit of social work, restoring her virginity to a healthy young woman who had absentmindedly lost it.

'How's it going?' Mascaranti asked.

Only when he had lit the gas did he look at him, and reply, 'Fine.' He lowered his voice. 'Did you check downstairs?' He went to the window which looked out on the courtyard, but withdrew almost immediately: in the courtyards of large cities, the spring air is filled with the smell of stones and rubbish and cooking, which is not very inviting, especially at night.

Mascaranti said yes, he had checked, he had the two-way radio in his pocket, he was really happy about that: this was life, this was work, being able to talk to Sergeant Morini, who was in the Via Pascoli with his squad, simply by taking the two-way radio from his pocket.

'Call me when it boils, but don't come in,' he said to Mascaranti, and went back to the surgery and the virgin. She was still smoking, she had lit another cigarette.

'I was almost falling asleep in this heat.'

'Would you mind getting on the couch?'

'All right. Can I smoke?'

He nodded, and stood watching her, without turning away, as she took off her suspender belt and slip. 'Go on.' She put the suspender belt and slip on the little table. From the cabinet he took a pair of rubber gloves and a little bottle of Citrosil, and poured the alcohol on his gloved hands.

'Will it take long?' she asked. 'Silvano told me it doesn't take long.'

'*I'm* the doctor,' he replied, moving the lamp in order to get more light.

'You lose your temper easily, I like men who lose their tempers easily.'

She was certainly friendly, with that tinge of outer Milanese dialect in the way she spoke. He began to examine her. It wasn't easy to see properly, this wasn't exactly a big operating room, he didn't have the facilities, he didn't even have a white coat, a white coat makes an impression, or at any rate he couldn't find it, where on earth had his sister Lorenza put it, but he had to carry on all the same, he had set out along this road and couldn't stop now.

'Have you had any diseases or infections?'

Calmly throwing the end of the Parisienne on the floor and looking up at the ceiling, she told him the name of the disease she had had. 'Can't hide anything from you doctors.'

He moved the lamp on the little table even closer, but it didn't give much light. 'Have you ever had an abortion?'

'Yes, three.'

'Abortions or miscarriages?' He thought the answer was obvious.

'Well,' she said sadly, slightly bitterly, 'only women who want children have miscarriages, it's those who don't want them who need dynamiting.'

He raised his head and took off his gloves. 'The procedure will only take a few minutes, but after it you'll have to lie here on the couch for at least two hours.'

'I'll have a nap,' she said. 'Mind if I smoke?'

'Go ahead.'

'I like smoking lying down. Can you get my cigarettes out of my handbag for me?'

Of course he could. He opened the little black bag in front of her – it was full to the brim, like a make-up case – and took out the yellow packet of Parisiennes and the lighter.

'Take one yourself.'

'Thank you.' He lit a cigarette for her, then one for himself. He had learnt to be a good actor: you had to, otherwise you'd drown. He'd even be able to join the Piccolo Teatro, Strehler[1] would refine his talents, but he already had what it took to be an actor. He continued with his playacting: 'When are you getting married?' He said it almost gently: if the girl wanted to seduce him before the operation, let her, it was all part of the performance.

'Don't remind me: tomorrow morning.' Lying there, her knees bent because the couch was too short for her, she smoked and blew the smoke towards the ceiling. Her black hair, not very long but thick, created a dark halo on the little white pillow: yes, she had a sour, slightly bony, slightly vulgar face, but she gave off intense waves of sensuality in the way she moved, spoke and behaved.

'You're getting married tomorrow morning?' His tone was not so much incredulous as resigned.

'Yes, unfortunately.' Another little cloud of smoke drifted up to the ceiling. 'Don't you have anything to drink? I mean something strong, to forget.'

'Maybe.' He went back to the kitchen. He must have a bottle or two of whisky left over from the time of Michelangelo's David,[2] and in fact there was one, one and a half, he took the half, and a glass, and looked at Mascaranti. Mascaranti was looking at the little bowl with the instruments in it.

'The water has just started boiling,' Mascaranti said.

'Let it boil for ten minutes, then call me.' He went back to the study and the girl was still smoking: even though the windows were open, all the smoke produced by this tobacco addict couldn't pass quickly enough through the closed shutters. 'I have whisky. Say when.'

'That's fine,' she said, propping herself on one elbow and taking a good swig. 'If only you knew how awful it is, a man can't imagine it.' She gave him back the glass.

'What is?'

'Getting married to a man who isn't right for you.'

It was true, a man couldn't know that.

'And that's not the worst thing.'

'What is?'

'Having to leave the man you like.' She gestured for a cigarette, and Duca gave her one and lit it for her and she continued, 'Silvano and I have been making love for a week. We know these are the last days we've got, and we feel really bad.'

This was nice, a romantic touch amid all the filth, if you could call it romantic. He gave her more to drink. Women are always the weak link in any chain. But then she said, 'Don't give me too much to drink, or I'll start chattering and then I'll be here for more than three hours.'

'Leave it if you don't want it.' Another brilliant piece of acting, pretending to walk away with the glass.

'No, please, if you had to get married to a butcher to-morrow morning, you'd want to drink a lot too,' and she made him give her back the glass, and this time, too, she took a big swig, paused, took another big swig, then sat there pensively, holding the glass in her hand.

This could be useful, knowing that she was about to marry a butcher. It wouldn't take Mascaranti more than half an hour to find out who, among the men getting married the following day, were butchers: there couldn't be all that many of them, there might only be one, *the* butcher.

'Listen,' he said, 'I'll turn out the light and open the shutters for a while, too, that way we can let out some of the smoke.'

'I'm sorry, I always stink the place up with my cigarettes.'

'Oh, no,' he said to her gently, in the darkness, opening the shutters onto the mild Milanese night, 'it's just that this apartment isn't well ventilated.'

'Since you have the window open, give me another cigarette, already lit.'

'Don't you think you smoke too much?' he said: she still had the other cigarette between her fingers, he could see the glow of the embers. In this filth, you had to be careful. The visitor known to him only as Silvano Solvere had sent this girl ahead to sound him out: she wasn't born yesterday, there had to be a purpose behind all the nonsense she was spouting and the odd way she was behaving. He mustn't make a mistake, he really couldn't afford to make any more mistakes in his life.

'Thank you,' she said when he had given her the lighted cigarette, 'I'm starting to get quite excited, being here in the dark with a handsome man like you.'

Her words made him feel a bit nauseous, but also made him want to laugh at the insolent confidence some people had in other people's innocence. 'Not me,' he said.

'All right, but don't get angry, otherwise I might feel even more excited, I told you I like men who get angry easily.'

The way she said this gave him pause for thought: he was no longer so sure that it was a trap, or that they were testing him, trying to see what he was made of.

'It's been boiling for ten minutes,' came Mascaranti's voice from the hall.

Duca closed the shutters and switched the light back on. She was completely naked.

'You didn't need to do that,' he said harshly. 'Cover yourself.'

'Go on, get angry, I like it.'

'Stop that or I'll throw you out.'

'Yes, yes, throw me out, throw me to the ground.'

He always got the rare specimens, the *trouvailles*, the collector's items of society. This time, an uncontrollable nymphomaniac. He went to the couch, grabbed her hair, lifted her head, and hit her with the edge of his hand, but not hard, at least not too hard, on the forehead, between the eyes and above the nose. A slap wouldn't have worked, it would only have excited her even more, instead of which the blow made her sigh, and she relaxed onto the pillow, she hadn't fainted, but the dizziness had stemmed the outpouring of her libido and stopped her from protesting, at least for the moment.

'Put these back on. I'll be right back.' He picked up the bra and slip she had thrown down on the floor amid the cigarette ends and went into the kitchen.

When he came back with the little bowl of sterilised instruments, she was dressed in her underwear and sitting on the couch. 'What did you do to me? I feel dizzy, I feel like I do when I'm in Rome and eat a lot of lamb and drink a lot of wine, and afterwards I feel sick, like this.'

'It'll pass soon, keep sitting on the couch.' He put the bowl down on the little table, moving aside the suspender belt and the slip. Then he opened his leather case, which was on the chair behind the little table – an elegant little doctor's case, a gift obviously, from his father, with all the instruments a doctor needed, and a section for emergency medicines – and took out a couple of tubes and a small box, things he had bought as soon as it had been decided that he would do this prenuptial procedure.

'Another cigarette and another drink,' she said querulously. 'It's passed, I feel fine, but you must teach me what blow you used.' She sounded like a sportswoman in the gym, eager to learn.

5

The packet of Parisiennes was finished, but she had two more in her handbag. He passed her an unopened packet, along with the lighter, and another glass of whisky, then, instead of getting ready, took a chair and sat down in front of her. 'I'd like to know if it's really necessary for you to have this procedure.'

She looked at him in astonishment, almost as she had when he had hit her, but immediately recovered. 'Just do it.' There was no warmth in her expression now, only hostility.

It was better that way, he preferred enemies. 'All right. Lie down.'

'Will it hurt?'

He put on the gloves and again sprayed Citrosil on them. 'No.'

'I'm sorry for the way I answered you.'

Without replying, he transferred the anaesthetic from the phial into the syringe, disinfected her side with alcohol, and massaged it.

'If you only knew what I've been thinking about all evening,' she said.

Still not replying, he sunk the needle into her young skin. It was in a sensitive spot, and she gave a little start. 'That's the worst it'll hurt,' he said: that was another reason he wasn't a good doctor, he felt too much pity for his patients, he really wanted to take care of them, to cure them, to help them even when, as in this case, it was a murky and dangerous piece of nonsense, and he actually felt their pain: someone like that shouldn't be a doctor, they should go to the park and read the newspaper.

'All evening, even before coming here, I've been thinking of running away with Silvano, he's thinking of it, too, I don't want to marry that man, and I didn't even want to have myself sewn up again, it's nonsense, but he believes in it, if I'm not a virgin he'll take one of the knives he has in the shop and cut me, he's told me that more than once, and I don't want to marry someone as stupid as that, I want to be with Silvano, but I can't.' She cursed, using a very vulgar swear word. 'You can never do what you like in life.' She cursed again, and now she was talking almost in dialect. 'So tomorrow morning I'll put on a white dress, what do think of that? Doesn't that take the biscuit, me in a white dress? Her laughter made her jump a little on the couch. He opened the tube containing the local anaesthetic. 'Keep still.'

'I'd like a drink.'

All right, let her drink, the booze plus the anaesthetic would send her to sleep. He gave her the glass, waited until she had had enough, even gave her another cigarette, then bent down again to finish the local anaesthetic.

'And you know what's even worse? The village. It's one thing to leave someone you like and marry someone you find ridiculous. But then I have to go and live there, in his village, the village I ran away from as a child, because I couldn't stand it, and it isn't even a real village, it's just a group of four houses, they don't even have the courage to call it a hamlet, they say Ca' Torino di Romano Banco a Buccinasco, by the time you've finished writing it your pen has run out of ink. Have you ever been over that way?'

With the tweezers he took the instruments from the bowl. 'If I hurt you, tell me.' He checked her sensitivity by touching her: she did not react, the anaesthetic had taken effect. 'Where exactly is it?' he asked. He could start now, and he did.

'What? You mean you've never heard of Ca' Tarino, or Buccinasco, or Romano Banco?' She was calm, motionless, only her voice was increasingly vulgar and tinged with dialect, and there was a tone of real bitterness in it. 'It's in Corsico, in other words, you go to Corsico from the Porta Ticinese, you go all the way along the Ripa di Porta Ticinese, you know I'm going to get completely sloshed this evening, and then you go down the Via Lodovico Il Moro, with the stinking water of the Naviglio Grande beside it, then you take the Via Garibaldi and keep going until you get to Romano Banco, that's where my fiancé has his butcher's shop, but he has another one in Ca' Tarino, and also, and this is where it gets interesting, he also has two shops in Milan and brings the meat in without paying duty on it. They've never caught him, he's made millions like that, hundreds of millions, I think he could buy the Galleria in Milan if he wanted.'

'Am I hurting you?' he asked. It wasn't easy to see, in that light, but it was all he had.

'No, I don't feel a thing, I'd like to have a drink, can I sit up?'

'No, you can't sit up, and don't drink for now, it'll all be over in a few minutes.'

Her head lay on the hard pillow, surrounded by a halo of black hair, and she waved her arm over it in a desolate, vulgar way. 'I don't care if I spend a few minutes or a few hours here. After tomorrow I'm going to have to spend all my life there, the first lady of Ca' Tarino, just like Jackie Kennedy, except that she got the White House. Can I at least smoke?'

'No. Keep absolutely still.'

'All right, I won't smoke. Fortunately Silvano is going with me tonight, all the way to Corsico. If it wasn't for this nonsense we'd make love again.' Despite the anaesthetic, which was relaxing her and making her talkative, her erotic impulses were still strong. 'If you only knew what Ca'Tarino is like in winter, it's always foggy, you feel soaked through, and in spring it's worse, with all the mud. When I was a child I played with the other children and all I remember is a lot of mud. To go to Romano Banco I'd have to wear boots, like the men who work in the irrigation ditches. And every season is worse than the last, even when it's really warm it rains, you can't go out of the house, and where would you go anyway? When television came the first person to install it was my fiancé, the butcher. The whole of Ca'Tarino would go to his house to watch it, but he'd pick and choose, he'd invite my parents, so I'd go too, and that's how we ended up engaged. In the dark he'd put his hand on my knee, then move it up, and as soon as he could he asked me if I was a virgin, and with that hand on my leg and my mother close by I was a bit annoyed so to make fun of him I said, yes, I'd been keeping myself specially for him. And then he told me that if I really was a virgin he wanted to marry me, and that in the meantime he'd send me to Milan, to one of his butcher's shops, to be a cashier, so did I want to become engaged to him? I didn't have to think about it a lot, he was the king of Ca'Tarino, and Romano Banco, and Buccinasco, and Corsico, and I was the daughter of a peasant, I slept on a straw mattress, my arms were covered in insect bites. How could I say no?'

She swore again. He had finished, but she was saying interesting things, so he pretended to continue. 'Keep still.'

'And so I was stuck. He took me straight to Milan, put

me on the cash desk, and told everyone I was his fiancée. In the evening he'd come and pick me up in his car and take me home, he cares a lot about what people think. In the car he'd ask me for all kinds of things, and in the end I had to yield, except for my virginity, because that's something he thinks is the cherry on the cake, to be kept for last, but he didn't want people to know anything because then they'd talk, and so he always got me back to Ca' Tarino by ten and handed me back to my parents. And he's always trusted me, that's why I feel a bit bad about it, not only because I cheated on him, but also because of the money. I started with the money straight away, because seeing all that money coming into the shop, I couldn't resist, before I got engaged to him a hundred lire was a big amount for me. I learned the system very quickly, and every day I put away thousands of lire, because nobody can imagine the money that comes in to a butcher's shop, it's near here, you know, in the Via Plinio, all I had to do this evening was walk here from the shop. He isn't driving me back tonight, he's not supposed to see the bride the night before the wedding, plus he's having his stag party. I told him not to worry, that I'd come back with Silvano, because they're friends, he's the one who introduced Silvano to me. I'd already strayed a few times, being there all day behind the cash desk, in the butcher's shop, a lot of men come in to do their shopping, though you wouldn't think so, and every now and again there were some really handsome assistants, I can't resist, if they insist it goes to my head, but he's jealous of the assistants and when they're too handsome he sends them away, but always after I've had my way with them.' She laughed.

'Keep still, or I'll hurt you.'

She was quite drunk now. 'And one evening he picked me up from the shop with Silvano, he said he was a friend of his and we went out to dinner together. We went to Bice's in the Via Manzoni, and when we were in the restaurant, he looked a bit too much like a butcher in comparison with Silvano who's such a gentleman, I really liked him straight away, he went to my head.'

So there was nothing for him to worry about. Apparently, she got excited very easily with everyone.

'We ate and drank everything they had, and in the end Bice herself came to our table and served us liqueurs and even sat down with us for a while, and she was really nice, and very polite to my fiancé, but he was already drunk, he told her he was a butcher and criticised the meat, he told her the meat he could supply her with was better than the meat she got sent from Tuscany, and Bice was so kind, she let him talk, and then she stood up and told him he was really nice, but he wasn't, he'd made a complete fool of himself.'

Duca dabbed with the cotton wool and stood up. 'There, it's all over, now I'm going to give you a pill.'

'I want a drink,' she said languidly, 'and a cigarette.'

'All right, but don't move, stay there with your legs down and closed, like that.' He took out the pill, and poured a good serving of whisky into the glass. 'I'm going to raise your head now, but I want you to keep your pelvis still.' He put a hand on the back of her neck and raised her head. She was smiling, but in a sisterly way now, all desire spent. 'Put your tongue out.' He put the little pill on her tongue and the glass of whisky between her lips. 'Slowly, you have to avoid coughing.' If she coughed she would undo the repair he had just made.

She drank slowly, but she drank quite a bit. 'It isn't a sleeping pill, is it?'

'No, it's an analgesic, it kills the pain, so although you'll start to hurt a bit, you shouldn't feel it.'

'I'd like to smoke.'

'Yes,' he said – he already knew that, he had already put the cigarette in his mouth to light it and then give it to her – 'but swallow your saliva if you feel like coughing, you mustn't cough, and if you really can't stop yourself, cough with your mouth open.'

He took the cigarette out of his mouth, and she took it greedily, and greedily smoked it, two or three gasps. 'Then I wanted to go home, but he said no.'

He waited for her to continue, but she took another couple of drags, and then he lit a cigarette, too, a Parisienne. All the cigarette ends on the floor really bothered him, but the bother passed as soon as she started speaking again.

'After the way he'd behaved with Bice I didn't want to go with someone as drunk as that, and compared with Silvano, well, there was no comparison, when I was with Silvano it was like being with a prince, but my fiancé was drunk and like all drunks he wanted to keep going. Our car was in the Via Montenapoleone, but he wanted to go to Motta's in the Piazza della Scala. God, that was embarrassing, he tried to joke with the waiter, he took out a wad of ten-thousand-lire notes, it might have been almost a million, and said, "Keep the change," how about that, eh? Finally Silvano managed to take him outside, very politely, I remember it so well, that first evening I saw him, he must come from an aristocratic family, although he doesn't let on, and in the Via Montenapoleone, the car was parked just in front of that jewellers' shop and then my fiancé, it was so embarrassing again, started going *tr–tr–tr–tr–tr* as if he was firing a machine gun, but so loud that a lady on the other side of the street screamed and she started walking away very quickly and stopped only when he started laughing.

Then Silvano bundled him into the car and we managed to leave, but when we got to Corsico he wanted to get out and drink some more, and Silvano told me to let him drink, even urge him to drink, because it was the only way to calm him down, so we made him drink and he fell asleep on our laps, and by the time we got to Ca' Tarino he was fast asleep and Silvano took him upstairs while I waited in the car, and then he came down again and we went on a bit further in the car and then we made love and it was better than the first time I'd ever made love, in fact the real first time was with him, I'll always remember it.'

He put a hand on her forehead. 'I'm going to turn out the light now and open the window, it's hot.'

'Oh yes, I'd like that, it's nice here.' Through the open window you could see the green of the trees with the light of the street lamps behind them. 'Can you give me a bit more whisky?'

'Yes, I'll go and get it,' he said and went out, into the darkness, guided by the faint light coming from the kitchen: she had already drunk half a bottle, she should have been asleep, but she must be used to it. In the kitchen, Mascaranti, who could never stop writing, having nothing to write, was doing crosswords. Duca opened the little cupboard and took out the bottle of whisky. 'Ask Morini if there's anybody watching outside.'

Mascaranti took the two-way radio from his pocket, pulled out the antenna, and turned the button to the minimum volume to avoid static. 'Hello, hello, hello,' he said, making fun of Morini, 'hello, over.'

'I'll give you "over",' Morini said.

'Roger. Have you seen anybody about? Dr Lamberti says there may be someone watching. Over.'

'I haven't seen anyone.'

'Thanks, talk to you soon.' He turned to Duca. 'He says there's nobody about.'

Duca took the corkscrew and opened the bottle, went back into the dark surgery, and looked for the glass in the dark.

'How nice,' she said, 'look, the light of the street lamps behind the leaves of the trees.'

Yes, she had already said that: obviously she had a taste for poetry, as well as a taste for men. He poured a generous serving into the glass. A pity she'd stopped talking: he couldn't insist or she'd start to suspect. 'Drink, but slowly, and wait for me to lift your head.' He supported her neck with his arm and with his other hand moved the glass close to her mouth. Now, with his eyes accustomed again to the dark, he could see her eyes, wet with drink, shining in the light from the window, and he watched her drink avidly: an anaesthetic makes you thirsty.

'A cigarette. If you only knew how much I like smoking lying down.'

He lit another cigarette for her. A pity she'd stopped talking about her own affairs, about Silvano and the butcher.

The cigarette glowed in the half-light. 'Listen, with the job you did, I'm really going to be a virgin tomorrow night?'

'Yes,' he said.

'What a laugh!'

'Don't laugh, please.'

'No, I'm not laughing, but you men are such idiots.'

Anything, provided she started talking again. Yes, idiots, what else could they be?

'We women are sluts, but you're just idiots.'

He liked this sweeping verdict: on one side the sluts, on the other the idiots, that's the world, there you are. But talk, please, start talking again, tell me about your butcher, about your prince Silvano.

'I'm sorry,' she said, smoking in the darkness, lying down, the way she liked, 'you have to be idiots, I can be a virgin and still have been with two hundred men, and when you think about the things my fiancé wanted in the car, as an advance, things you couldn't imagine, what kind of virginity is that?'

Don't talk about virginity, talk about your fiancé, he was begging her, sitting on the stool by the window. Talk, talk.

'You make me laugh, all of you.' Her voice was getting blurred. 'As soon as I see a pair of trousers, I get the urge, but I also feel like laughing.'

Duca saw ash fall from her cigarette, and he stared at that point of light, waiting for her to speak again, but there was silence and in the silence he heard heavy breathing. He got up and went to the couch and saw that she was asleep. He angrily stubbed out the cigarette, although it was still alight. He left her alone and went into the kitchen. According to the alarm clock with the pink dial and the second hand in the shape of a hen, it was after ten.

6

At half-past, after helping Mascaranti to solve almost all the crosswords, he heard a noise in the surgery and went to see.

She was sitting up on the couch. 'What time is it?' she asked.

'Twenty to one.'

'I was in a deep sleep, I feel as if I slept the whole night.'

It was better that way. He went and closed the shutters, then switched on the light, and her red slip burst into flame.

'Can I go?'

He approached her. 'Get off the couch, slowly, and try to walk.' After all, he wasn't a specialist in certain kinds of work, he might have made a few mistakes.

She got down, slowly, walked up and down the cramped surgery, without suspenders her black stockings slowly slid down her slim legs, and she swayed a bit, but as a joke, because she was smiling at him, and even shaking her head to make her dark, smooth hair fall straight on her neck. 'So it's all right?'

'Do you feel any pain?'

'It burns but only a little bit.'

'Any discomfort?'

'Not really.'

Congratulations, Dr Duca Lamberti, you're a good hymenologist: after all those years of study, all those years when your father ate almost nothing but mortadella – you're from Emilia Romagna, you should like mortadella – and all those books you read, and Esculapius[3], at last you've made it, now you have a future in front of you, as a great restorer. He covered his face with his hands, almost as if he was sleepy. 'Lift a leg, slowly, as high as you can.'

'It's like a gymnastics lesson,' she said, doing as he said, very smoothly, showing off: she was like a cat on a roof.

'Does it hurt?'

'No.'

'Lift the other leg.'

Her black stocking slid down to her calf as she shame-lessly lifted her leg, shamelessly raising the short slip and looking him in the face.

'Do you feel any pain?

'A bit of discomfort, but not very much.'

He picked up her handbag and took a cigarette from the packet of Parisiennes.

'What time are you getting married?' he asked.

'At eleven, so that everyone can be there, the whole of Romano Banco and the whole of Buccinasco, and the whole of Ca' Tarino, and they're even coming from Corsico.' In the meantime she had put on her knickers and then her suspenders. 'The little church in Romano Banco is lovely, you should come and see it, you know he arranged for traffic police on motorcycles? They're going to stop all the traffic, from the Naviglio all the way to Romano Banco, you don't know what it's like when someone like my fiancé gets mar-ried in a place like that.' She might have been talking about some tribe in the Mato Grosso. 'Even the mayor is coming, and tonight there's actually a lorry full of flowers coming from Sanremo, what do you think of that, all the way from Sanremo! He made me phone Sanremo, to make sure they were coming at the hour he said, at four in the morning, so that the priest and the people in the oratory will have time to decorate the church. Actually I'd quite like it, if I wasn't thinking about Silvano.'

She took a cigarette from her handbag, lit it, took the red dress coat from the chair on which she had thrown it, put it on, still with the cigarette and her lipstick in one hand, and did her lips, looking at herself in the big mirror from the handbag.

'Can I make a phone call?' she said, pursing her lips.

'In the hall.' He opened the door for her, switched on the light, and pointed to the phone.

She dialled the number calmly, right there in front of him. She had no secrets from him: only stupid people bother with secrets, with ciphers and codes and special signals. With her eyes shining, as if she really had slept a whole night, she stood there next to him as she spoke into the phone, and smiled at him, wide awake.

'Ricci's pastry shop?' She winked at him. 'Signor Silvano Solvere, please.' With the little finger of her right hand she touched the corner of her right eye. 'That's the pastry shop that did my wedding cake, they're delivering it to Romano Banco, it must be taller than I am, it cost two hundred thousand lire, and Silvano has gone there to have a drink and wait for me, it's where we always meet.' She stopped the chatter and became serious. 'Yes, I've finished, I'm getting a taxi now.' And she hung up immediately: Silvano couldn't have been much of a conversationalist, at least not over the phone.

'Can I call a taxi?' she asked, being by the phone. 'I don't remember the number anymore, do you have a directory?'

'86 71 51,' he said, and watched as she dialled.

'Imola 4, in two minutes,' she said, putting the receiver down. Every gesture she made was shameless and vulgar.

'I'm going straight down, thanks for everything.' She could have been a guest taking her leave after a tea party.

'The case,' he said. That case, whatever it was, that he had seen as soon as she had appeared in the doorway.

She stood by the door, looking quite cheerful: she was the kind of woman who came to life after midnight. The hall was so small that looking at her he could see the specks of gold in her violet eyes. She looked wonderful, she looked so good in that red dress coat and those black stockings, she was very Cinemascope, something from a sensationalised, half-fictional investigation into the world of vice: *the photographic model comes out at midnight to go to the brothel from which they've just called her*. It wasn't true, she was actually on her way to get married, he'd patched her up to be a virgin again so that she could get married, but that was the look she had, and as she did not reply, he repeated, 'The case,' and pointed to the surgery, where she had left the case, whatever it was.

'It stays here,' she said.

Mascaranti must be writing all this down. There was no point, but it did him good.

'Really?' he said.

'Silvano will come and pick it up tomorrow,' she said, 'after the ceremony, because he's going to be best man.'

Oh, so Silvano was coming to pick it up. That meant it was Silvano's case. Why was she leaving it here, was it because it had dirty washing in it and she could trust him with it, or else because it contained something compromising? These people didn't do anything for no reason. When you live like these people, he thought, there was a reason for looking on the ground rather than up in the air, only they'd trusted this woman too much. Or were they trying to frame him?

'Thank you, doctor, I don't suppose we'll see each other again.' She held out her hand. 'Oh, Silvano told me to tell you he'll settle up with you when he comes by.'

He opened the door for her, motioned her through and walked her downstairs to the front door of the building. *Settle up*: another seven hundred thousand lire. Two or three clients like this every month and he'd be fine, his sister would be fine, little Sara would be fine. Everybody would be fine.

'Again, doctor, don't wish me good luck because it brings bad luck.' She went out through the front door, in her red dress coat.

7

Sergeant Morini saw the girl in the red dress coat come out as he was holding the two-way radio to his ear and Mascaranti was saying, 'She's on her way out, she's wearing a red overcoat, she's taking a taxi, Imola 4, are you receiving me?'

The taxi hadn't arrived yet, but now it did, the usual boxlike Fiat Multipla, she got in with her beautiful, long, young legs, she got in harmoniously, and Sergeant Morini sitting beside the driver of the normal, respectable black Alfa Romeo, which did not look like a police car, said to the driver, 'It's that piece of stuff there.'

There were two other officers in the back, both in plain clothes, but they looked so timid and weary, you wouldn't have thought they were police officers.

'Roger, Signor Mascaranti,' he said into the radio, tongue in cheek.

Then the Fiat with the girl in the red dress coat inside it left the Piazza Leonardo da Vinci and immediately turned into the Via Pascoli. At that hour it was almost impossible to follow a car in another car without being noticed, because there was hardly any traffic, apart from the usual Vespa roaring like a jet or the usual overbearing lorry. The best thing to do was keep behind the Fiat without worrying about being noticed, it didn't matter if they suspected they were being followed or not, the fact was, they had to follow them and they would.

And after the Via Pascoli, buried in the velvet of the

night and the brownish green of the large old trees swollen with spring foliage, the Fiat turned into the Via Plinio, nervously drove the whole length of the street, with dozens of closed shops on either side, shot across the Corso Buenos Aires, zoomed into the Piazza Duca d'Aosta: she couldn't be going to the station, could she, she couldn't be catching a train? That would make pursuit difficult, but no, the Fiat rushed down the Via Vittor Pisani, again all the shops closed, a feeling of night, only towards the Piazza della Repubblica were there a few lights, a bit of life.

'He's put his indicator light on,' Morini said to the driver. 'He's stopping in front of the pastry shop, pull over.'

And the girl in the red overcoat, as Mascaranti had called it, because he couldn't have known it was actually called a dress coat, got out of the taxi and walked straight into the Ricci pastry shop.

'Get out, Giovanni, there's an exit in the Via Ferdinando di Savoia, she may be trying to give us the slip.'

One of the two timid, weary officers in the back dashed out of the Alfa Romeo, but quietly, and entered the pastry shop almost immediately behind the girl, but with an absent-minded air, a bit like a drug addict who has just got up and is now hoping for a dissolute night.

She had just entered when a tall, almost aristocratic man dressed in a light grey suit, a white and pink shirt and a greyish pink – in other words, salmon-coloured – tie came up to her, took her gently, almost tenderly, yes, that was the word, tenderly, by the arm, and walked back outside, under the arcades. The waiters were clearing the tables, the tablecloths were trembling in the stormy wind, and at the traffic lights, which were green, a dark Simca was parked, even though the lights were green, and in the car were two prostitutes, the older one at the wheel, the younger one in the seat next to her, close to the window, and this one was smiling, though discreetly, at the few single men coming out of Ricci's. If they had known they had a police car behind them they would have moved on even if the lights had been red, but Sergeant Morini was in the S. squad, not the vice squad, although he had been in the vice squad and had been involved in quite a few roundups, which had made him a hate figure to all the ladies of easy virtue from Rogoredo to Rho and from Crescenzago to Muggiano, from the arcades in the Piazza del Duomo to the Piazza Oberdan. And there, in the Piazza della Repubblica, you could actually see the sky, the black sky, swollen with wind and crossed by lightning flashes, and soon they would hear the rolls of thunder, which Sergeant Morini always told his two-year-old daughter were big horses in the sky hurrying to their mothers, which was why they were making all that noise.

'Look, driver, look, they're getting into that Giulietta.' An olive green Giulietta that went really well with the red of the girl's dress coat and the dove grey of the man's suit. 'If they put on speed I don't know if you could keep up with them.' Nobody could ever keep up with a Giulietta, not even an old, worn-looking one like that.

But the Giulietta didn't put on speed, on the contrary, it went like an ambling horse, frisky but holding back, the driver and the girl in the red dress coat could be seen talking inside, and they crossed the whole of the Piazza della Repubblica, climbed onto the ramparts of Porta Venezia, and after Viale Maino, and the Viale Bianca Maria, and the Piazza Cinque Giornate, Morini started to get irritated. Despite the skill of the driver it was almost impossible for the people in the Giulietta not to have realised that there was an Alfa Romeo following them, unless, he thought, they were hand in hand, her head on his shoulder, letting Providence do the driving. But they weren't such mystical people, he thought: they knew they were being followed, but for the moment they were pretending they weren't and weren't putting on speed. They might lurch forward suddenly when the moment came and disappear.

So he said to the driver, 'Don't keep too far from them, or they'll get away at the first turning. I don't care if they realise we're following them.'

And the night ride continued, after the Piazza Cinque Giornate the Giulietta came down off the ramparts for some reason, drove down the Viale Montenero, Viale Sabotino, which looked like a stage set thanks to the late hour, the emptiness, the flashing yellow lights at the crossroads, the last cheap bar open – its neon sign *Crota Piemunteisa* seemed to tremble, deprived as it was of the letters *r*, *u* and *a* – then the Viale Bligny and the Viale Col di Lana, in other words the whole ring of old Milan, pieces of which still remained, architecturally preserved or occasionally rebuilt for the tourists, those ramparts on the terraces of which valiant men at arms had once apparently stood watch. Sergeant Morini didn't like any of this, and as soon as the Giulietta, which was still ahead of them, had crossed the Piazza 24 Maggio, and turned onto the Ripa Ticinese and the old road, the one to the right of the canal, he contacted the S. office at Headquarters.

'I know it's late, but that's no reason to fall asleep. This is Morini, in case you're still awake and it's of any interest to you. Don't fall asleep again and take this down: I'm on the Ripa Ticinese, I'm following a Giulietta, license number MI 836752, inform all cars in the vicinity, I'll keep calling back with my position.' He hung up and looked again at the red lights of the Giulietta, which was still running ahead of them, although not exactly running, it fact it was going very slowly, along the narrow road to the right of the Alzaia Naviglio Grande.

Morini was middle-aged. When he had first come to Milan the Navigli were not yet covered and in the Via Senato there were still painters painting the dark, dense waters of the Naviglio. He was only a boy in those days, so small and bony that they called him the little hunchback, and he swallowed it because in Milan you had to swallow it if you wanted to earn your living, working as a delivery boy in a tavern in the Via Spiga, spending all day carrying flagons and bottles of wine, and he also did many other jobs until he joined the police, that was his world and he made a career of it, because he liked order and clarity, you're either a cop or a robber, and so he got to know all of Milan, all the streets, all the different neighbourhoods and the kinds of people who lived there, and was quite familiar, maybe house by house, field by field, with the roads to the left and right of the Naviglio Grande.

'Here it comes,' he said to the driver, blinded by the lightning and stunned by the thunder as the storm was unleashed, apparently right over their heads. He started the windscreen wipers under the sudden torrent and, without switching on the headlights, continued to follow the Giulietta.

'This is Morini,' Morini said into the radio. 'I'm on the Alzaia Naviglio Grande, on the way to Corsico and Vigevano, I'm still following the Giulietta license number 836752, I just need to know where the nearest car is.'

'It's in the Via Famagusta, the driver says he's right behind you.'

'Tell him to do his work, I'll call him if I need him,' he shouted to drown out, if possible, the roar of the thunder.

The Giulietta had not stopped, but in the driving rain

it had put on its headlights now and slowed down, it was probably not even doing thirty, and it was going quite carefully, because on that narrow road, with the canal so close without any protection, and in that weather, it would have been stupid to go any faster.

'It's a hurricane,' one of the men in the back sneered, and Morini laughed softly and sharply. Where were those two going, on this road, and in this weather? They had almost reached Ronchetto sul Naviglio, in a real hurricane of rain and wind and thunder and lightning, and a solitary tram passed, improbable and empty, on the road on the other side of the canal, almost wrapped in lightning, and at that moment the driver said, 'There's another car coming towards them.'

'Stop,' Sergeant Morini said. It was as if he knew the exact measurements of the road they were going down. There were two roads with the canal in the middle, neither of them was much of a road, but the one on the left where the tram was passing was at least wide and between it and the canal there was a little rail which might not hold much back, but it was better than nothing. The road on which they were, on the other hand, could hold two cars, at least in theory, one in one direction, one in another, and by the canal there was no protection, and every now and again a drunk walking along it fell in: that was the disadvantage of the Venetian style.

The Alfa Romeo stopped, overwhelmed by all the flashes of lightning, not that it could have done otherwise anyway because the Giulietta was slowing down, as if about to stop.

'Be careful,' Morini said, his face suddenly illuminated by the headlights of the car coming from the opposite direction, and these were his last words before the frenzied *rat-a-tat*, made somehow even more explosive by the scouring rain: the green Giulietta, in front of them, instead of stopping, seemed to tremble, pitilessly illuminated by the headlights of the other car, swaying as if drunk.

'They're shooting a whole machine gun volley at them,' Morini said, and he could clearly see every bullet from the submachine gun hitting the Giulietta and bouncing off it like spray in the deluge of rain illuminated by the headlights.

'Turn off all the lights and let's jump out,' Morini said, but it was pointless: the Giulietta, maddened by the discharge of bullets, gave a great roar and jerked forward, trying to get out of the ray of light, but there were only two ways for it to go, on the right was the wall of a house, and on the left the canal, and the car first smashed against the wall, then bounced, headed for the canal, and fell in. The lights of the car in front, the car from which the volley had come, now lit up the Alfa Romeo, but the Alfa Romeo was empty and the men, despite the deluge, were sheltering it. Suddenly the other car came straight towards them, as if intending to ram them, and Morini fired, but there was nothing they could do: the other car came within a centimetre of the Alfa Romeo, passed it, accelerated with a roar that seemed louder than the thunder and disappeared before they could do anything but fire a few futile shots into the storm-swept darkness.

Now soaking and dripping, unafraid of the rain, Morini ran towards the canal where the Giulietta had fallen. 'Bring the car closer and put on the headlights,' he ordered the driver.

But it was pointless. For several minutes the headlights illumined the rain-swept waters of the Naviglio Grande at this point close to Ronchetto sul Naviglio, but there was nothing to be done, the girl in the red dress coat with the long, youthful legs and her elegant companion in the grey suit had been ferried into another universe, a universe of unknown and mysterious dimensions.

8

As soon as the wind came up, Duca Lamberti went and closed all the windows in the apartment, then came back to the study and together with Mascaranti took another look at the suitcase the girl had left. It wasn't really a case, it was more like a crate or a small trunk, it wasn't leather and the metal corners looked very solid, too solid for such a small trunk.

'I'd like to open it,' he said to Mascaranti.

'It won't be easy,' Mascaranti said.

Duca stood up and fished in the glass bowl containing the instruments he had used on the girl, took two of them and tried them in the small lock of the case. 'I thought it'd be harder,' he said, standing up again and looking for another instrument in the bowl. 'This should do it.' He inserted it in the lock and slowly pushed.

'But those are surgical instruments,' Mascaranti said, regretfully.

Not Duca: he wasn't regretful as he pushed the thin little instrument that looked like a bradawl into the lock, because he had already decided that all this – the instruments, the bottle of coloured or colourless Citrosil, the whole pharmacological Tower of Babel from which to choose the right medicine – just wasn't his world any more. He didn't hate it, but he was leaving it, saying farewell to it, and these instruments could just as well be used to force a lock, or even to open a tin of sardines.

And while the thunder rolled terribly and the rain beat against the shutters, he forced that lock and lifted the lid and they saw a layer of dark wood shavings.

'How did you do it?' Mascaranti said, admiringly.

He didn't reply. He threw the shavings onto the floor. Beneath it was greaseproof paper, the colour of iodine, folded the way it was in big boxes of chocolates. He unfolded it, beneath it were more shavings. Then he stopped and lit a cigarette. He was making a mistake again, he couldn't afford to make a mistake, and yet he was still making them. Why didn't he keep out of things like this, why didn't he become a pharmaceuticals salesman? Why didn't he go and see his sister and Livia[4] and his niece in Inverigo?

'What do you think is inside?' he said to Mascaranti.

'Something fragile, I suppose, with all these shavings.'

Why not crystal glasses for pink champagne? But he didn't say anything and took away the shavings and threw them on the floor again. Beneath, there was a dark cloth, as he had expected. It looked like the kind of cloth used to wash floors, but it was sticky to the touch, because it was soaked in grease.

'It can't be,' Mascaranti said, starting to understand.

'It is,' he replied, lifting the cloth the way a stripper throws off her last undergarment.

Mascaranti stood up from his chair and knelt on the floor by the case, looking without touching. 'It looks like a dismantled submachine gun.'

'It *is* a submachine gun.'

Mascaranti kept staring at it, as if he couldn't believe it. 'It isn't a Browning, a Browning is bigger.'

'No, it isn't a Browning, a Browning weighs nearly nine kilos, this one isn't even seven.' He took out one part, the barrel. The second part was the central body with the chamber, the two parts fitting together like the pieces of a children's game, and the third part was the breech, with a false grip, which also slotted in very smoothly, because of all the grease. And finally, under another layer of wood shavings, the magazines. He inserted one vertically into the chamber. 'It can do thirty shots per magazine, ten more than a Browning, and two more than a Bren.' The bottom of the case was full of magazines. The bullet was a calibre 7.8, a higher calibre than other submachine guns. He put the bullet back and looked carefully down the barrel: there seemed to be eight striations, which meant the speed of firing must be at least eight hundred metres a second. 'This gem is a Skoda,' he said. 'Everybody thinks they only make cars these days but they must have kept some of their military sections, here it is, it's a very small mark: *CSSR*, which means, if I remember correctly, *Ceskoslovenska Socialisticka Republika*. This is the best submachine gun in the world, it can be hidden under a coat, and it has the power of a small cannon. You hold it like a bicycle pump, like this, you pull back the false grip with your right hand and the weapon discharges a hundred shots a minute and more. Remember a Bren, which weighs ten and a half kilos, can't do more than eighty shots a minute. You let go of the grip and the gun stops. It cools in the air, look.'

'Don't shoot, Dr Lamberti.'

He would gladly have fired the gun, very gladly: there was never any lack of targets. Instead of which he carefully dismantled the gun and put it back in place, almost the way he had found it, but without trying to hide the fact that he had handled it, he didn't see any point in hiding that. He looked at his greasy hands, and went into the little bathroom. 'Mascaranti, get out the coffee and the percolator and make us a bit of coffee.' Mascaranti liked coffee and was good at making it. It took Duca some time to wash his hands clean, he had to use the bathroom tile detergent, and there were still marks on his fingers, then, with the thunder pealing convulsively outside, he went into the kitchen, sat down in the little corner where he had done the crosswords with Mascaranti while the girl had slept, and where Mascaranti was now grinding the coffee in a grinder that was not so much old as historic.

'Which grocer did you get this coffee from?' Mascaranti asked as he ground the coffee. 'I'll go and shut him down.'

'From your boss Superintendent Carrua's grocer.' Another unpleasant aspect of his situation as a former doctor, currently unemployed: Carrua's suppliers, from the grocer to the butcher, were also his. Lorenza, when she was in Milan, didn't have to do anything except make a phone call and place an order. What should he call that? A loan, a gesture of friendship, charity? He and Lorenza were content to place their orders, without calling it anything.

'Superintendent Carrua knows about police matters, and nothing about anything else,' Mascaranti said didactically.

For a while the thunder was muffled and distant, the hurricane was subsiding. In the near-silence the grinder rasped domestically, good-naturedly, reminiscent of the kitchens of long ago, the ones with fireplaces. Duca slumped onto the chair and stared at the percolator on the stove, the livid, motionless little flame, a substitute for the brilliant, burning, reddish, dancing flames of a fireplace.

'Let's assume a small part of what the girl told us is true,' he said, still staring at his imaginary fireplace, the silence growing around them, because the storm, the hurricane, was almost over.

Mascaranti stood up with the grinder in his hand. 'I've

gone mad. I put the percolator on without any coffee in it.'
He shook his head, turned off the gas, and waited for the
percolator to cool down a bit.

'Let's assume a small part of what the girl told us is
true,' Duca repeated.

'Yes,' Mascaranti said.

'She said, if she was telling the truth, that one of her
fiancé's two shops in Milan is near here, in the Via Plinio,
and she walked here tonight.'

Mascaranti emptied the percolator, unscrewed it, put
the coffee in the filter, screwed it up again, relit the gas
and put the percolator over the little flame. 'That may well
be true.'

'Let's assume it is. She arrived here with the case.
Which means she had the case with her when she finished
work, she left the shop with it and came here.'

'That's possible,' Mascaranti said, 'but she could also
have left the shop without the case and gone to pick it up
from somewhere where it had been left.'

No, he thought, we have to use Occam's razor,[5] we have
to be economical with our hypotheses, and the right hy-
pothesis was the most economical. 'I don't think that's very
likely. First of all, this other place where she may have left
the case would have to have been somewhere between the
shop and here. Then it would have had to be a place she
could trust, you don't leave a case like this in a bar or in the
apartment of some casual acquaintance. And it'd be odd if
she found a place like that halfway between the butcher's
shop and here.'

Mascaranti nodded, his eyes still on the percolator. 'But
if she had the case with her in the shop, then her fiancé, the
butcher, must know what it is, because it's unlikely she'd be
able to keep a case like that hidden from her fiancé.'

'That's what I was thinking,' Duca said. 'It isn't certain but it's very likely. A woman is quite capable of hiding her lover's photograph in her husband's wallet if she has to, but if she can she'd rather avoid it. So let's assume she has the case with her in the shop, and that her fiancé knows it's there.' He opened the window because the storm was over, it was only raining now. He breathed in the damp air of concrete and rubbish from the courtyard, then sat down again. 'And let's also assume that her fiancé, the butcher, knows what's in the case.' He looked at the gas flame, half closed his eyes, thinking of the sparks rising, long ago, through the hoods of fireplaces, and imagining that those sparks were rising now from the little gas flame. 'In fact, let's assume that he was the one who gave the girl the case, in other words, that the butcher gave his fiancée a submachine gun to bring here. Nobody would ever think a girl like that was carrying a submachine gun. Then the case is deposited here, in the apartment of an honest if censured professional, and at a suitable time someone comes to pick it up.'

Mascaranti continued to nod, then stopped in order to flip over the percolator. Then he started nodding again as he went to fetch the cups and the sugar bowl.

Then Duca said, 'Mascaranti, you heard what the girl said before?'

'Yes, I heard, but I didn't see,' Mascaranti said, smiling ambiguously.

'The girl said her fiancé made lots of money, hundreds of millions even, with the meat he brought in to his shop in Milan without paying duty.' Sadly, the gas had been switched off, and the flame was gone. 'I don't think you can make hundreds of millions cheating on duty,' he continued patiently. 'Do you?'

'Not really,' Mascaranti said, pouring the coffee.

'But do you think you could make that much money by importing guns like the one in that case?'

Mascaranti nodded and handed him the cup of coffee and then the sugar bowl.

'And do you think these are weapons of war?' He put in the sugar, stirred it, and waited for the reply.

Mascaranti put in the sugar and stirred it, and as he was stirring it, sitting there beside him, with the alarm clock ticking in the rainy night and the second hand in the shape of a hen swaying with every tick, he pondered unhurriedly. 'No,' he said. He sipped a little of the coffee and nodded to indicate that it was good. 'I mean, even a rolling pin for making pasta could be a weapon of war, but you couldn't mount a real attack with that kind of gun, at most some kind of commando action.'

'Or something similar, like a robbery,' Duca said. He tasted the coffee. 'It's good like this, it shouldn't be too strong at night.' He stood up and went and opened all the other windows in the apartment. In Lorenza's bedroom, the lid of the steriliser in which Sara's dummies were left to soak was off. Every night he saw the lid was off and every night he forgot to put it on, and Lorenza had been away for now ten days now. How embarrassing! He took the lid and put it on the steriliser, then looked for the cigarettes he had in the pocket of his jacket which was hanging in the hall, the plain national brand, not for export, and went back into the kitchen. Mascaranti was carefully washing the cups.

'Or else it could be a sample,' Duca said, sitting down behind him. 'If someone's looking to buy wholesale, you open the case and show him the sample, explain that it's the latest model, and sell it at a reasonable price.'

Mascaranti dried his hands on the tea towel hanging next to the sink. 'So we're dealing with middle men in the arms trade.'

'Maybe,' he said, simultaneously shaking his head, 'maybe, but that's not the heart of the matter.'

Then the telephone rang. He stood up and went into the hall. It was Sergeant Morini. He listened to his story, and it didn't even take long to listen to, because Morini was as laconic as Tacitus and the couple's terrible death – blinded by headlights, riddled with machine gun fire, driven so mad that they threw themselves in the canal – became, in Morini's description, terse, formal, official, which made the story even more chilling. When the call was over, Duca stood there looking at the telephone, and at the wall, and gave a shudder of disgust.

9

After the storm, the sky over Milan, because Milan does have a sky, became even bluer than the sky over the Plateau Rosa,[6] and beyond the buildings, from the roof terraces, the snow-covered mountains were clearly visible. The man at the petrol station in the Piazza della Repubblica, where Mascaranti had stopped, was wearing sky blue overalls. He was keen, he didn't read the newspapers and didn't know anything, every night in Milan a number of people die, more than during the day, and for the most diverse reasons, from bronchial pneumonia to a machine gun slaying in the Ripa Ticinese, and he couldn't mourn them all, and besides, not all of them were worth mourning. Nobody had ever tried to rob his petrol station, and so his world had a normal, liveable, even happy dimension. Duca Lamberti looked at the meter on the petrol pump, the triumphant sun, the vivid spring green of the geometrical little lawns in the Piazza. At this very moment, the girl in the red dress coat was in the morgue, without her coat, and in another cold chamber was her unfortunate companion, and these images had no meaning in a normal, liveable world like that of the man in the petrol station.

'I'm just popping over to Ricci's pastry shop,' he said to Mascaranti, and he crossed the Via Ferdinando di Savoia, obeying the traffic lights, went in under the arcades of the skyscraper and then into the pastry shop.

The image of the girl lying in the frozen chamber was wiped out by the counters of that venerable temple to confectionery and tea and ice-cream, where half – or all? – of Milan came whenever it could for the ritual of the aperitif, the boxes of pastries that husbands took home to their wives and children on Sundays, and the bottles of French, Greek, German and Spanish wine displayed, slightly tilted, in a window, liquid delights that were hard to fathom if your palate was accustomed to table wines.

'Police.' He flashed an ID, which was actually Mascaranti's.

The polite, well-built man looked at him uncertainly through his glasses, held his arm out, made a kind of bow and led him towards the back of the shop.

'Are you the owner?' Duca asked him. He was being excessively meticulous: after all, even he came here every now and again, and he recognised the man.

'Yes, I am.'

'I need some information. I'd like to know if a wedding cake was ordered here.'

'We get lots of orders for wedding cakes.' Through his glasses the man was looking at Duca without either fear or curiosity, but with refinement, a gentleman looking at another gentleman.

'This is a wedding cake that was supposed to be sent to a little village near Milan.'

'I'd have to look at the order slips,' the gentleman said, his expression indicating that he was starting to get a little irritated. 'Do you know who ordered it?'

'No, the cake was supposed to be sent to Romano Banco, in the municipality of Buccinasco, near Corsico. It could have been ordered by anybody.'

These geographical indications were a bit excessive,

and the owner of the pastry shop continued to look at him coolly through his glasses, without saying anything.

'I'm told it was a cake that cost two hundred thousand lire.'

The expression behind the glasses was now one of incredulity. 'Well, they might make a cake like that for the Queen of England.'

Duca smiled: he liked this man, whose behaviour could not be faulted. 'Maybe they were exaggerating. Let's say a hundred thousand.'

'As I said, we have to look at the order slips.'

They looked, and they found the slip for the cake, which was in fact a cake for thirty-five thousand lire, because the girl who was now in a cold chamber in the morgue had had, when she was alive, a childlike tendency to exaggerate, which was how thirty-five had become two hundred, and the cake, which didn't even weigh ten kilos, had been taken, three days earlier, in a Ricci's delivery van, to Trattoria dei Gigli in the Via dei Gigli in Romano Banco, in the municipality of Buccinasco, and the cake had been paid for in advance by cheque, as was shown on the slip, a Bank of America and Italy cheque, number 1180 398, and it had been ordered by someone genuinely Milanese, at least to judge by the name, Ulrico Brambilla, who would have been the bridegroom if there had actually been a wedding, and who owned butcher's shops in Milan, Romano Banco and Ca' Tarino.

Duca went back to his car and sat down next to Mascaranti, who was at the wheel. 'The cake was ordered and sent.' He would have liked to know what had happened to the cake, however modest, only thirty-five thousand instead of two hundred, it must have been a good solid cake of about ten kilos, only one one-hectogram slice per guest, with a hundred guests to eat it. But the wedding had not taken place.

'Let's go to Romano Banco,' he said to Mascaranti. 'We can go by way of Inverigo.' It was a poor attempt at humour, but Mascaranti understood: to get to Romano Banco you don't go by way of Inverigo because it's in the opposite direction, but it was ten days since Duca had last seen his sister, ten days since he had last seen little Sara, ten days since he had last seen Livia with the M-shaped and W-shaped scars all over her face.

The journey to the Villa Auseri was like advancing directly into the sun.

'Is this it?' Mascaranti asked.

Yes, this was it: Lorenza was already behind the gate, holding her child by the hand. They were fine, they were lovely, the girl's cheeks and bottom were firm, and Lorenza's ponytail looked good against the light green hilly background of the Brianza.

'Livia's stayed in her room,' Lorenza said.

It was the least she could do: someone with seventy-seven scars on her face, at the corners of her eyes, the corners of her lips and on either side of her nose, couldn't do much else besides stay in her room, even after all the plastic surgery. With Sara in his arms, he crossed the garden of the villa, more aristocratic in style than most in the Brianza, and entered the main room.

'Where are you taking me, uncle?'

Because he was, after all, an uncle. 'We're going to find Signorina Livia.' He climbed the stairs which led to the upper floor, he knew that Livia had seen him from the window and was waiting for him.

'I want to play with Signorina Livia,' Sara said, 'but she doesn't want to.'

'Signorina Livia's a bit tired,' he said. The second door on the right along the corridor opened and Livia said, 'This is all very sudden.'

'I've only got a minute,' he said, standing there with Sara in his arms, looked closely at Livia: seventy-seven scars don't disappear in ten days, or even in ten months, or ten years.

'It's not good, is it?' she said. She meant: *my face isn't good.*

He said, kindly but brutally, 'No.' Livia Ussaro preferred the truth to a fool's paradise, even if the truth cut like a guillotine, and she even smiled as if he had told her that she was really beautiful.

'Leave me the child and go and see your sister,' she said, smiling: the plastic surgeon had done a good job, Livia could actually smile, you might think she had only had a slight case of smallpox.

'All right,' he said. He put the child down. 'Go and play with the Signorina.' He took one step forward. 'I have a job to finish, I hope to finish it soon, then we can go to the sea, the doctors said the sea will do you good.' Not even the owner of all the oceans of the world, the God of the seas, the creator of the waters, could ever erase those seventy-seven scars, he knew that.

'I'm fine here too, don't worry.' She took the child, led her into her room, and immediately closed the door.

He couldn't do anything, he couldn't tear limb from limb the person who had embroidered that monstrous tracery of scars on Livia Ussaro's face, the law doesn't allow you to tear anyone limb from limb, it doesn't permit personal vengeance. He descended the pleasant staircase of the pleasant villa, and put an arm round Lorenza's shoulders.

'Why don't you stay here, what work do you have?'

He looked at her tenderly, he didn't want her to see all

the hatred seething away inside him. 'It's nothing important,' he lied, 'but they may put me back on the register, and I have to see some people, you know, I have to explain what happened.' It was Lorenza's greatest wish that he should be a doctor again, but he was much less keen on the idea. Pierced by a ray of sunlight falling radiantly over the hollow of Lake Segrino, he got back in the car, and through the window stroked Lorenza's face. 'Better go a bit faster,' he said to Mascaranti, 'we're late.'

10

Midday isn't the best time to cross Milan by car, there may not even be a best time, and people actually avoid crossing it if they can. Mascaranti started counting the traffic lights in the Viale Fulvio Testi and by the time he got to the Porta Ticinese there had been thirty-two. As in a slow-moving children's carousel they did a half circle around the Piazzale 24 Maggio in a line of cars four or five deep, and had time to admire the wet dock of the port of Milan. Some said it was the fifth largest port in Europe in terms of the weight of goods that passed through it, which was mostly sand and stones: that might well be so, he thought. 'Let's take the right bank,' he said to Mascaranti, meaning the right bank of the Alzaia Naviglio Grande, the one that couple had taken, the girl and Silvano, the late couple, just three days earlier, in the storm. Now there was sun, and mountain air. They immediately identified the spot where it had happened: the asphalt still showed the tracks of the breakdown lorry that had fished out the car, and Mascaranti, having got out, saw immediately on the wall of the house the chipped plaster from where the bullets had passed close to it. Duca looked at the water of the canal. Why had Silvano and the girl taken this narrow road? If they had taken the left bank, where the road was wider, they would have been able to escape that deadly machine-gun attack. And how on earth did the people who had fired at them know they would be going along the right bank? Whoever it was must have known the time, too. They seemed to have known a lot of things.

He got back into the car and they continued on their way towards Romano Banco, driving slowly because he wanted to get there no earlier than half past one, when Ulrico Brambilla the butcher would probably have finished eating, he didn't want to disturb him over lunch. When they got to Corsico, they crossed the bridge onto the other bank, then drove through Corsico. A sign at the end of the Via Dante said that Romano Banco was on the left. The broad tarred road went partly between fields and partly between houses, both small houses and attempts at skyscrapers, then another sign indicated that they were entering Romano Banco and that it was forbidden to sound motor horns.

'The church, go to the church.'

Mascaranti drove towards the little bell tower through broad streets of scattered houses.

Yes, Duca thought, he must really have ordered a lorry full of carnations from Sanremo: next to the little church with its unremarkable little bell tower, so dull and dreary as to be quite touching, you could still smell the carnations, the sickly scent of carnations still seemed to hover over the old houses around the church. Without even getting out of the car, they turned onto the main street. After asking a couple of passers-by, they found the house of Signor Ulrico Brambilla, a small one-storey villa with a few centimetres of garden in front, which wasn't really a garden, just a strip of ground with patches of green.

'Signor Brambilla, please.'

The thin, black-clad woman, who was not old – there was still a vestige of femininity in her sallow face, her blue-circled eyes with wrinkles at the corners – said in an anxious voice, 'He isn't here, he's left.'

Ah, so he had already left.

'Where did he go? I'm a friend of Silvano's.' There were some people he didn't like having as friends, but they had been friends in a way, hadn't they? Between them they had money matters, girls to be 'cured', and even submachine guns: that was a kind of friendship.

The name Silvano had the effect on the woman he had hoped it would, she turned pale and looked at him, then at Mascaranti, and moved aside to let them in. As soon as they entered, they saw it was a simple rustic house: with all his millions, Ulrico Brambilla had left the house as plain as it must have been when he had bought it, he who bought everything, who had bought half of Ca' Tarino, both houses and land.

'I don't know where he went,' she said. She looked scared: the name Silvano seemed to have scared her.

The first room they came to was a combined living room and dining room, where they probably never ate, they almost certainly ate in the kitchen. There was a rectangular table in the middle, chairs on either side of the table, a hand-embroidered centrepiece in the middle of the table, and there was also a sideboard and a dresser and a wall clock and a floor of shiny red tiles and a stiff little sofa, a kind of long chair for three people, on which they sat without being invited, while the woman in her black peasant dress, almost a regional costume, but with a low neckline, looked at them.

'I have to talk to Ulrico,' he said, in the pleasant, somnolent gloom of the dining room: Ulrico must be a man with his head screwed on, he hadn't employed either an architect or an interior decorator. Not having ever seen him, Duca felt like laughing when he called him Ulrico. 'It's about a serious matter.'

This, too, had an effect on the woman. She couldn't have

been fifty yet, when she was younger she must have been what a Milanese would have called a handsome figure of a girl. But a kind of anger in her overcame the effect his words had had, and she said, 'More serious than what's happened? He was supposed to get married, instead of which his fiancée drowns in a ditch, it was such a blow I thought he'd end up in the cemetery, too. Anyway he left, I even told him to go away for a while.'

'And who are you?' Duca asked her impudently, wickedly.

'I'm his assistant,' she said, 'his assistant in the butcher's shops, here and in Ca' Tarino.' Then she insisted on adding, 'The cashier,' which made her sound more important.

That was notable – in fact, it was what in texts on arithmetic is defined as a notable product. Ulrico had a younger assistant, something of a nymphomaniac, in his shops in Milan, and a mature assistant for his shops outside Milan.

'I also keep house for him,' she said proudly, satisfied she had got them to understand what she wanted them to understand.

She kept it very well, Duca thought: the red floor tiles were well polished, not unpleasantly reflective, they were old-fashioned, warmly intimate, no dust, no smells, nothing out of place, if she kept Ulrico as neat and tidy as this, Ulrico was a lucky man.

'I have to talk to Ulrico,' he said again, in an even tone, neither threatening nor insistent. 'It's very important.'

She sat down, moving one of the four chairs at the table, and suddenly a ray of sunlight came through the plain curtains at the half-open window, hit the shiny surface of the table, although not strongly, and was reflected on her face, bringing out the circles under her eyes, the little wrinkles, the tiredness of her skin. Proudly, she did not move from that reflection, she scorned it, haughtily exposed herself to it in all her decay. 'I don't know where he's gone.'

It was an interesting conversation: he kept saying that he wanted to talk to Ulrico, and she kept saying that she didn't know where he'd gone. So he decided to raise the stakes. 'Silvano left me something, Ulrico knows what it is.'

She fell into his little trap, and her face stiffened in the reflection. 'I don't know anything about that.'

I don't know anything means a lot of things. It means that you know something, but you don't want to say it, want to make it seem in fact as if you don't know anything. How crafty some people are! But now he knew that she knew.

'I can't keep that thing in my home,' he said to her, but politely. He was starting to feel a bit embarrassed: despite everything, her age, her experience, her peasant guile, she still retained, as so many women do, a genuine innocence. And indeed she now put her other foot in the trap. 'He's supposed to be phoning me today, I'll tell him.'

This was important. Ulrico Brambilla would be phoning, whether or not the woman knew where Ulrico was, he would be phoning. She probably didn't know, he probably hadn't told her where he was going, and he might not even be staying too long in one place. Did that mean he was running away? If so, why? There are a lot of reasons to run away, one of them being grief: if your fiancée ends up in a ditch, as the woman in black had put it, downgrading the Naviglio, you might well close up your four butcher's shops – although Carrua was of the opinion that Brambilla had more, registered in other names, obviously – and go and mourn somewhere far from other people. But maybe Brambilla hadn't run away for such a nice reason. You can also run away because you're afraid. Afraid of someone.

'Yes, do tell him,' Duca said, still sitting, bolt upright,

on the little dark green sofa, next to Mascaranti. 'We'll stay here, and when he phones tell him we need to talk to him, and that we have to hand that thing over to him.'

She stood up. 'This isn't a station waiting room,' she said. She spoke good Italian, with the barest touch of a local intonation, in fact, that was the extraordinary thing, she wasn't an intellectual, most definitely not, but she was something better, she was intelligent. Her eyes were tired, they suggested liver problems and a difficult menopause, but there was an intelligent look to them. And as she was a woman, her intelligence drove her to be domineering. 'Get out,' she said with sudden anger. 'If you have something to tell Signor Brambilla, write to him.'

Why not? We can write him a postcard. Duca didn't like either what the woman said or the way she said it, and he stood up and moved around the table until he stood facing her. 'All right, we'll go,' he said, looking straight at her, his eyes saying, *All right, if that's the way you want it, it's your funeral.* 'Let's go,' he said to Mascaranti.

But when they got to the door, she stopped them, remorsefully. 'If you want to wait ...' Despite her sallow complexion, her face turned slightly pink. 'I only said that because you might have a long wait, I don't know when he's going to phone.'

He did not even look at her. 'Too bad for him,' he said. He asked Mascaranti for a piece of paper and a pen, wrote down his name and address and telephone number as clearly as he could and gave it to the woman. 'If he's interested, he can write to me or come and see me.' They left the house, aware that she was watching them through the half-open door and was making a note of the car, might even be taking down the licence number. Let her. In fact, it was what they wanted.

'Let's go home.'

That meant crossing the city again, but everything has an end, even a journey from Romano Banco to the Piazza Leonardo da Vinci. And the case was still in his apartment, still dark green, still with the metal corners that made it look like a trunk. As soon as they got inside they opened it, they didn't trust anything any more, they were on the scent of a big gang and they didn't want to lose the opportunity to meet them, to have a sitdown, wasn't that what they called it? Eye to eye. And an eye for an eye, and seventy-seven scars for seventy-seven scars.

'It's like a rose,' he said to Mascaranti, crouching by the case as it lay open on the floor. 'Sooner or later a bee will come buzzing around it.' He wiped his hands on the wood filings. 'And while we wait, let's go back to the beginning and take out all the files.'

PART TWO

The principle of the bone saw is very simple: it is a serrated steel band wound around two spools, almost like a film projector. Part of the band remains exposed for a length of thirty or forty centimetres, and when a bone is pushed against the serrated edge of the band as it rotates at high speed, the bone is neatly severed. It is also used to carve the bones of large Florentine chops, which are then cut further with a little hatchet, or in any situation where a butcher needs to divide a bone into two or three pieces.

1

There were four files, and files can be dull and even repulsive things, especially after you've looked through them, document by document, three or four times, or five, especially on a spring day like today, a day when Milan had never been so beautiful, soft blades of sunlight cutting gently and incredibly through all the rooms in the apartment, showing up the dust, the dirty windowpanes, the lost sheen of the brass door handles. But Duca and Mascaranti kept their heads bowed over the kitchen table and those fine, thick, pale brown files.

Technically, there had been three falls into the water. The first went back almost four years. A young couple, a woman of twenty-four named Michela Vasorelli and a man of twenty-nine named Gianpietro Ghislesi, plunged into the Lambro, at the Conca Fallata, just after the Cascina Sant'Ambrogio. A murky episode, isn't it, Superintendent Carrua? Isn't it, Sgt Mascaranti? Isn't it, Lady Justice? The owner of the car, Attorney Turiddu Sompani, who was with them, was arrested, having got out of the car and let young Ghislesi drive even though a) he didn't have a licence, b) he was completely drunk, and c) he was shouting out that he wanted to drive across the river. Many witnesses had heard the girl who was with him scream, and had tried in vain to prevent him. Attorney Turiddu Sompani had been unfortunate and had come up against a tough young examining magistrate who dragged him to court, accusing him of culpable double homicide, and dropping major hints that it was not culpable but voluntary. Unfortunately, they were unable to give him more than two and a half years.

Then almost four years had passed and there had been a second fall. Turiddu Sompani, who had not been out of prison for even a year, and an old friend of his, Adele Terrini, fell into the Alzaia Naviglio Pavese two weeks ago. Here, his impatience with repetitions started to irritate Duca, and the irritation reached its height with the third fall. A fine-looking figure of a man named Silvano Solvere, and a lady friend of his, Giovanna Marelli, in black stockings and a red dress coat, were machine-gunned on the road running alongside the Alzaia Naviglio Grande and ended up falling into the canal, where they drowned inside their car. The incident had been witnessed by Sergeant Morini's team, so there were no doubts about any of the details, and there were plenty of details right there in one of the thick files. He reread them all, one by one, and his irritation became unbearable. The most irritating aspect was that the three events were linked by one person: Turiddu Sompani. The first couple had gone into the Lambro while they were out with Attorney Sompani, then Sompani himself had gone into the Alzaia Naviglio Pavese with a lady companion of his, and finally the third couple were friends of Sompani's, the young man in the grey cardigan even introducing himself to Duca by saying that he had been sent by Turiddu Sompani.

It was also irritating that the protagonists of these three incidents were all such dubious figures. Of the first couple, the woman, Michela Vasorelli, had been, as was clearly stated in her file, a prostitute, while the man, Gianpietro Ghislesi, was officially unemployed, and unofficially a pimp, not very unofficially because he had been arrested twice for pimping, but thanks to Attorney Sompani had got off scot free.

The second couple had the thickest file of all. The notes on these two amounted to a kind of sacrilegious bible of immorality. First, because ladies always have to come first, there was Adele Terrini. One irritating detail was that Adele Terrini, a young lady in her fifties, had been born in Ca' Tarino, which coincidentally – though he didn't believe in coincidences, supposing that he believed in anything – was also the birthplace of the other young lady, the one on whom he had performed a hymenoplasty and who had died, or rather, been killed only a few days ago. Life really was amazing: two women born in Ca' Tarino, one more than twenty years before the other, but both, within little more than a week, drowned in their cars.

But the more obscure, more repulsive member of this second couple was the man, Turiddu Sompani. The obscurities started with his name, especially his Christian name, Turiddu, because Turiddu is a Sicilian diminutive, and there was no reason in the world why he should be called Turiddu, having never had anything to do with Sicily. Even the surname wasn't the correct one. Turiddu Sompani had made his appearance in Italy after September 1943 and all his documents had been issued by Republican Fascist authorities, or by the Germans. In one of the files there were the photocopies of many documents, including the certificate granting of Italian citizenship to Jean Saintpouin, with the name Turiddu Sompani in brackets, born in Vannes, Brittany on July 12, 1905. Why a Frenchman, a Breton, should be called Turiddu, why he had taken Italian citizenship at such an unusual time as September 1943,[7] was unclear, but there were other documents that dispersed some of the thick clouds surrounding this Lawrence of Lombardy: photocopies of a Fascist Party membership card, then a photograph of Sompani, taken in the mountains, bearded and with a handkerchief around his neck like a partisan, a small card issued by the SS command in Milan, a universal safe conduct – with that card nobody could stop him, let alone search him – issued, as could be seen from the stamp, by *Ober* something or other, at the Hotel Regina in Milan in June 1944. There was also – just to cover every eventuality – a letter from the Curia thanking their devout friend Turiddu Sompani for his intervention on behalf of political prisoners.

At this point, Mascaranti muttered through his laughter, 'All he needed was a card from the synagogue and a letter from Eisenhower, and he would have been protected on all sides.'

But the most touching document was a small receipt from the University of Pavia, which indicated that Jean Saintpouin (*Turiddu Sompani*) had paid all his university fees and had graduated in law. Then there was the most menacing document: the weapons permit. The photocopies had been made, with great meticulousness, by the men in Morini's team, and showed all the pages of the little book, which was a kind of historical gallery of stamps and visas. Issued by police headquarters in Milan at the end of 1943, the permit had then been certified by the Fascists, then by the Wehrmacht, on a special sheet stuck to the book, with a large swastika stamped on it, which also bore, in thick ink and Gothic writing, an authorisation by the SS command, signed by the usual *Ober* whatever. As if that was not enough, there was also another sheet of paper, unstamped, from the Resistance Council, dated November 1944, authorising the person in question to carry arms, which meant that if he'd wanted he could have gone around with a cannon, because he had permission from the partisans. And so it went on: on June 11, 1945, the Allied command in Milan authorised Turiddu Sompani to *carry on his person arms such as revolvers, pistols and others, for the purpose of self-defence*: this was how it was expressed by the interpreters and translators of the period, chosen from among former dishwashers from Wyoming who claimed to speak Italian and former lemonade vendors from the Via Caracciolo in Naples who said they could speak English.

All these dry, repulsive documents already said quite a lot about the man, but there were others that were more subtly indicative: the police may be empirical but they are also highly analytical and have a fearsome memory. Of this Breton who had been naturalised as an Italian for reasons obscured by the chaos of war, and who had suddenly emerged from that chaos, the police had religiously conserved a number of indelible descriptions. In 1948, just before the elections, a sizeable quantity of arms had been found in his house, notably anti-tank grenades, old-fashioned rifles, and four dozen Lugers. In his defence he stated that these arms had been given to him by the partisans and that he was about to hand them in to the authorities: an impudent excuse, but the authorities were too weak to do anything but accept it. There were notes about his sending girls to North Africa; he had defended two married couples from Chiasso who had been accused of smuggling medicines containing drugs, had got them acquitted, then had himself been denounced for being involved in the same smuggling operation but had got off due to insufficient evidence. There was a bit of everything. In his legal practice, if it could be called that, a fifteen-year-old boy had worked as a messenger, and the boy's mother had gone to the local police and stated that the lawyer was corrupting her son, with the help of his mistress, Adele Terrini. The accusation was contemptuously rejected, and the local chief inspector was humiliated by the statement of an angelic Emilian prelate who personally vouched for Attorney Turiddu Sompani's moral rectitude. In addition to pederasty, drugs, and the exporting of prostitutes, there was also violence against women. His own mistress, Adele Terrini, had been admitted to hospital with an unusual wound: the bone in her right leg, commonly called the shinbone, and more officially the tibia, had been broken almost in half, not to say shattered. Signora Terrini had refused to say what had happened, but the police, being naturally suspicious people, thought she had been kicked by her friend Turiddu Sompani. On another occasion, in a café, screaming drunkenly, he had undressed a humble prostitute who had not greeted him with the due respect, and the only reason he hadn't stripped her completely naked was that the waiters and the other customers had stopped him. Having been taken to the police station, he had switched from accused to accuser and claimed that the poor, innocent prostitute had stolen a cigarette lighter he had left for a moment on one of the tables in the café. Once, on a train, he had been found in the toilet with a fourteen-year-old girl who was on her way to Milan to study with the Northern Railways. He had saved his skin this time too: the girl's father, to avoid scandal in the newspapers, pretended to believe Attorney Sompani, who declared that he had gone to the toilet, had found the door left open, and as soon as he had seen the girl had turned to walk away, only it was at that exact moment that a soldier had appeared and stupidly started shouting at him: *You dirty pig!*

According to one small but in its way significant document, Attorney Turiddu Sompani claimed only a million lire in taxable income and, apart from that, it was not clear what he lived on, clearly not on the income from his work, since a search in his office had established that he had last handled an actual case in 1962. And this was the man who, together with his companion Adele Terrini, had at last left the world stage by drowning in the Alzaia Naviglio Pavese.

And then there was the other drowned couple, a couple Duca knew personally, having had the honour of a visit from Silvano Solvere, then another from the woman he loved, Giovanna Marelli. There were some interesting things in the files about both of them. Silvano Solvere had no criminal record, but police informers had several times suggested that he was involved, as some kind of organiser, in various robberies: he had even been picked up at the time of the robbery in the Via Montenapoleone, and then released for lack of evidence. He was a salesman for one of the biggest detergent companies and, apart from these hints from the police informers – including his being a pimp, according to the notes – there was nothing against him.

There wasn't much about his lady friend, either, although what little there was in the file was fairly significant. Born in Ca' Tarino, when she was twelve her parents had been requested by the Carabinieri to keep a closer watch on their daughter, who seemed to be excessively friendly, in a not disinterested way, with a number of elderly gentlemen in the area. Subsequent to this appeal by the Carabinieri, the father of the twelve-year-old Giovanna Marelli had apparently beaten his daughter so badly that she had run away, it was believed that she had worked clandestinely as a maid in Milan, although that was doubtful, but in any case she hadn't put in another appearance in Ca' Tarino until she was twenty, for her mother's funeral. Picked up in Milan one evening and subjected to a medical examination, she had been found to be suffering from gonorrhoea. Later, the Carabinieri in Buccinasco recorded that she had been hired by Signor Ulrico Brambilla for his butcher's shop in Milan. But what did the authorities, what did the law know about her sinister links with the sinister Silvano Solvere?

It was all so nasty as to be quite nauseating. 'The usual settling of accounts,' Carrua had said, almost throwing the files at him. 'Take this stuff and study it, and you'll see what it amounts to, some kind of stupid feud. Turiddu receives orders to execute that couple, Vasorelli and Ghislesi, for something or other that they've done, and he drowns them in the Lambro, but the couple must have had friends, they can't do anything to Turiddu while he's in prison, but after he's been out for a while they throw him in the water as well, along with his lady friend. Ah, say the others, Turiddu's friends, you killed our Turiddu. In that case, we'll kill your Silvano and *his* lady friend. And what do you think will happen now? I'll tell you. Someone will say: Oh, so you killed our Silvano and his lady friend? Then we're going to kill somebody or other. And you know what I say? I say, let them carry on. Why should I go to the bother of tracking them down and arresting them when all they'll get, thanks to their powerful masters, is a six-month suspended sentence, whereas if I let them carry on they'll kill each other? Let them get on with it, the Naviglios, the Lambros, the ditches, the Conca Fallatas are all theirs, in other words, long live the feud!' He hadn't laughed, that would have been vulgar and he hated vulgarity, he had simply smiled at his scurrilous witticisms. 'Are they rival gangs?' Duca had asked.

'I never said anything about rival gangs,' Carrua had said, irritably. 'You're an intelligent man, you should have realised we're not dealing with rival gangs, but deviant individuals. In a big gang, people do all right, they make a lot of money, but some are tempted to set up for themselves, to do a bit of work outside the syndicate. It's a suicidal temptation, because a boss can't allow any kind of deviation, and when it comes to punishment he has no truck with half measures, his penal code has only one article in it: *Kill them.* It's the shortest code in the world and its only article doesn't allow for objections. So why should I bother about them? You deal with it, you can be a one-man crime squad if you like. If you succeed, I'll get you a job here, that's what you want, isn't it? But if you do succeed, what will the gang do to you? Which canal would you prefer to drown in? Well, you've chosen your path, you're a visionary like your father and I can't change you, bring me some of the gentlemen and ladies who make up this fine community and I'll reward you well.'

He needed a good, solid, concrete reward, so he would bring Carrua all the gentlemen and ladies he could. It shouldn't even be too much of an effort, all he had to do was stay here and wait. Of course, waiting could sometimes be more of a bother than running around, yelling, doing things, but he was capable of anything, even of waiting. He got up from the kitchen table, nauseated by all those documents, and went into the hall. The only thing he was happy about was that the green case was still there in the hall, he had put it where it could be seen by anyone, even if they were just standing in the doorway, they wouldn't even need to come in. Beautiful case from far away and which would like to go further still, stay here and we'll see who comes looking for you, I really need to know who's looking for you.

2

On 8 May, Mother's Day, a very serious-looking young lady appeared, obviously honest, obviously very Milanese, even though she spoke standard Italian, dressed in rather good taste, in a dark green tailored suit, with brown hair which went well with the suit, and a dark brown handbag just like her hair. She immediately told him, with admirable Milanese honesty, that she was pregnant, she had had a urine test and unfortunately there was no doubt, and she also told him that she was unmarried, and that she did not want the baby. Then, to encourage him, she told him that she was the owner of a perfume shop, right here, in the Via Plinio area and that a girl, Signorina Marelli – did he know her? – had told her that he was a good doctor who could help a woman in difficulty.

Good. She might, Duca thought, have had the delicacy to come to him on a day other than Mother's Day. But these were subtleties. 'Do you mean Signorina Marelli, the assistant from the butcher's shop?'

'Yes,' she said, happily. She must have been close to thirty-five, she wasn't alluring in any way, but someone, perhaps out of politeness, had made her pregnant.

'Did you know that Signorina Marelli is dead?' he said, but only out of idle curiosity, without even looking at her, looking rather at the beautiful green light that came from the window, like the light reflected off a pine grove high in the mountains – and yet, incredibly, they were in Milan.

'Oh, yes, I do know, poor thing, they've even closed the

butcher's shop, that's why it came into my mind,' she said, unaware of her own immorality. 'As soon as I read the newspaper I thought: if only I could find that doctor.'

'Why, did Signorina Marelli give you my name?'

'No, all she said was, my doctor in the Piazza Leonardo da Vinci, and you're the only doctor here. I was lucky to find you so quickly.'

Yes, very lucky. He remained silent, looking at her every now and again, but only briefly, he preferred to look at Mascaranti who was listening out in the hall. In the end, she could hold back no longer.

'My mother is quite elderly, she has a bad heart, if she found out about this, not to mention what people would say ... I have means, you know, you mustn't think I want to take advantage of you, poor Signorina Marelli could tell you if she was alive, the shop is small but I earn enough, otherwise you'd tell the tax people, we women spend without thinking when it comes to creams, lipsticks, nail polish, things you wouldn't believe, there are maids who spend all their wages in my shop, so just name your price, oh, no offence meant, doctor, I'm sorry.'

Her anxiety, long repressed, seemed quite sincere, but he had long ago decided to ignore sincerity and other similar virtues. 'How long had you known Signorina Marelli?' he interrupted her coldly. She had died, had Signorina Marelli, in her red dress coat, and she had died a virgin.

'You know,' she said, intimidated by his angry tone, 'the butcher's shop is there, my shop is here, and Frontini's is there.'

'Frontini's café?'

'The café and pastry shop, yes, I love the panettone there, it's better than all the others, you know. We used to meet there in the morning for a cappuccino and in the afternoon for another cappuccino, and sometimes also for an aperitif, but mostly she came to my shop for nail polish, it was an obsession, she bought nail polish in every colour, though she always left them natural in the end. She once told me she only put on nail polish for the butcher, that the butcher liked painted nails, but only when she was with him, she would paint her nails the oddest colours, sometimes each nail a different colour, but then afterwards she always left them natural. And so we became almost friends, in fact very good friends.'

She was getting confused, because of the way he was looking at her, she didn't know if she had been almost friends or very good friends with the girl from the butcher's shop. 'And did Signorina Marelli tell you why she came to me?'

A few patches of pink appeared on her otherwise wan face. 'I'll be honest with you, you know, she did tell me, not to speak badly of the poor girl, because she's dead, but she also told me a lot of things that took me by surprise.'

'And what did she tell you she came to me for?' He continued to stare at her, hardly taking his eyes off her even for a moment.

'But, doctor, you know.'

'I want you to tell me what Signorina Marelli told you.'

She was uneasy now. 'She told me she was supposed to be getting married to the owner of the butcher's shop, this was something she'd told me before, and she also told me she didn't like the idea because she was in love with someone else, the man who died with her, but that the butcher was an opportunity for her, and that he wanted her to be a virgin, otherwise he wouldn't marry her, she wasn't a virgin and so she'd found a good doctor who would see to everything.'

So he was a good doctor who saw to everything. He

stopped staring at the poor woman and everything inside him smiled. These crooks can do whatever they like, there's always some crazy woman who blabs, who goes around telling tales. 'And what can I do for you?'

'Listen, doctor, if you don't want to do it, tell me, you know. I already told you, this is quite a delicate matter, even for a woman.'

He broke off listening to her and called, 'Mascaranti!' From the hall, where he had been listening religiously, Mascaranti came into the surgery almost softly. 'Mascaranti, please, show the young lady your ID.'

This was unexpected, it wasn't logical to let them know that they were with the police, but he obeyed all the same.

'Have a good look,' Duca said, 'we're with the police. Don't be afraid.' But the woman *was* afraid, he had the impression she might even faint.

'But aren't you a doctor?' She was breathing in little gasps, as if the air was lead. 'The caretaker told me you're a doctor.'

'Calm down,' he yelled to stop her fainting. 'I am a doctor, or I was a doctor. But right now you have to help the police.'

Alone, between those two men suddenly revealed as policemen, she turned into a child. 'I have to go back to the shop, it's late, I've left my mother alone, she's elderly, she can't cope.' She got up, holding her handbag clumsily in both hands, her face was green, but it was only the reflection of the spring light coming in through the window.

'Sit down,' he ordered.

Perhaps his voice had been louder and harsher than was strictly necessary, but she gave a start, actually jumped. 'Yes, yes, yes,' she said like a child, 'yes,' and she sat down, and at the same time started crying.

The best way to calm someone who is crying is to give them orders. 'Show me your papers,' Duca said.

'Yes, yes,' she said, crying, and started looking in her handbag. 'All I have is my driving license, but I have my passport at home.'

Duca looked at the licence for a moment (twenty-nine years old, though she looked older: like many Milanese women who work, she overworked and ended up looking like that) then passed it to Mascaranti. As you have to be gentle with women who are expecting, he gave her a little speech: 'You mustn't be afraid, we only want to know something about that girl, you know a lot more than you've told us, and you have to tell the police. For example, go on with that story about the nail polish, it interests me, you said she even painted each nail a different colour, but she didn't go out in the street like that, did she?'

'No, can you imagine?' She had stopped crying. 'It was only for her man.'

'Her fiancé, the owner of the butcher's shop?'

'That's right,' she said, starting to become really involved in the subject. 'She told me about all the things he wanted her to do, except give up her virginity, you know, I realised she wasn't exactly a virgin, from some of the things she said, anyway he liked her to stroke him with her nails painted different colours, that made an impression on me, and other things I really can't repeat, but you know, you can't choose your customers, but I didn't think she was really a bad girl.'

No, whoever said she'd been a bad girl? An instrument is neither good nor bad, it depends on how you use it, you can even choke someone with a rosebud if you push it far enough down his throat. So the butcher, among other things, was a fetishist, a kind of chromatic fetishist: nothing bad about that, we all have our little quirks. But this twenty-nine-year-old woman who looked thirty-five through overwork must know other things. 'And did you ever meet the other man, the one who died with Signorina Marelli?'

She glanced at Mascaranti, who was sitting next to the window, looking like a pensioner writing his memoirs, the story of his life, with that little book in his hand and that horrible pink plastic ballpoint pen between his fingers. She couldn't have imagined that he was taking down everything she said: she didn't have much of an imagination about police matters. 'Signor Silvano?' she said. 'Yes, once.'

'At Frontini's, perhaps?' he suggested.

'Oh, no,' she burst out, surprised at such naivety, 'do you think they wanted to be seen together so close to the butcher's shop, where the assistants would tell the boss everything? No, it was because of a case.'

Suddenly the spring stopped coming in through the window, at least for him and Mascaranti, even though the word she had used was so simple, so bland, that she could not have imagined the effect it caused.

'One evening, leaving the butcher's shop to go home, she came into my shop with a case and asked me if I could keep it until the following morning, when her Silvano would drop by to collect it.'

'And so the next morning, Signor Silvano came to your shop and picked up the case?'

'Yes, he was really a handsome young man, I started to understand why she wasn't so happy about being engaged to the butcher.'

What women understand by *handsome young man* never has anything to do with morality. Not all women, not Livia Ussaro: he needed her, sometimes sharply, but she didn't want to talk to anyone any more, about anything, not even about abstract subjects, not even with him, after all she was a woman, and seventy-seven scars on her face can make a woman a bit depressed. 'And what did he tell you: "I'm Silvano"?' he said, dismissing Livia Ussaro from his mind.

'Something like that, yes, first he asked me if Signorina Giovanna had left a case for him, and I said yes, and then he told me he was Silvano, but even if he hadn't told me, I'd already guessed it was him.'

He was clearly of great interest to women, that fine figure of a man, Silvano Solvere. But it isn't right to speak ill of the dead. 'Mascaranti,' he said, 'get me the photograph of Signor Silvano from the file.'

It wasn't a very good photograph, the one Mascaranti brought, and it might not have been a good idea to show it to a pregnant woman, but apart from the fact that there were no amateur photographers at the morgue, just simple functionaries who captured in all their cold nakedness the corpses who had ended up on a marble slab, the discovery of the truth had precedence over such delicacy. 'Is this Signor Silvano?' It might not even have been a good idea to show a woman a naked man, but this was the only photograph they had of him.

She took a good look at the photograph, obviously the image she had inside her of the handsome young man was better than the one she was looking at on the glossy 18 × 12 black and white photograph without margins, but it was immediately obvious that she had recognised him, even though it took her a while before she said, 'Yes, that's him.'

'Mascaranti, the case,' Duca said, giving Mascaranti the photograph, and after a minute Mascaranti came back into the surgery holding the green case, or small trunk, with the beautiful shiny metal corners. 'Was the case Signorina

Marelli left in your shop, the one Signor Silvano later came to pick up, anything like this, by any chance?'

'Oh my God, it's the same one, I'm sure it is.' She was extremely surprised. 'That's Signor Silvano's sample case, isn't it?'

So the girl in the red dress coat had led her to think the case contained Signor Silvano's detergent samples. That was only natural: she certainly couldn't have told her the truth. Nor did he tell her the truth now. 'Yes, it's a case for detergent samples,' he lied bluntly and gave the case back to Mascaranti.

'How long ago was the case left with you?' he asked after a moment.

'Quite a while ago, at least two months,' she said confidently, Milanese women are confident when it's a matter of dates or figures, 'my mother was still in Nervi because it was too cold here.'

Two months. He looked at the cuffs of his shirt and realised that they were frayed, but you had to use old shirts for as long as you could. The problem of his wardrobe aside, two months earlier Signor Silvano had gone to pick up the case from the shop selling perfumes, cosmetics and so on, but two months earlier the Milanese lawyer Turiddu Sompani, originally from Brittany, was still alive.

'Did you ever see him again after that?'

'No,' she said, 'but the evening before Giovanna died, she left the case with me for a while, yes, for a couple of hours, then came and picked it up again.'

'Now listen.' It was true that it was Mother's Day and she was a mother-to-be, but he had to carry on, at all costs. 'I get the impression she told you quite a lot about her relationship with Signor Silvano.'

She nodded. She seemed to be taking more of an interest now, in the situation, the drama, the adventure: the Milanese sometimes have an unsuspected taste for strong-arm tactics, police methods, interrogations. She liked it, it took her away a moment from her shop, from her mother, from her situation as an unmarried woman absent-mindedly seduced and not even abandoned,[8] but forgotten, mixed up with someone else: her seducer must have wondered every now and again, 'Who was she, that night? Was it that one or was it this one?' And so she stopped crying, she wasn't even afraid any more, she wanted to help, she was the kind of citizen who helps.

'She told you lots of things, even quite delicate things,' Duca said didactically, 'so it's quite likely she told you where she met Signor Silvano.' In an attempt to clarify things he went on, 'She lived in Ca' Tarino, near Corsico, and every evening she had to go back home, it was usually her fiancé, the owner of the butcher's shop, who drove her home. By day she had to be in the butcher's shop, at the cash desk, so maybe she told you when it was that she saw Signor Silvano?'

But she had already understood. 'There were days when the owner of the butcher's shop had to go away,' she explained, informatively, 'sometimes he was away five or six days, and that was when they saw each other.' She paused for breath, engrossed in her role as a collaborator in the discovery of the truth. 'She'd leave the assistants alone in the shop, and go with him.'

'And did she tell you where they went?'

'They didn't always go to the same place, and besides, she didn't tell me everything, but two or three times she mentioned a place she liked a lot, the Binaschina.'

'The Bi – ?' he echoed, he hadn't quite caught the word.

'The Binaschina. Yes, after Binasco, on the road that leads to Pavia, it's a bit further on, not far from the Charterhouse of Pavia. She told me such good things about it that I went there with my mother one Saturday last summer, it's a really nice place, and very close to the Charterhouse.'

'Is it a hotel?' he interrupted.

'Oh, no, it's only a restaurant,' she said, bowing her head modestly, then continuing with her endless *you know*s, 'you know how it is when they have regular customers, they must have rooms upstairs.'

Pleasant little places, in the middle of all that nature, all that greenery, with bedrooms upstairs, out of the way of the Milan road: you take your friend's wife there, or an underage girl, you have a nice lunch, because it's better to go there by day, that way it's even more innocent, and then you go upstairs, broadly speaking, just like that, and then, broadly speaking, you come down again and nobody can say anything about it. It was the kind of place you chose to go to, not a place you discovered by chance.

'Did she mention anywhere else?'

She tried hard to remember, then said, 'No, I really don't think so, you know, I don't have a very good memory, but if she'd been with him the day before, the day after she'd tell me so much about the Binaschina, she'd say the food was really good, but to tell the truth, that time I went there with my mother, the food wasn't so great, in fact the meat was a bit tough.'

He let her talk, it had been a more instructive encounter than it might have seemed, thank you, thank you, young lady of the cosmetics, Mascaranti had written her name down, but Duca didn't care about names. 'Thank you,' he said, quite sincerely, and then, equally sincerely, he started to give her advice, professional advice to start with: if by chance anyone came asking questions about Signor Silvano and Signorina Giovanna Marelli, she should immediately inform the police, she mustn't forget that, or the police would be angry. The next advice he gave her was more in the nature of moral advice, or not exactly moral, in practice they were more like threats – when you came down to it the expression 'I'll smash your head in' was more effective than a lot of highly ethical and noble phrases – he told her that if she was expecting a child, she had to keep it, for two very simple reasons: one, that if she had an abortion she could go to prison and then they would even take away her licence for the perfume shop; two, that in many cases – he was a doctor and knew what he was talking about – an abortion could, among other things, cause septicaemia, and septicaemia is a general infection, in case she didn't know, which not even modern medicine could keep under control. But when they were at the door, and before he opened it, taking advantage of the fact that it was Mother's Day, he told her, in a low, persuasive voice, that the child might be a boy, but even if it was a girl, in a mere twenty years or so, it could keep the shop going, why work so hard for a business if you don't have anyone to leave it to?

When he had got rid of the woman, he ran into the kitchen. The loved and hated files were still there, on the shelf of the larger dresser.

'Mascaranti, show me the map of the spot where Turiddu Sompani's car fell.'

They both grabbed the Breton's file and there they were, the maps, along with the photographs of the car being lifted from the water. The spot where Turiddu Sompani's car had fallen into the Alzaia Naviglio Pavese was almost halfway between Binasco and the Charterhouse of Pavia.

'Let's go and have a look,' he said to Mascaranti.

3

At the moment, there wasn't much to see. It was only twelve, and despite the sun and the clear sky and the tender, resplendent expanse of green and the acute sense of spring, so rare in Lombardy, the place, seen from the outside, had the discreet air common once upon a time to high-class brothels. From the road you couldn't see anything at all, then, once past the curtain of trees, the road led to an open space, with a sign saying *car park*, but even here you couldn't see the brothel itself, you had to go further, on foot, past another little barrier of trees, and then there it was, apparently innocuous, a bit of folklore, architecturally horrendous, its style a mixture of a lower Lombard farmhouse and a Swedish Protestant church.

It was midday, exactly midday. They went in. At that hour nobody came to greet them, it was too early, everyone was in the kitchen preparing the food. They had to go through two doors, very heavy ones, and the opulence of the doors with their decorated bronze handles half a metre long were already clear evidence that whoever owned these doors earned a comfortable income.

'I don't think there's any point trying to pass ourselves off as customers,' Duca said, 'they won't believe us.' He was starting to feel very much a policeman.

The main room could – if you were trying to be funny – be called pretty. It was done up like a stable or cowshed, there were saddles, cartwheels, heaps of straw on the ground and hay in the mangers lined up against the walls. But, tactfully, neither the saddles nor the spades nor the cartwheels took anything away from the spotless white tablecloths, the trolleys filled with hors d'oeuvre and fruit, and the little mustard-yellow velvet chairs. The place had the look of a stable without any of the disadvantages, rustic lamps hung from the ceiling, a little barrow stood in a corner crammed with sorghum broomsticks, but everything was very clean, well hoovered, and the few copper pans displayed here and there testified, in their bright sheen, to the general cleanliness (hygiene is so important, after all, especially where you eat).

'Really despicable,' Duca said.

Nobody had come to greet them and there was nobody to be seen. Through the three large open windows birdsong came in along with the light, but from somewhere close by that must have been the kitchen, you could hear banging: they must have been beating a piece of meat, or chopping something with a knife. Then an old man came out, short and thin and pink, wearing black trousers and a white shirt with the sleeves rolled up and no hat of any kind. He looked as if he had a lot of experience and an uneasy conscience, because he did not approach them as if they were likely customers, but with the uncertain look of someone who doesn't know what the doctor is about to tell him: hay fever or neoplasia?

'Your ID, Mascaranti,' Duca ordered. And as Mascaranti showed the old man his ID, a number of white-clad waiters, slender but rather well-built, appeared behind the old man, and even two female cooks with white caps like ice bags on their heads, they looked very nineteenth-century, Duca was reminded of Toulouse-Lautrec for a moment, was Toulouse-Lautrec also a Breton, like Turiddu Sompani? He tried to remember, no, he wasn't a Breton, he was probably a Gascon.

With all those waiters standing behind him in long white aprons, as if they were at the Moulin Rouge, the old man looked at Mascaranti's ID and said 'Yes,' he was probably quite familiar with the police, he did not smile, he was not servile, that *yes* was even a little cold and stiff.

But Duca shook him, warmed him. 'We need to talk to you. Let's go upstairs, to one of those rooms you rent by the hour.'

The old man liked his clarity, he liked it in a bad way, even his skull turned pink. 'Everything's above board here,' he said and then repeated, 'Everything's above board. The rooms upstairs are for my daughter and my son-in-law, and apart from that there are two more for the cook and the waitresses. We close at one in the morning and the girls can't go home alone at that hour.'

No, of course they couldn't. Not in such virginal surroundings. 'Yes,' Duca said, 'let's go upstairs to talk,' and he took him by the arm and pushed him, physical contact is more effective than any words could be, it's like a kick. 'Mascaranti, you stay here and keep an eye on these people, and on the phone.'

Reluctantly, the old man led him upstairs. To do so you had to go out in the garden, so that a couple would look as if they were leaving, instead of which you turned right and went through a small, very ordinary wooden door, so ordinary that no one would have thought of opening it, and behind the little door there was an ordinary little staircase, just one flight, but on the walls hung – who would ever have thought it? – fox hunting prints.

'Show me the rooms,' Duca said, with delicacy, not boorishly like a policeman, gripping him by the elbow and pushing him up.

The old man showed him the rooms. He explained that

one of them was his and his wife's, it was very elegant and very clean, nothing exceptional, except for the bathroom: in such a rustic restaurant, with the downstairs room got up like a stable, a Pompeian bath like this jarred somewhat.

'This is my son's and daughter-in-law's,' the old man said in the next room. It was a copy of the first room, except that the furniture, apart from that in the bathroom, was of lighter wood, and not suitable for a long stay.

The three rooms for the waitresses did not have double beds, only two small beds next to each other, so close that it was hard to see why they were not joined, and there was no bathroom: each room had a wash basin with a bidet beneath it, modestly covered by a pink or sky blue or yellow towel. The blinds on the windows were permanently lowered, creating, even at midday, a languid atmosphere of sin, but in the third of the three waitresses' rooms – or what the old man had indicated were the waitresses' rooms – Duca raised the blinds and the sunlight came flooding in.

'Right, let's talk here,' he said to the old man, and closed the door.

'Everything's above board,' the old man said, 'the Carabinieri have been here and they found everything in order. I have competitors who talk about me, even in Milan, trying to ruin me, but it's all above board here, I don't do what those bastards say, I do well enough with the restaurant, I don't need to rent rooms by the hour.' He wasn't pleading, and he wasn't exaggerating: he was right, he was the owner of a restaurant that had been checked by the authorities, he was small and old and completely bald, but he had his own repulsive form of nobility: it was obvious he was being protected and that was why he wasn't afraid.

Duca would have to get the truth out of him.

He sat down on one of the two little beds, and even

sitting down he was almost as tall as the old man. 'I only want some information,' he said, sounding very calm, very democratic, almost constitutional, not at all the kind of policeman who tortures suspects. 'You have lots of customers, and you can't remember all of them, I know, but do you by any chance remember a certain Signor Silvano? Silvano Solvere? Obviously you don't remember him, with all the customers you have.'

To his great joy, the old man shook his head, no, he didn't remember. In fact he even got slightly annoyed. 'How could I? I don't know the names of my customers, people coming to a restaurant don't give their names.'

'I was thinking,' Duca suggested, 'that this Silvano Solvere might possibly have been called to the phone, and that way you would have found out that particular customer was called Silvano Solvere.' He kept repeating the name, with constitutional politeness, respecting the constitution, which guarantees the freedom of the citizen from any abuse of executive or judicial power.

'That might have happened, but who remembers all the names?' the old man said, increasingly calm faced with this policeman who was so well-behaved, he didn't even seem like a policeman.

'You're right, of course,' Duca said, 'but how about Attorney Sompani, Turiddu Sompani? Maybe you remember him.'

Benignly, the old man pretended to make an effort to remember, he knitted his brows until they were thick with lines like the rails near a terminal. 'I don't think I've ever heard of him.'

Duca nodded, understandingly, and stood up, on his feet he was almost twice as tall as the old man, but the old man didn't seem to be afraid. He really needed to get the truth out of him now, and fast. The mistake that crooks make is to deny everything, they're so stupid, if you ask them, 'How many fingers do you have on your right hand?' they say, 'I don't know, I don't know a thing.' That's how they give themselves away.

'You see,' he said, going to the wash basin and turning on the cold water tap, Attorney Turiddu Sompani and a lady friend of his, Signora Adele Terrini, are the two people whose car fell into the canal, the Alzaia Naviglio Pavese, one kilometre from here, not even that. I thought they might have had dinner here, and besides, I thought maybe you'd read the papers, that you were interested in an accident that happened so close to your restaurant. But maybe you don't read the papers?'

He was too old and crafty to rise to the bait, he did not go so far as to deny that he read the newspapers, but his denial was more subtle: 'Every other day there's some kind of accident on this road, as there are on all the roads, am I supposed to remember all of them, and remember the names of all the people involved?' He smiled, he was so sure of himself, he *had* to be protected.

'So you don't know anything about Silvano Solvere or Turiddu Sompani?' Duca said without looking at him, because he had bent down to take one of the two towels from the bidet, a portable bidet, there was a blue towel for men and a pink towel for women, and he took the blue one, put it under the jet of cold water and soaked it thoroughly. He didn't like doing what he was about to do, on such a glorious spring day, with the smell of sun-warmed earth at last entering this chamber of sin, but the old man had not left him any alternative, the old man took other people, and the police in particular, for cretins, for mental retards, he took the law and civil rights as jokes that had nothing to do with him, because he believed he had protection that was much stronger than the police and the law, and so, advanced in years as he was, he had to be taught to respect the law and the police: even on television they always said it was never too late.

Without losing his temper, he went up to the old man, who was watching, curious and bored, gently grabbed him by the back of the neck with his left hand, while with the right he simultaneously, instantaneously blocked his nose and mouth, his two channels for breathing, with the wet towel.

The old man tried to kick but Duca kept him still and laid him down on the bed, face up and with one knee bent. Four seconds had passed, the old man could hold out for forty seconds, maybe more, there was still time. A wet towel – they were of very fine terry cloth – sticks better and gives better insulation: air can neither leave nor enter the lungs.

'Now look at me,' Duca said, all politeness gone, only the threat left, 'if you don't answer my questions the way I want, I'll keep this rag over your mouth. I don't have any desire to suffocate you, but if you don't indicate that you're going to talk, I'll keep right on. And the worst thing is if you resist, at your age you'll have a heart attack, even if I take the towel away you'll breathe but as soon as you start breathing again you'll have a heart attack. I'll give you some advice as a doctor, because I'm a doctor as well as a policeman: agree to talk right now. Twenty-five seconds have already passed, it doesn't bother me if you die of a heart attack, I'll just say it happened suddenly, and you won't be able to deny it from the other world, and all your protectors, with all their power, won't be able to bring you back to life, in fact they'll be happy: one less accomplice to worry about.'

He lifted the hand with the wet towel, because the old man had nodded. He let him recover, threw the wet towel on the bidet, turned off the tap, went back to the bed and took the old man's pulse. The old man's face was no longer pink, but had turned lilac, he was like a dripping lilac. His pulse was agitated but quite regular, his breathing was questionable, his lips were also slightly lilac. Duca had said all that to scare him, but they had indeed been closer to a heart attack than might have been expected. He lit a cigarette and went to the window while the old man recovered. When he turned, his face hot with sun, he saw that the owner of the Binaschina was starting to look almost human again. 'Lie back and let's talk a bit,' he said to him. He had no intention of killing an old man, although he didn't make any distinction between killing old men or young men or whatever in order to find out the truth, not because he cared a lot about the truth, which was, after all, an abstruse abstraction, but simply because it would take him to the people who could do anything but were never seen, and he wanted those people to go to prison, and he wanted everybody to know and see that they were in prison. 'So, do you know Silvano Solvere?'

'Oh, yes,' the old man said, humble and modest now. 'He often came here.'

'Alone or in company?'

'Almost always in company.'

'What kind of company?'

'A girl.'

'When you say a girl, do you mean always the same one, or different ones?'

'No, always the same one.'

'What was she like?'

'Tall, brown hair, a pretty girl.'

He had tried to avoid raising his voice and getting angry, but people are too stupid. 'Don't make me lose my patience,' he cried, raising his fist over the man's face, 'you know perfectly well it's the same girl who died in the car with Silvano Solvere, machine-gunned by your protectors, the bastards who protect this little business for you, this little knocking shop for idle Milanese.'

'Yes, yes,' he said, really scared – it must be unpleasant to be old and defenceless against a mad policeman – and he blinked and instinctively turned his head away from that threatening fist. 'I was about to say that, it's her.'

'Who?'

'It's his girlfriend, Giovanna Marelli.' He should have said *it was*: you had to make a bit of a distinction between the living and the dead.

'So Silvano Solvere and a girlfriend of his, Giovanna Marelli, came here,' Duca said, calming down. 'What did they come here to do?' It was a curious question, but with crooks you had to ask unusual questions.

'They came to eat.'

Of course, you go to a restaurant like the Binaschina to eat. 'And then?'

The old man hesitated, but finally admitted the sin. 'They came upstairs.'

'And then?' Duca said. He saw him move. 'Don't get up, you'll only feel sick. And think carefully before you answer.'

'Then what?' the old man moaned. 'I don't know what you mean. Then they went away, that's all I know.'

He seemed genuine, but with some people you can't trust *seems* and *appears*. 'Try and tell me everything, at your age the heart is fragile.' He went to the wash basin and turned on the tap. 'And don't scream, that'll only make it worse, everything will be worse as long as you trust your protectors more than you trust the police.'

He did not scream. He watched, with eyes that had grown round, as Duca soaked the towel, and his breathing became agitated again, and his words were agitated too, when he spoke: 'He'd come here with the girl every now and again, like everyone else, most often by day, like everyone else, but sometimes also in the evening, that's all I know, really, I know the name because he had a lot of phone calls, as you said, they called him on the phone, and that was how I found out his name was Silvano Solvere, but that's all I know.'

Abruptly, Duca turned off the tap, and without a word approached the bed with the blue towel, which was soaking wet now and dripping water.

Wisely, the old man shook his head, and wisely he opened the last secret cabinet of his complex soul: 'They recommended him to me.' He must know all about people who intend to kill, at his age and with the kind of company he had kept, and maybe he had seen a determination to kill in this policeman's eyes, he hadn't expected to come across a policeman like this one.

'What do you mean, they "recommended" him to you?'

'Some friends phoned me and said to treat him well.' He even smiled, in his terror, because now it was no longer a question of fear, but of terror: a wet towel can be more terrifying than a revolver.

'And who are these "friends"?' he asked the old man. Then he did three things: he dropped the towel on the floor, took the false owner of the Binaschina by one arm and gently raised him to a sitting position on the bed, and finally took from the pockets of his jacket a ballpoint pen and the only piece of paper he had in his possession at the moment, a coupon from the previous week's football pools, in which he had scored four. 'Write down the names and addresses of the people who give you these recommendations.'

'I don't know anything, I only saw them three times in three years, I only know the telephone number, when I need them I phone them.'

'Write down the telephone number.'

The old man wrote the number on the coupon.

'Try to remember it correctly and don't make a mistake, if you tell me later that you made a mistake I won't believe you.'

The old man shook his head sadly. 'I know when I can cheat and when I can't,' he said, wearily, and lay back down on the bed, really worn out, morally too. 'I'm a cook, not a criminal, I've never gone looking for trouble, I've always been a good cook, I keep the sauce for the lasagne on the stove for almost a week, night and day, I used to get up three times a night to look at it, that was how I made my fortune. This thing about the rooms just kind of happened, it's the most I've ever done, and it isn't even my fault, it's the customers, after eating they say they've eaten so well, and drunk so well, they don't feel like driving, could I provide a room, just so they can lie down for a moment, if I said no, they'd declare war on me, they'd tell all their friends and acquaintances that the food here was lousy and the prices ridiculous, once I started with all that I had to continue, I couldn't help it, I'm old, I want to be left to work in peace, you don't know what it's like, how could you, the customers are wild animals.'

Duca let him pour it all out. The man, he thought, wasn't basically wicked, he was actually quite interesting: he had character, he liked money, like everyone, but also philosophy, he was a bit despicable, a bit of a pimp, a bit of a criminal, but also a bit Socratic. But Duca needed concrete information, not digressions.

'How did you meet these "friends"?' he asked. One thing was for sure: the wet towel had persuaded the owner of the Binaschina to tell the truth. It might not be a particularly praiseworthy system of education, but it got results.

'They came here once, three years ago. I'd only just opened, and the Carabinieri had already closed me down because they'd found a couple upstairs. The place was closed, but they knocked at the door and asked to come in.'

'And then?'

The old man's breathing was irregular and his lips even more lilac, and Duca didn't want him to die before he'd told him everything.

'Ask them to bring up a coffee, a strong one.'

'I haven't drunk coffee in twenty years, because of my heart.'

'You'll drink it now.' There was a little intercom between the two beds, a nice touch, it was there so that the owner could warn the couple, if the police came, at least to get dressed, or so that the couple could order a stirrup cup before the sin started. 'A ristretto, right away,' he ordered the thin, false little female voice that answered him.

And then those three men had come in, even though the restaurant was closed, and they had looked surprised and said, 'This is such a lovely restaurant, we've heard a lot of good things about it, we came here to have a nice meal, and yet we find it closed, how come?' He had explained that, unfortunately, the Carabinieri had found a couple in one of the rooms, and not only had the restaurant been closed down, he was also about to go to prison. 'No, what are you saying?' one of the three men had said. 'If they had to close all the places that give lovers a helping hand, they'd have to close everything, they'd have to close the whole of the Po Valley, but don't worry, we have friends, we'll see to it.'

'And then?' Duca asked with childish insistence.

And then the three had been as good as their word: two days later he had been issued a provisional licence to reopen the restaurant.

'After just two days?' Duca said, politely incredulous.

'Just two days.'

Just two days. There were poor but honest people who had to wait six months for a licence to sell fifty kilos of rotten apples from a cart, and in two days, despite the Carabinieri, the police, the local authorities, these people managed to get a place that was publicly a restaurant, but actually a brothel with a restaurant car and sleeping car attached, reopened. Duca gritted his teeth and tried to stay calm. 'Did it ever occur to you,' he said, 'that the pimps who came along to save you were the same people who'd previously informed on you?'

The word *pimps* pleased the old man: he probably didn't like them very much himself either, these protectors of his. 'Yes, I realised that almost immediately, nobody does anything for nothing, but they were so good to me, all they said was that every now and again they'd recommend somebody to me, and that I should treat that person well, even if he didn't have any money, and that they'd pay me later.'

And indeed, they had phoned him every now and again, to inform him that a brown-haired man, in a grey suit and a small mourning button in the buttonhole of his jacket, would arrive with a girl, also brown-haired, dressed in such and such a way, and that they needed to stay for a couple of days, but without being too conspicuous, and it hadn't taken him long to realise that they were using his restaurant as a base, but he had also realised that he couldn't say no, unless he had wanted, if not to die, to have all his bones broken, one by one. They had even told him once, at table, about someone who hadn't been a friend, according to them, and so one of them, who was a bit highly strung, had broken all his bones, one by one, and as they were telling him about this person who hadn't been a friend and whose bones they had broken, they had stared at him without batting an eyelid, so that even if he had been a cretin he would have understood.

And then the old man told him everything, because he was old and desperate, afraid of death but exhausted with the burden of living, he told him that every now and again people came there and left a case, and then other people came and took the case away.

'And what did these cases look like? Were they always the same? Were they green, not made of leather, with metal corners?'

'Yes, yes,' he said, 'yes, yes, twice they were exactly like that.'

There was a knock at the door. Outside stood a waiter, almost two metres tall, bearing a small tray with a little cup of coffee and a bowl of sugar on it. Duca took the tray. 'Thank you,' he said and almost slammed the door in the giant's face. 'Is he one of the waiters who were forced on you by your friends?' He helped him to sit up on the bed, put a single spoonful of sugar in the coffee. 'The coffee takes effect quicker if you don't put in too much sugar.'

'But what about my heart?' He was almost as afraid of the coffee as he was of the wet towel.

'I said drink.' He put a hand on the old man's shoulder and moved the cup closer to his lips. 'So, was that waiter a friend of your friends? Drink first and then answer.'

Under duress, the old man drank the coffee, then said, 'There's another one as well. There are two of them. They don't even know how to wash the dishes, in fact they don't wash them, they don't do anything, they just keep an eye on me.' He gave a weary, colourless smile. 'Can I lie down?'

Duca helped him to lie down. 'So,' he said, 'about those cases.'

Yes, those cases, he told him all about them, docile now, sincere. Silvano Solvere had come several times, yes, four or five times, with cases, and yes, twice they were green with metal corners, like small trunks, but the other times they were old leather cases, or ugly-looking canvas cases.

'It's possible, then,' Duca said, 'that inside these big cases were those other cases with metal corners that look like small trunks.'

The old man gave a polite, contented smile. 'You know that's what I thought too.' It was an easy thing to think, because the craftier they are, the stupider they are. Craftiness is one of the forms of mental deficiency: lacking in intelligence, cretins try to compensate by playing little games. And then the old man told him that Silvano Solvere would leave his case there and say, 'A friend of mine will come and pick it up,' and he didn't even tell him what this friend of his was called, or what he looked like.

'And then?' Duca said. The doors of truth were opening.

And then Attorney Turiddu Sompani – the Breton naturalised as an Italian with the Sicilian Christian name of Salvatore, which then became Salvaturiddu and eventually Turiddu – would come and pick up the case left by Silvano Solvere. He never came alone, but always with a woman, either very young women, so young that they looked like his granddaughters, because he must have been around sixty, only they were the kind of granddaughters who went upstairs with him to the rooms, or sometimes – this was how the owner of the Binaschina put it, sternly – his old whore.

'Maybe,' Duca said, 'that was the woman who died with him in the accident in the canal, very near here.'

'Yes, that was the one.' On the evening of the accident, he said, they had been there having dinner, Attorney Turiddu Sompani, his old lady friend, and a young guest, also a woman. He did not smile when he said *accident*, he repeated the word Duca had used, *accident*, as if he hadn't noticed the hint of irony: in fact he had noticed it, but didn't want to get involved.

'Was it always Silvano Solvere who came here to leave a case, and was it always Attorney Sompani who came to pick it up?'

'Yes, that's what always happened,' the old man confirmed and, having revived a little thanks to the coffee, sat up again on the bed. 'But they also came without leaving cases, or without picking them up, and they never paid.'

Those cases certainly went on quite a tour, starting at the butcher's shop, from where a girl, now deceased, poor thing, would take them to a perfume shop, and from the perfume shop a certain Silvano Solvere would take them to the Binaschina, where a certain Turiddu Sompani would come and pick them up and nothing more was heard of them. One evening the tour had been extended, the girl had taken the case from the butcher's shop to his apartment, the apartment of the doctor who was supposed to put her back together again for her wedding, and from there Silvano Solvere should have come to collect it and take it to the Binaschina. But he had not been able to collect anything, because that same night death had collected him from the

Alzaia Naviglio Grande, along with the girl. So the case had stayed with him, Duca.

'How do you feel?'

'Better.' The coffee had given the old man a little bit more energy.

'Now tell me what the other waiter who works for your friends looks like.'

'He's as tall as the one who came here with the coffee, and he's fair-haired, those two are the tallest people here.'

'All right, we're going to leave those two free.'

'Oh, no, you have to get them off my back or they'll kill me as soon as they find out I've talked.'

'But they have to know that you've talked,' Duca explained, gently. 'You have to phone those people, your friends, as soon as possible and tell them everything that happened, tell them the police came, tell them they threatened to choke you with a wet towel if you didn't talk, and that you had to tell them everything, apart from the two foot soldiers who are pretending to be waiters. Letting those two go free and informing your friends immediately of the police visit will be the proof that you're on their side.'

He was starting to understand, but he was not convinced. 'But if I phone them, they'll get away.' *And what's the point of that?* his eyes added.

'Of course, that's what I want, I want them to get agitated, to think their cover's been blown.' He shrugged. 'I don't want to waste time arresting them, they'll only be free again after a month. They have to get away and leave Milan in peace for a little while.'

He wasn't being honest at all, but sometimes, with some people, honesty is an expensive luxury. What he really thought was that the old man's friends would realise that he had come to an arrangement with the police and would want to take revenge, but in order to take revenge they would have to come and get him, and in order to get him they would have to come out of their lairs.

'Oh, of course they'll get away,' the old man said. 'But before that they'll do something nasty to me.'

'I don't think so. Anyway you'll be protected, if they come here to hurt you they'll get more than they bargained for.' Abandoning him to his uncertainty, his bitter puzzlement, Duca abruptly left the little room that had seen so many scenes of love, went down the little staircase with the English – or almost English – prints, went out in the garden, and then back into the luxury stable. The Toulouse Lautrec-style waiters and waitresses were all there, sitting at the longest table, watched over by Mascaranti, and from the way Mascaranti was glaring at them, it was as if he was keeping them at bay with a revolver.

'I took everyone's names and details,' Mascaranti said, in a low voice, 'I stopped them from making any phone calls, and I sent away a few customers who wanted to come in.'

'Now send them all back to work and say goodbye.' He went out into the warm sun, walked to the car park, and got back in the car. He preferred not to drive, if he didn't have to, and he sat down next to the driver's seat. Mascaranti arrived a moment later.

'Where are we going?'

'The Charterhouse of Pavia,' Duca said. 'I haven't been there for a long time.'

'I've never seen it,' Mascaranti said. 'I've heard it's very beautiful.

4

It was very beautiful, but it was closed: they had forgotten, in their absent-mindedness and because of the glorious spring weather, that even charterhouses have schedules, and all they could do was walk around the walls of the Charterhouse. Beyond those walls, invisible, were the great cloister with the cells around it, and the temple with the choir at the far end, and the small cloister with the library and the refectory, the old sacristy with the famous ivory polyptych – who was it by? no, they couldn't remember – and a whole other universe, so totally different from our universe of today. And having done their little tour, they went back to the little square, where there were a couple of trattorias. Duca chose the less rustic of the two: he didn't trust rusticity.

'Let's make a phone call and have a sandwich.' On the phone he informed Carrua that they had found the syndicate's base, the Binaschina, he told him about his conversation with the old man, omitting to mention the towel.

'In a couple of hours I'll send some men to keep an eye on the place,' Carrua said. And so the Binaschina became another trap.

'Thanks,' Duca said.

'You're welcome,' Carrua said, humorously, then in a darker tone, 'But be careful not to make any mistakes, not only can you not make a mistake with those people, you can't make a mistake with me.' That final *me* sounded like an elephant's trumpeting. Then he hung up.

At the non-rustic restaurant, with a few attempts at elegance and modernity, opposite the closed Charterhouse of Pavia, it proved quite difficult to obtain two sandwiches with salami and pickled peppers: they didn't want to lower themselves to such a small order. The barman, the waiter and the woman owner, who was at the cash register, all dragged their heels, until Mascaranti went into the kitchen, said he was from the police, and that he wanted two sandwiches with salami and a little slice of pickled pepper but right now, not for the August bank holiday, and at the word *police* the sandwiches almost leapt like flashes of lightning from the hands of the kitchen staff, and Mascaranti went to the cash register, paid the owner for the sandwiches and the two bottles of beer and went to the car, where Duca was waiting for him and where they ate, with the doors open, in a corner that gave a vague sense of a green hermitage, beneath a row of little trees with clear, childish green foliage.

As he ate his sandwich, Duca read the two newspapers from the day before that he had found in the car. The front page of *La Notte* said: *Lured by His Lover, Killed with Scissors and Thrown in the Lake!* There was even an exclamation mark. The *Corriere d'Informazione*, on the other hand, preferred to present the news like this: *Drawn into a Trap by his Lover, Strangled and Thrown in the Adda*. In other words, what was missing was the detail of the scissors, which was relegated to the summary, and there was also a divergence of location and method: *La Notte* said that the murder victim had been thrown into a lake, whereas the *Corriere d'Informazione*, mentioned the Adda, which was a river; the *Corriere* said the man had been strangled, while according to *La Notte* it was the scissors that had killed him.

'We don't carry knives, sabres and swords anymore,' Duca said, 'so we kill with whatever we find close to hand.

If we're in our car we take a screwdriver from the glove compartment and plunge it into the neck of the person who's just overtaken us on our right. If we're at home, in a healthy domestic environment, we choose scissors from among the household tools, and with fifty or sixty stabs we finish off the friend who hasn't given us back the money we owed him.' The salami was very dubious, and the pepper tasted slightly of turpentine rather than oil, but that was nobody's fault, was it?

On the inside pages, in the Milan city news, there were the usual little items of the day. One of the headlines in *La Notte* was *Bride Posed for Three Thousand Pornographic Photographs*. Another was *Skull Found – may be that of the Singing Cobbler*. The *Corriere d'Informazione* reported, but without giving it much prominence, the news of an assault on an optician's shop in the Via Orefici, the headline said: *Hunt is on for Armed Drug Dealers*. For two film cameras and a radio, a trio of young idiots had actually opened fire, risking life imprisonment.

Duca finished the pitiful sandwich, drank his little bottle of beer, and shook his head. 'Some people haven't yet understood that Milan is a big city,' he said to Mascaranti. 'They haven't yet understood the change of scale, they still talk about Milan as if it finished at the Porta Venezia or as if people didn't do anything else but eat panettone or millet cake. If you say Marseilles, Chicago, Paris, those are real metropolises, with lots of criminals, but not Milan. Some stupid people don't think of it as a big city, they still look for what they call local colour, cafés with braziers, weigh houses, and maybe even steam trams. They forget that a city with a population of nearly two million has an international, not a local feel, a city as big as Milan attracts criminals from all over the world, madmen, alcoholics, drug addicts, or simply desperate people in search of money who get hold of a revolver, steal a car and jump on the counter of a bank shouting, "Everybody down on the ground!" just as they've heard you're supposed to do. There are many advantages to the increasing size of the city, but there are also changes that give us pause for thought. These settlings of accounts' – he refused the cigarette Mascaranti was offering him – 'should really make us stop and think. There are armed gangs organised militarily, with members ready for anything, with a whole series of strategic bases and hideouts, spread all over the place. We found the Binaschina by chance, but how many bases must there be like that within the borders of the province of Milan or even outside, but still in this big sweet cake called Milan? Milan is where the money is and this is where they come to get it, by any means possible, even with submachine guns.' He shook his head again. 'And now, talking of submachine guns, let's go back home. One of these days they'll realise I have their gun and they'll come and ask for it. I want to live until that day.' He clenched his fists, then looked at Mascaranti to indicate that he should get going. A pity, but he would come back to the Charterhouse another time. When they got home, the green case with metal corners was still there, in the hall, perfectly visible. It was the first big trap, and maybe the fox would fall into it. The case must be of interest to lots of people, and in fact other people did come.

The first was that black-clad woman with her hair in a bun, the woman from Romano Banco who didn't know anything. He had been right to give her his own address: time had passed and she had made her mind up, and here she was, having come straight from Romano Banco, not old, and yet already old.

When she arrived, it was late afternoon and almost hot,

just a slight breath of heat. In the Piazza Leonardo da Vinci, imponderable white flakes were flying in the sun, and Duca and Mascaranti were watching them when she rang the bell. Duca went and opened the door and when she had come in she looked at the case on the floor, it was so clearly visible, and she seemed to recognise it, and it looked as if she was about to cry, but she didn't, she said, 'He hasn't phoned again, I haven't heard from him, I don't know what's happened to him.'

Duca led her into the surgery and sat her down. 'I need to know everything, otherwise I can't help you.' He looked her straight in the face, but without harshness, because he could see she was suffering. 'I'm not a friend of Silvano's, I'm with the police. There's a lot we already know, but we need to know everything.'

The word *police* took her aback, but the surprise only registered on her face: it was as if the skin of her face quivered, like the skin of horses. Then she started crying.

5

Then she started speaking. She had stopped crying, because you don't cry in front of your confessor, and that was what she wanted to do now, urged on by her own anguish and the way Duca was looking at her: to confess. The police knew a certain amount about her, that her name was Rosa Gavoni, that she was born in Ca' Tarino, forty-nine years ago, which meant there were three famous women from Ca' Tarino: Rosa Gavoni, the girl dressed in red named Giovanna Marelli, and Adele Terrini, the woman who had ended up in the Naviglio Pavese together with Turiddu Sompani, Ca' Tarino really was a centre for important people; but now she told them what the police did not know and could not have documented. She had known Ulrico, Ulrico Brambilla, the powerful butcher, since he was three years old and she was twelve and she was the one who looked after him in the fields around Ca' Tarino, just as all the girls of five or more looked after the smaller children, because the mothers were either washing, or in service, or in the factory. Both their families were very poor, like all the families in Ca' Tarino, but they were the poorest of the poor, and by the time he was six he was already well-known as a thief, skilfully stealing hens and taking them to his mother.

Nothing might have happened between them, partly because of the age difference, if it hadn't been for the war. When, after 8 September 1943, the Germans arrived, he had to hide and he had become the Scarlet Pimpernel of the Corsico area, of Buccinasco, Romano Banco, Pontirolo, Rovido. Every night he slept in a different house in his personal resistance zone, and they were happy to put him up because he was a handsome young man, he was thought of as a young stud. Several girls and even a few married women had strayed into sin with him, and even she, Rosa Gavoni, had sinned, but out of love, she said, not out of carnal lust like the others: she actually used the words *carnal lust*.

When the war was over, Ulrico Brambilla, the young stud – as she confessed it, her yellowish face went red and she lowered her eyes with that bluish halo around them – had quickly got rich by supplying girls to the American soldiers, especially blonde girls for the Negroes, and underage girls for the older officers. It was a nasty business, but she had only learnt about it later, when he had opened a butcher's shop in Ca'Tarino and stopped doing that work, which even he hadn't liked.

'Are you sure he really did stop?' Duca asked. He had probably continued: a butcher's shop was a good cover.

Yes, he had stopped, Rosa Gavoni fervently assured Duca, his one concern was his butcher's shop and the butcher's shop did so well that he had immediately opened another in Romano Banco, and then another in Milan, and then one in Buccinasco. She had helped him a great deal in his work, she had been close to him throughout the years, she had been everything to him, his maid, his cashier, his manager, she had even been like a wife, and indeed he had sometimes talked about marrying her, but then he always seemed to forget, and she did not insist: she knew she was nine years older than him, she knew she had faded prematurely, and when he had got involved with Giovanna Marelli, she had not even despaired, she had only asked him if, after he was married, he would keep her on as cashier in one of his shops, and he had generously told her he would, because she was old and couldn't go back to Ca'Tarino after the scandal of living for so many years with a man who was not her husband.

All this, thought Duca, had its interest – humility and resignation can reach hysterical heights in some human beings, and she, Rosa Gavoni, had spent more than twenty years with a man who had abused her in every way, paying her poorly, and when he found another woman, all she had asked was that he shouldn't fire her but keep her on as a cashier – but what he really wanted to know about was the cases. He went to get the case from the hall and opened it on the floor in front of her. 'This,' he said, nervously lifting the barrel of the submachine gun, 'I want to know about this.'

She knew. She said she hadn't known anything at first, only that he, Ulrico sometimes went to Genoa in his car and came back in the evening with a case: it was often green like this one, but there were other kinds too. Then one evening he had got drunk, he had started crying and told her that he was scared, very scared, and she had pitifully asked him what he was afraid of and in the end he had told her.

So this modest, weary, humble woman knew everything about these dangerous activities: in his drunken, scared state the man had confided his heavy secret to her. Now to see if she really knew everything. 'When did this business with the cases start?' Duca asked.

She replied immediately, without any anguish, a polite, precise, meticulous Lombard who knew what she was doing and wanted to do it well. 'Just under three years ago.'

So it had been going on for quite a while. 'Why did Ulrico have to go to Genoa to get those cases?'

'Because they came in from France.'

'From Marseilles?'

'Yes, from Marseilles.'

A little flash of light: Turiddu Sompani was an ex-Frenchman, an ex-Breton, and the provenance of the weapons was French.

'And who did Ulrico have to hand these cases over to?' He already knew, but he wanted to see if she confirmed it.

'To Silvano.'

'And who did Silvano have to take them to?'

'A lawyer named Turiddu Sompani.'

Yes, the woman was telling the truth. Now to see if she knew more than that. 'And who did this Turiddu Sompani have to take them to?' He couldn't have kept all those weapons for himself, in his personal armoury.

'Even Ulrico didn't really know,' she replied immediately, 'but he was very scared, because Silvano had told him once the things ended up in the Alto Adige.'[9]

So that was what this bunch were up to: transporting guns through Italy to supply terrorists. He felt disgusted, but he had to go on. 'And why did Ulrico agree to this work? He made a lot of money from it, I suppose?'

Her eyes, inside the blue halo, glittered with disdain. 'Not a lira, and he wouldn't have agreed even if they'd offered him a billion lire, but they forced him.'

'How?'

'He told me they were people who had done a lot of favours for him at the end of the war, and later saved him several times when he did something not quite above board and if he'd refused they'd have ruined him, or worse.'

Duca looked at Mascaranti. 'Did you hear that?' Yes, Mascaranti heard everything perfectly well. 'I want you to phone Carrua immediately, this is something he has to look into.' Mascaranti nodded. 'Tell him this. Provenance of the weapons: France, Marseilles. Final destination: terrorists in the Alto Adige.' What a bunch of crooks! 'Route: Ulrico Brambilla collects the material in Genoa, from persons unknown, he passes it on to Silvano Solvere through his fiancée Giovanna Marelli, and Silvano Solvere passes it to Turiddu Sompani, who gets it to the Alto Adige through the base in the Binaschina. A perfect plan, because nobody would suspect that weapons for terrorists, submachine guns, explosives to blow up pylons, would be passing through Italy. And what's more, we don't know anything – not even their nicknames – about the bastards at the starting point in France, the ones supplying the weapons, or the other bastards at the finishing point, the ones who hand them over to the terrorists. But that's something he'll have to find out, I don't want to get involved, because otherwise ...' He looked at the case on the floor, the magazines were in it, no, you can't, you can't, the law forbids you to kill the bastards, the ones who betray everyone, especially those who always have to have a defence lawyer, a regular trial, a regular jury and a verdict inspired by the desire to rehabilitate society's misfits, although you don't need permission to spray a couple of patrolling Carabinieri with bullets, or shoot in the mouth a bank teller who's taking his time handing over bundles of ten-thousand-lire notes, or firing a submachine gun into the middle of a crowd in order to get away after a robbery, that you can do, but giving a punch in the face to some son of a bitch involved in all kinds of nasty business, that no, the law forbids it, it's bad, *you haven't understood Beccaria*[10] *at all*, no, he, Duca Lamberti, hadn't understood *On Crimes and Punishments* at all, he was a rough character and had no hope of becoming refined, but he would have liked to meet these bastards and punch their faces in. 'And please tell Carrua that I'm only interested' – in passing, he grabbed one of the little white flakes of pollen which in those incredible days were sailing in the air between skyscrapers, trams and trolleybuses, trying in vain to inseminate cement and asphalt and aluminium – 'that I'm only interested in those falls in the water.' He opened his hand, and the pollen wasn't there any more, or rather, he hadn't caught it at all, it was in fact still sailing gently through the room, his abortive medical surgery that was now a secret, anonymous, unauthorised police office.

6

And while Mascaranti phoned, Duca again looked at the black-clad woman, Rosa Gavoni. Maybe he was too suspicious towards people, but was there any reason, a single one, to trust them? 'Why have you confessed all these things to me?' he asked the woman, looking her straight in the eyes. 'When we find Ulrico, he'll go to prison for arms smuggling, and they may find other things, it's unlikely he'll get less than ten years.'

She was a precise Lombard. 'But at least he'll be alive. And if they've killed him, the police will get those responsible.'

She was beyond reproach. 'Why did Ulrico run away after his fiancée and Silvano Solvere were killed?'

She shook her head gently, now that she had unburdened herself of all her secrets. 'I don't know. He closed up all the shops, sent the assistants on holiday and then left. I was in Ca' Tarino, and he said, "Close the shop and stay at home, and I'll phone you".'

'And did he phone?'

'Yes, twice, he asked me if anyone had come looking for him, I told him no, the same day he phoned me again and asked me the same question, and I gave him the same answer, because nobody had come for him, then I wanted to know why he was doing this, what he was afraid of, but he told me that he would phone the day after.'

'That was when we came,' Duca said.

Yes, that was when they had come and she had told them that she was expecting a phone call from Ulrico, but

Ulrico hadn't phoned again and she was afraid, because if Ulrico hadn't phoned, that meant that something had happened to him.

'Like what?' He had to be merciless. 'Do you mean they might have killed him?'

She nodded, and her face quivered a little: it was the thought that they might have killed Ulrico that had driven her here, to see Duca and Mascaranti, and it didn't matter if they were friends of Silvano's or policemen, as long as they could do something for Ulrico.

'You know him well,' Duca said. 'Do you have any idea where he may have gone when he left home?' A woman knows a man's habits, his impulses, his vices, even without knowing anything specific, and she, Rosa Gavoni, might give them a lead that would help them find Ulrico Brambilla. 'Just say the most stupid thing that comes into your mind. Could some other woman have put him up?' During the war he had been a local Scarlet Pimpernel, escaping German roundups, and now, to escape other enemies, he might have found other pretty women and girls to put him up.

'No,' she said. 'The only other woman was Giovanna. She was all he talked about, she was the only person he wanted to be with. I know him.' She raised her head, proud to know him, even in her humiliating position as a woman who had not been loved for years but who still loved. 'When he settles on one, there's no one else.'

So where was he hiding? Not in hotels, where he would be too exposed and his enemies could easily find him. 'When he phoned, did you think he was calling from Milan? Or was it a long distance call?'

'No,' she said, lowering her head pensively. 'In fact, I could hear him quite well.' And anyway, with direct dialling, you couldn't tell the difference between local and long distance calls any more.

'All right,' he said, getting to his feet. 'Go home now and wait. If anyone comes, phone me. If they put you in a position where you can't phone, leave a clue.' He thought for a moment, looking at her: she was listening without fear, she understood the danger, but wasn't afraid of it, as long as Ulrico was safe. 'Leave a light on, for example, move a chair, drop an ornament, the house is so tidy that we'll immediately understand the signal.' When they were at the door, he said, 'From now on, we'll phone you every three hours. Help us, and we'll do everything we can to find him.'

By the time he had closed the door behind the unfortunate Rosa Gavoni and gone back to his surgery, the setting sun had set the Piazza Leonardo da Vinci ablaze and a bright flame-like light entered the room, together with two more white flakes of pollen. This time, he managed to grab one when he opened his palm. It was in his palm, and it seemed like nothing, but it was a nothing from which a plane tree might come, or one of those huge trees you see photographs of in encyclopaedias, which form canopies through which cars pass. 'Mascaranti,' he said.

'Yes?' Mascaranti said, coming in from the kitchen.

'What did Carrua say?'

'He said okay, he'll look into the arms.'

'Anything else?'

'Yes.' Mascaranti hesitated, but only for a moment, his face gold in the reflection of the setting sun. 'He said to be careful, these are nasty people.' There was a bitter irony in his tone, even though it was very serious.

He was being very careful, he thought. 'Mascaranti, let's go and grab a sandwich and buy the newspapers.'

'I know a trattoria near here that's quite cheap,' Mascaranti said: he was tired of meals consisting only of sandwiches.

'All right, then. I'll change my shirt.' In the chest of drawers in his room there was one last shirt that wasn't too bad, his sister Lorenza had said, 'Keep it for important occasions, because after that one you don't have any others.' He wasn't sure if lunch with Mascaranti was an important occasion or not. He decided it was, took off his shirt with its threadbare cuffs and put on a new one, took out his royal blue tie and then realised that he had to change his suit as well, fortunately, his only decent suit, of the three he had, was also blue, he went in the bathroom and with the electric razor shaved his rough, masculine facial hair. Scoundrels and betrayers, betrayers of everybody, they sold their own mothers and their own daughters, their own country, their own friends, every word they said was false, they had one hand over their hearts and the other on the handles of the knives in their pockets. 'Mascaranti,' he called as he was finishing shaving.

Mascaranti came into the bathroom, looking calm, almost lordly.

'You have to tell me the truth,' he said. 'Do you think we should drop this whole thing? Remember what Carrua said. They'll kill each other. The more they do that, the better it is. What do we care if A was killed by B or by C or if B killed C or D, when A, B, C and D are all as unsavoury as each other? Tell me the truth, Mascaranti: shall we stop or shall we carry on?' He continued moving the shaver over his chin because the rough, masculine hair on his chin was rougher and more masculine than he had anticipated, every now and again he wished he could be like the ancient Romans, the best shaved people in history, using wax, the kind that women use for the hair on their legs.

'Dr Lamberti, you're not asking that seriously,' Mascaranti said formalistically.

He abruptly took out the plug for the electric shaver, said irritably, 'I don't ask questions as a joke,' and scrupulously rewound the cord. 'You must know the proverb.'

'What proverb?'

'He who lives by the sword dies by the sword.'

'Then we die by the sword.' Mascaranti could actually be witty.

Duca gave him a small, not very happy smile, put the shaver away, poured a little lavender in the hollow of his hand and rubbed it into his hair: it was long, almost half a centimetre, he had never been so negligent, but without his sister he couldn't even get to the barber's. He left the bathroom. 'You can play the hero if you like, but this evening I'm buying you a farewell dinner.' He had no desire to get himself bumped off by some hired killer. Yes, of course he would have liked to uproot all the weeds, but why did he have to uproot them by himself? And what could he really uproot, when you came down to it, when you put one in prison and three others were let out, when you put them inside and someone much more powerful got them out again, maybe because, as he had read the day before in the *Corriere*, *His state of health would not withstand a custodial sentence*? How was it that someone could kill ten people, then, because he's poorly and the air in the San Vittore isn't good for him, they commute his life sentence and transfer him to Nervi and even let him eat fish soup in little restaurants on the promenade? Was he supposed to put himself in danger of being riddled with bullets like a bird for the sake of these invalids? 'I'll take you to a place where we can have a good meal, let's go to Prospero's.'

It was a trattoria near the church of San Pietro in

Gessate, he had been there with his sister and niece after Epiphany, little Sara had miraculously behaved herself, in the sense that after a huge plate of tagliatelle with butter she had fallen asleep, sinking into the paradise of relaxation caused by the tagliatelle, and she hadn't made another sound and they had put her back in the pushchair like a toy dog, and they too had eaten very well, and he had promised Lorenza that he would do everything he could to get himself put back on the medical register, and he had also promised her that he would take no further interest in these police matters: it made no sense, after studying for so many years to be a doctor, to then start running after call girls and car thieves. He had promised her, and now he was going back there to remember that promise, which he intended to keep.

'It's Friday,' he said to Mascaranti. 'Let's have fish.'

They ate like men – spaghetti with clams, fried fillets of cod with pecorino cheese – and while they were eating they read the afternoon papers, because they were men but also bachelors and didn't have wives to hold a conversation with over dinner. They read that at 10.30 that morning there had been an eclipse – the headline was *Dark Sun* – although they hadn't even noticed it, and they read that anti-doping checks for the Giro d'Italia had been abolished, so everybody could take whatever they liked and when somebody won a lap the reporters no longer asked them what gear they had used on the climb to San Bartolomeo, but what pill they had managed to get hold of. When they got to the pecorino, after reading that modern Japan has a European face and that after pop music at mass there might next be pop music at funerals, they were pleased to read *Bank Robber Caught in the Spotlight*: an automatic camera in the bank had taken the photographs, published by the newspaper, in which you could see a big idiot pointing a gun at the cashier and in another photograph the idiot escaping with a bag full of money. According to the caption, he had been arrested, thanks to these photographs, just an hour later (Atlanta, Georgia, United States).

'Mascaranti, can you take me to Inverigo tomorrow morning?' He would spend a few days with his sister and Livia and try to forget all these things.

'Yes, of course,' Mascaranti said.

'Then take the case with the submachine gun to Superintendent Carrua.'

'Yes,' Mascaranti said.

'And tell him I'm dropping this business and that he can go ahead himself.'

'Yes, I'll tell him.'

Duca exchanged the pages of the newspaper with Mascaranti, and as soon as the brandy arrived, he drank slowly but without stopping until he had finished the generous glass, then realised that he had taken the literary page and read, again with real pleasure, a review, entitled *A Doctor of 2,000 Years Ago*, of a book about Hippocrates by Mariano Vegetti, published in Turin, 6,000 lire, and re-read with genuine, deep pleasure a quotation from the Corpus Hippocraticum: "In acute diseases, you should first observe the countenance of the patient, if it be like that of a healthy person in health, and especially if it be like his usual self, for that is best of all. But the opposite is the worst, such as: a sharp nose, hollow eyes and sunken temples; ears cold and contracted and with the lobes turned outwards; the skin of the forehead rough, stretched and dry; the colour of the face green or livid." And he too, two thousand years later, was a doctor, even though they weren't allowing him to be one, he would buy the book, and then, as they say, move heaven and earth to be put back on the medical register and so he would start again, and even his father, from the grave, would be happy to see him say once more, 'Cough, say 33,' and measure the blood pressure, because for his father that was what medicine was: prescribing the right syrup to get rid of a cough.

He looked at his watch: the restaurant was emptying, it was ten o'clock, maybe it wasn't too late to phone Inverigo. He left Mascaranti alone and went to the telephone on the cash desk, and beside the cash register stood a pleasant lady who was taking the thread from some beans, and as Inverigo was available by direct dialling, he dialled the prefix, 031, and then the number and then he heard the manly, low and deeply aristocratic voice of the incredible butler from the Villa Auseri.

'Signora Lamberti, please.' Strictly speaking, his sister was Signorina, as she was unmarried, and a functionary in the town hall of Milan could have reported him for false pretences.

'*Just a moment, sir.*' He gave exactly the answer that butlers give in films, in real life he had rarely heard anyone say Just a moment, sir. And instead of his sister's voice, he heard the voice of Livia Ussaro. 'It's me, Signor Lamberti, Lorenza and Sara have already gone to bed.'

Signor Lamberti: after receiving seventy-seven cuts on the face, from forehead to chin, from one cheek to the other, all because of him, Duca Lamberti – it was his colleague, the surgeon at the Fatebenefratelli who had tried to put her together, who had informed him of the number, because he had had to count them, which he, Duca, had not had to do – after all that, Livia did not feel close enough to him to dispense with the terminology *Signor Lamberti*. 'I just wanted to hear your voice,' he said.

Silence, a silence that breathed kindness, the silence of

a woman wrapping herself in a man's kind words as if in an expensive fur. And at last, very sweetly, very courageously for someone as formalistic as her, she said, 'I wanted to hear your voice too.'

He looked at the woman who was taking the thread from the beans, and feeling herself being looked at she raised her head and smiled at him. 'And I also needed your advice,' he said.

Again that breath of kindness: 'It isn't easy to give advice.'

This miracle of kindness and surrender was possible because, at least in calls between Milan and Inverigo, videophones hadn't been invented yet, in other words, they could still talk without seeing each other, and over the telephone she could emerge, in those few minutes of conversation, from the abyss of her desolate state as a victim, an aesthetic outcast, and again became a woman like any other, she felt that she could, with her voice, do what every other woman is able to do with a man.

'It isn't really advice, it's a game,' he returned the smile the woman behind the cash register gave him and with his eyes asked for a bean and took it and crushed it between his fingers, just to perpetrate violence on something, because violence against people was prohibited by the law.

'A game? Really?'

'The thing is,' he said, 'I have to make a choice.' It was pleasant to crush a bean between your fingers, your fingers felt rough but clean and gave off a cool, bitter smell of spring. 'I'll say, heads or tails, and you have to choose either heads or tails.'

'But then you must tell me the choice you have to make.'

'No, Livia, if I tell you that, it isn't a game any more. You just have to say heads or tails. Heads is one of the two things I have to choose, tails is the other, but you mustn't know what it's about.'

'Then I have to toss a coin.' There was a smile in her voice.

'Yes, are you ready?'

'I'm ready.'

'Heads or tails?' The woman with the beans smiled, because she was listening good-naturedly, and he too smiled, waiting for Livia to reply: heads meant being a doctor, choosing a sensible profession, a normal, quiet life, while tails meant being a policeman, playing cops and robbers.

He heard her sigh. 'Tails.'

He did not reply immediately, then said, 'Thanks.'

'Signor Lamberti,' she said, 'when we have to choose between two things it's because we prefer one of the two more, even though it's not as sensible as the other. At least tell me if tails was the thing you preferred.'

'Oh, yes,' he replied almost before she had finished speaking: exactly the thing he preferred, even if it was the less sensible of the two.

The next morning Mascaranti said to him, 'So let's go to Inverigo.'

'No,' he said, 'let's stay here, next to that case.'

Mascaranti saw him pointing at the case, out there in the hall, as soon as you opened the door everybody could see it, and he did not ask if he had changed his mind, he did not say that he knew, he was an intelligent man and said only, 'Yes.'

And they started waiting again, the thief catcher and his assistant, in the kitchen, that way they were near the precious case, exactly the way that, on safari, you stayed near the goat you were using as bait and waited for the lion to arrive. And the lion arrived.

7

She was a lioness. Anatomically so tall and brown, with those white boots over black cowboy-style trousers and the white jacket held together just over the breasts by a big black button in such a way that on either side of the button the breasts swelled as if to advertise them, she might even be considered beautiful. But the vulgarity of her face, of the slightest expression of her face, the vulgarity of her slightest gesture, even the way she held her handbag, the vulgarity of her voice, reminiscent not of a region, because it was too vulgar to be a dialect, but of army barracks where the recruits converse in obscenities, or the waiting rooms of syphilis clinics where the patients tell each other their life stories, that was the kind of vulgarity she evoked, and in spite of her height and brownness and sex appeal it was repellent.

'Dr Duca Lamberti?' she said as soon as Duca had opened the door to her, and as she said it, she looked at the case, because the case was right there and it was impossible not to see it.

'Yes,' he said, letting her in, while Mascaranti appeared from the kitchen.

'I'm a friend of poor Silvano's,' she said, and there was something very vulgar in that *poor Silvano*, as if she was trying to convince him of the depth of her grief at Silvano's death.

'Oh,' Duca said, not coldly: there was even a touch of happiness in his voice, he sensed that the safari had begun.

'He left a case here, and I've come to pick it up.'

Duca pointed to the case in the corner. 'Is it that one?' he asked, and only a stupid lioness could not have noticed the irony of the question.

'Yes,' she said, oblivious.

Duca crouched next to the case and opened it, lifted some of the wood filings, took out the grip of the submachine gun and showed it to her. 'With this?' he said.

'Yes,' she said, going closer, still oblivious.

'You can check it's all there, if you like.'

His great politeness made the woman, in all her obliviousness, play the lady. 'Oh, there's no need.'

He closed the case again. 'Then take it.' He held out the case and she took it.

Mascaranti was watching. Duca went to the door, as if to open it, instead of which he turned the key three times to close it and said, 'Mascaranti, show her your ID': the police ID, the thief catcher's ID.

Mascaranti took his ID from the pocket of his jacket and showed it to the lioness, and standing there with the shiny white handbag in one hand, and the case in the other – it was so heavy that the veins on the back of her hand had already become swollen with blood – she took a good look at the badge, almost as if she was a connoisseur, and even glanced at Mascaranti's face to compare it with the photograph, then, gently, but with a face that, even under the very vulgar make-up, which suited her, became distorted with anger – lionesses easily get angry – put the case back down on the floor, spat in Mascaranti's face and said, 'Filthy bastards, you're always screwing us, just like your …' indicating an unmistakable male attribute.

'No, Mascaranti,' Duca said, stopping Mascaranti's left arm, which was rotating like an Indian club, a fraction of a second before it landed a lethal slap on the lioness's face. 'And you, give me your handbag, I want to see your papers, I don't like talking to people I don't know.'

The lioness spat at him, too: we each use whatever means of communication we possess, and in her case the principal means seemed to be her saliva glands. Duca was able to avoid this communication only by a fraction of a millimetre, but he was unable to prevent Mascaranti hitting the girl this time.

It was a nasty slap: she did not cry out, but her mouth suddenly sweated blood and she slammed against the wall and would have collapsed on the floor if Duca hadn't supported her.

'I told you no, Mascaranti!' he yelled angrily.

'I'm sorry,' Mascaranti yelled back, 'but I don't like people spitting in my face and I don't like them spitting at my friends either.'

'Let's stop shouting,' Duca said, 'and while I'm here I forbid you to use violence.' He lowered his voice a little. 'I want to be the only one to use it.' He supported the woman, who was dazed, her mouth covered in blood, and took her into the kitchen and led her to the sink. 'Clean yourself up.' He gave her a napkin, found a half-finished bottle of whisky, and poured a little bit of it into a glass. 'Wipe your mouth with this.'

She wiped her mouth a bit, and drank the rest, took a small mirror from her handbag and examined her teeth: she had withstood the blow quite well, and had broken only one canine.

'Filthy bastards,' she said, looking at her tooth.

'Sit down and drink some more,' Duca said. 'You can finish the bottle if you like.'

She sat down. She was a bit tottery, because she was still

in shock, and her left cheek was swelling. He poured the rest of the whisky into the glass, filling the glass almost to the brim, until the bottle was empty. She immediately took the glass and drank: she drank the whisky as if it was cold tea.

'There's still some blood coming out,' Duca said, 'clean yourself up and in the meantime I'll get you some ice.'

'Filthy bastards,' she said, and stood up and went and washed herself.

He approached her with the ice holder, took out three or four cubes, managed to break them with a fork, filled a spoon with the fragments and said, 'Keep this in your mouth.'

He spoonfed her as if she were a baby, and she stared at him, trying to make it clear to him with her eyes – in fact she made it very clear – that the only thing she wanted to do was spit the ice back in his face. 'I'm sorry,' he said, sitting down, 'but you shouldn't have provoked us.'

Every now and again there was a wavering in the look of hate she gave him: his politeness, the kind way he spoke to her, couldn't have been familiar to her and puzzled her. She stood up, spat the now melted ice into the sink, sat down again, her black hair turning bluish in the ray of sunlight that fell on her head, took a big gulp of whisky, cleaned her lips with the tissue, checked that her mouth was no longer bleeding, and said, 'Filthy bastards.'

This was a problem that had sometimes vaguely exercised Duca: how to instil obedience in a woman, how to get her to cooperate. Duca considered the use of force on a man perfectly fair and reasonable. If you ask a man, 'Excuse me, do you know who killed that old fellow?' and the man replies, 'I don't know,' a series of slaps, or even kicks, may suddenly remind the man as to who killed the old fellow and even make him reply, 'I did.'

But for reasons – instincts, rather – that must have been completely irrational, he felt himself incapable of using force on a woman. An ancestral sense of chivalry perhaps, because if a woman can kill – and the one facing him now would certainly have killed him if she had been armed, and would have done so without hesitation, killed him or Mascaranti or both – then that woman should be prepared for the reactions of the person she is ready to kill, as well as all the punishments consequent on her ability to kill. But despite this geometrical demonstration, he hesitated to use force on a woman. If he used it, in three minutes he would know everything he needed to know, everything she knew, but he refused to do so.

'Listen,' he said.

'Filthy bastards,' she said.

She was a woman who would yield only to violence, Duca thought, looking beyond the woman, at the view of the shabby courtyard afforded by the kitchen window, and given that he did not want to use violence, that meant she would not yield.

'All right,' he said, then: 'Mascaranti.'

He was also there in the kitchen, the ray of sunlight that had hit the head of the lioness, in continuing its trajectory, came to rest on Mascaranti's dark brown tie as he leaned against the dresser. 'Yes, doctor.'

'Please phone the house and tell them to come and get this lady. Warn them that she spits and resists.' *The house* meant Headquarters.

'Yes, doctor.' Mascaranti went out into the hall to phone.

'Filthy bastards,' the woman said.

'All right,' Duca said, 'you've gambled away your freedom. If you'd listened to me, in half an hour I'd have let you go free, we have no real interest in arresting a nonentity like you. I only wanted to know two things from you: the whereabouts of the friend who sent you here to pick up the case, and the whereabouts of Ulrico Brambilla. You just had to tell me those two things and I'd have let you go, we don't have room in prison for nobodies like you.'

She repeated her one phrase, arrogantly lighting a cigarette with an eye-catching gold Dunhill lighter.

'Very well,' Duca said. 'In a quarter of an hour you'll be in a cell and I assure you that you won't get out again for four or five years. There's criminal conspiracy, there's arms trafficking, and whatever else we find, and even though you aren't the head of the gang, you won't get out until 1971 or '72.'

Mascaranti came back to the kitchen and said, 'I've phoned, they're on their way.'

She looked at the two of them, drank, took a drag on her cigarette then repeated her phrase.

'Dr Lamberti,' Mascaranti said, 'I can't resist.'

'Then go downstairs and wait for the car,' Duca said in a low voice. 'When it comes, come back up with the officers and take the girl away.'

'All right, doctor,' Mascaranti said, and as he went out, the girl said her phrase after him and he stoically refused to turn round.

Duca stood up, took a glass and filled it with water from the tap: it wasn't exactly water from a mountain spring, but the effort to control yourself makes you thirsty. 'It hurts to sacrifice yourself like this for a cretin like your friend. And I'll tell you why he's a cretin: because he lets you walk around dressed like that, disguised as a gangster's moll or a chorus girl on a TV variety show.'

'Filthy bastard,' she said. She drank the whisky, lit another cigarette, and touched her swollen cheek every now and again.

'We're talking about arms trafficking,' Duca said, 'betrayal, complicity with terrorists, multiple killings. Turiddu Sompani throws a couple in the Lambro, Michela Vasorelli and Gianpietro Ghislesi, then someone, maybe Silvano Solvere, throws Turiddu Sompani in the Naviglio, then someone else, maybe your friend, throws Silvano in the Naviglio, and we could let you all carry on, and in a few days they'll kill your friend. As you see, I know something about you people.'

Strangely, she said nothing, just finished drinking the whisky remaining in the glass.

'And your friend sends you here, in a white Opel, dressed like a gangster's moll. I'm surprised the police didn't stop you, just seeing you at the wheel of that car. When we saw it from the window, we thought, here comes the secretary of Murder Inc.'

She did not repeat her phrase, she looked at him with hate, but remained silent. Mechanically, she picked up the glass but it was empty. 'Isn't there any more?' she asked.

'I'll send for a bottle immediately. What kind do you prefer?'

She looked at him with hate, but also with uncertainty, she didn't like to be mocked, but looking at him she realised he wasn't mocking her. 'I'd prefer a Sambuca,' she said.

The entryphone was right there in the kitchen, he asked the caretaker to send Mascaranti to buy a bottle of Sambuca and fifty grams of unground coffee. 'Emphasise that: unground.' The girl might want to chew a few coffee beans with the Sambuca. He lit a cigarette. 'But the stupidity of sending you here, to pick up a case with a submachine gun, as if it was a tin of biscuits! No way is that an operation for a woman. To crown it all, we're with the police, and so you've fallen into a trap, but even if I'd been "straight" and not a filthy bastard of a policeman, do you think I'd have given the case, just like that, to the first woman who comes and says she's a friend of Silvano? At least two men should have come to pick up a case with something like that in it, two armed men, not a girl.'

'He couldn't come himself,' she said, 'not now.'

'Then he should have waited until he could, unless he's an idiot.'

For the first time she lowered her eyes.

'And the stupidity of all of you killing each other! Turiddu Sompani was an important man for you people, and so was Silvano Solvere, so why did you kill them? And who's going to kill you now? I never give advice, but as long as you hang out with idiots, things are going to go badly for you, just as they are now, falling into the hands of the police because of an idiot, and with the certainty of years and years in prison. And prison's not a good place to be. But I can still give you a choice: you have a valid passport, here we are, let's see' – and from the back pocket of his trousers he took the ten-thousand-lire notes that Silvano Solvere had given him before that delicate operation – 'twenty, twenty-one, twenty-two, twenty-three, twenty-four, twenty-five, this is two hundred and fifty thousand lire' – he had spent the rest – 'it's all I have, if I had more I'd give you more, if you answer a few of my questions and if you take me to where your friend is, I promise you I'll let you go free, you can go to France, maybe you've already been there and have a few friends there. I promise you solemnly.' He looked at the money: it was the devil's money, let it go back to the devil.

Her face pitifully distorted by the swollen cheek, she smiled and said, vulgarly, 'I wasn't born yesterday.'

'I wasn't born yesterday either, to think I could deceive someone like you with a trap like that,' Duca said, and then he began to seethe because he too, when you came down to it, had a nervous system, just like Mascaranti, and he threw the twenty-five ten-thousand-lire notes down on the table and raised his voice: 'If I made you that offer it's because it isn't a trap. But go on, try and be clever, the prisons are always as full as Viareggio in high season, because you people are so stupid and ignorant. I'm telling you I'll let you go free, I'm giving you two hundred and fifty thousand lire and you can drive away in your white Opel, because we aren't interested in whores like you, but you won't believe me, you think it's a trap. If I wanted to lay a trap I'd lay a more intelligent one than that, wouldn't I?'

She spat on the ten-thousand-lire notes, making a grimace of pain as she did so because with her mouth swollen it hurt to spit.

'All right,' Duca said. He stood up and went and opened the door to Mascaranti, then came back into the kitchen with the bottle of Sambuca and the unground coffee. He poured the Sambuca into a clean glass and put a few coffee beans into the liquid. For himself, he poured some more water from the tap. 'I don't even need you. When you don't come back your friend will say, "Where's my baby, where's my white Opel?" And he'll come looking for it, I just have to stay here and wait, with that case there in the hall, for him to come here, for the case, for the Opel, and also for you, and I'll leave his Opel outside the front door, with a colleague posted next to it, he'll arrive and we'll grab him, you'll go straight to Police Headquarters, if that's how you want it, everybody has the right to reside where they like.' Keeping his patience was starting to tire him out: if he hadn't had ancestors who had won lots of chivalry tournaments, he would have got her to talk in next to no time.

'He's not that stupid that he'd come here,' she said scornfully.

'Oh, yes, he would,' he yelled angrily, 'because he needs to know what happened to his pretty girlfriend, not because he's all that interested in you, but because he'll suspect you've been arrested by the police, and he knows you'll talk in the end, in fact, we won't even have to lay a finger on you, but we'll make you talk, it's only a matter of time, it might take a week, or two, or three, but you'll tell everything, and so he'll come here to find out what happened to you. He'll be careful, but he'll come here, we'll get him and we'll make him talk.'

Vulgar and ignorant as she was, this argument got through to her. 'So I'm supposed to believe that if I talk, you'll let me go? With the money?' She took a coffee bean, crunched into it and laboriously chewed it with her good jaw, and then took a large swig of the Sambuca.

'Don't believe it if you don't want to,' he said in a low but exasperated voice. Then he had to get up because there was someone at the door. It was Mascaranti with two uniformed officers.

'They've brought the bandage,' Mascaranti said. One of the two officers was holding a big whitish roll, probably hemp, almost like a baby's swaddling clothes in the old days, only much longer. They had heard that they were coming to get a dangerous person, and a dangerous person, bound like a child with that bandage, wasn't dangerous any more, couldn't do anything any more, not even spit, because the bandaging began from the mouth, leaving the nose free for breathing.

The girl was smoking when Duca came back into the kitchen followed by Mascaranti and the two uniformed officers, and a kind of mushroom cloud of smoke was rising over her face and above her head, lit at a certain height by the ray of sunlight. She took a good look at Duca, then at Mascaranti, looked at the two officers then, with the cigarette in her mouth, took the bundle of ten-thousand-lire notes she had spat at a little while earlier, put it in her handbag and said to Duca, 'Send those filthy bastards away.'

Duca had to leap to his feet to stop Mascaranti, who had leapt forward. 'I don't care if I lose my job,' Mascaranti said, 'but I'm going to make the other side of that face swell up too.'

'Please,' Duca said, holding him back, and holding back the two angry officers with his eyes. 'Send the officers back to the house. You stay downstairs outside the front door and keep watch, especially on the Opel.'

Controlling himself heroically, Mascaranti said, 'Yes.' He turned to the officers and said, 'Come on,' and they left the kitchen with their bandage, and with anger seething in their bodies, because it's hard to earn so little, a few measly thousand-lire notes per month, and then hear a lowdown whore like her say words like that to them.

She waited until she heard the front door close, then said, 'You'll really let me go if I talk?' She poured herself some more Sambuca and put a coffee bean in her mouth and started laboriously chewing it.

'Yes, that's right.'

With the coffee bean in her mouth, the lioness said, 'Then fire away.'

They would betray anybody, their dying mothers, their pregnant daughters, they would sell their husbands and wives, their friends and lovers, their brothers and sisters, they would kill anyone for a thousand lire, betray anyone for an ice cream cone, you didn't even have to hit them, you just had to dig down into the muddy depths of their personalities, and what emerged was cowardice, corruption, betrayal.

He stood up and put the glasses, the Sambuca bottle and the coffee in the sink. 'You just have to take me to where your friend is now.' He took her arm and helped her up. 'You can't tell me much, but your friend can tell me a lot more, and your friend's friends even more. Where is he?'

The quarter litre and more of alcohol that she had drunk, at only 10.30 in the morning, had not had any effect on her, she must be armour-plated, she was steady on her feet and spoke clearly. 'He's in Ca' Tarino,' she said, 'in Ulrico's butcher's shop.'

8

He was indeed in Ca' Tarino, shut inside Ulrico's butcher's shop. Ca' Tarino is part of Romano Banco, which is a hamlet attached to Buccinasco, which is a municipality next to Corsico, which is so close to Milan, it practically is Milan. Originally, Ca' Tarino was a cluster of four farmhouses, arranged in a rectangle in the Basso Corsinese, between Pontirolo and Assago, but after the war they had lost the appearance of farmhouses, although not entirely, there were still fields around, although barely cultivated and then only in expectation of selling them as building land, there were muddy roads leading to the farmhouses, but there was also the tarred road that led to Romano Banco, and at the corners of the rectangle of farmhouses there were shops: the wine shop, which had once been called a tavern and today had a jukebox, the drugstore, the bakery that functioned as a small supermarket, and Ulrico Brambilla's butcher's shop.

The man was there, he was tall and well-built, in fact very tall and very well-built, with a handsome, feral face, very handsome and really feral, he looked as if he would easily win a beauty contest for bison, he was clean-shaven, but where the razor had passed the skin was dark purple, a kind of mask that covered his cheeks and chin between his long, thick sideburns.

He was very well dressed, and he was sitting on the marble cash desk. His grey trousers had turn-ups, and his embroidered red shoes, almost size 15, were English in style, might even have been English, his very springlike sky-blue jacket was of good cloth, also probably English, and his shirt, the one thing out of place, was of silk, probably the softest, heaviest silk on the market, a deep yellowish colour, too deep for the sky blue of the jacket.

The bison was smoking a cigarette, and in his hand the cigarette, even though it was king-size, looked miniature, a kind of little cigarette for gnomes. He must be a big smoker because the place was full of cigarette ends, not so much thrown on the ground, but strewn everywhere, above all on the counter, where various things lay in disorder: a metal hammer for beating chops, a wooden one with a handle, two or three knives of various sizes, a hook taken off the rack where the meat was displayed and the little chopper for breaking the bones of big Florentine-style steaks. Many other cigarette ends had finished up on the work bench, near the counter where the butchers cut the big quarters of beef to a commercial size, and there were cigarette ends on the wooden board, on the long marble table, between the big axes, the skewers for holding large pieces of lean meat, the electric bone saw and the mincing machine.

Even though it was half past ten on an exceptionally beautiful May morning all the lights were on in the butcher's shop, because the shutter was down over the main entrance and the back door was also closed. The lighting in butcher's shops is always very strong to bring out the red glow of the meat and all six lights were on, giving out a pitiless light like that of an operating theatre.

The huge man looked at the watch on his wrist – it was a solid gold Vacheron, almost as big as an alarm clock, but very flat – the watch said 10.37 and after seeing the time he passed a hand through his hair, or rather, through that black helmet, at least four centimetres high, that natural helmet that constituted his main claim to beauty, or so he thought, even though the expression did not match his little eyes bordered on the north by his heavy eyebrows and on the south by his vast, mountainous cheekbones. However, something must have happened inside him, as a result of looking at the time, because he jumped down from the cash desk, the cigarette now only half visible, as if it had vanished between his thumb and index finger, and went and looked through the pane of glass into the cold room.

He saw the usual quarter of beef poleaxed by the cold, the only piece of meat left there since, as a sign of mourning – or something else? – Ulrico Brambilla had closed up the shop and sent the butcher's boy on holiday, and then, as usual, he saw Ulrico Brambilla's bare feet, and then all the rest of his naked body, lying on the floor, all the way up to his face, or what had once been his face. The only way you could deduce now that it was a face was because it was above the neck, and still attached to the neck, but you had the impression the bison's fists had modified even its geometrical configuration, the bloodstained ears had been attached to the temples, the nose was only a huge swelling and the mouth like a clown's, going from one cheek to the other. One of Ulrico Brambilla's arms was lying on the floor in an inverted position, in fact it was broken, it had been broken almost an hour earlier, by a simple pressure of the bison's hands, it doesn't take much force, when you come down to it, to break an arm, even one as strong and robust as Ulrico Brambilla's, you just know have to know where to apply that force, and that was something he knew well.

Ulrico Brambilla was breathing and quivering: that gave the man a certain sense of pleasure, and his face with its purple beard relaxed a little with the pleasure, then he stopped looking through the pane of glass, went to the end of the workbench, where there were hooks, from one of which hung a white jacket, the kind that butchers use for their work, and on another hook was hanging a white apron, or what had once been white, now it was all stained, and he put on the jacket and the apron that reached down to his calves, carefully placing his sky-blue jacket over the handle of the glass door, beyond which was the lowered shutter, then retraced his steps, and abruptly opened the door to the cold room.

Ulrico Brambilla looked at him, he couldn't see him well because of all the congealed blood around his eyes, but he saw him, and fainted: he had once been a young stud, the Scarlet Pimpernel, he had been strong too, and killed oxen with a single blow of his big knife, during the war, when he had had to do his butchering clandestinely, but now he had met not so much a man as a stone breaking machine, and the mere sight of him at that moment was worse than a hammer blow.

The man took Ulrico Brambilla by one calf, and dragged him out of the cold room, dragged him over the white tiled floor, which was usually so clean but was now stained with Brambilla's blood. Then he took the little stool from behind the cash desk, moved it closer to that stiff, quivering body, sat down and said, 'Have you changed your mind? Are you going to tell me the truth?' Talking to a man who has fainted, you can't really except an answer, but he was suspicious, he did not believe he had fainted, let alone that he was dying, a man might pretend to have fainted or to be dying in order to trick you, but he wouldn't let anyone trick him and he gave him a slap on the stomach. Given the weight of the hand and the force of the blow, the only result he obtained was a spurt of blood from the mouth.

At this point he realised he was making a mistake, if he killed him he wouldn't get what he wanted. He lit a cigarette, and the smoke flew up towards the lights, the six small ones in the shop. He smoked almost half the cigarette, then threw it away, flicking it through the air with his thumb and index finger as he had been taught at whatever school of good manners he had attended, took Ulrico Brambilla by the armpits, lifted him into a sitting position and propped him against the wall.

He waited, but nothing happened. 'Don't play dead, you're not fooling me.'

No reply.

'I know you're not dead, you're only taking a breather, and then you're going to pull some trick, but you won't catch me.' He spoke with a strong accent from the countryside around Brescia. 'Open your eyes and talk. Tell me how you killed Turiddu.'

No reply: the hairy body of this man who had once been a young stud was perfectly still, with what the Nazi doctors had established in their experiments on the Jews as the stiffness of environmental thermal collapse. In the cold room it was only seven or eight degrees below zero, because that was enough for the normal preservation of meat, and a physique like Ulrico Brambilla's had withstood that modest degree of cold very well, but the bison had not reckoned with the fact that all the blows he had taken had affected Ulrico Brambilla's sensitivity, causing thermal collapse. The only method of re-establishing thermal balance and reviving sensitivity, or at least the quickest, most efficient method, as had been demonstrated by the experiments carried out by Nazi doctors in the extermination camps, was that of animal warmth through sex with a woman: the Jew who had been exposed, naked, for four hours to a temperature of fifteen degrees below zero, was revived, if he was not already dead, by the warmth of a girl, also Jewish to avoid any undesirable mixing of the races, and once he had regained enough strength to feel desire and had achieved an orgasm his thermal balance was re-established and if his heart was strong he recovered. This was why, during the war, when a German pilot fell into icy waters and remained immersed for a few hours before being rescued, the Luftwaffe were recommended to perform this so-called animal thermal therapy.

But the bison did not know these things. This man was playing dead, and he would show him that nobody had ever fooled him. 'Now let's see if you're dead,' he said. He lifted him again by the armpits and dragged him to the end of the workbench, keeping him more or less on his feet, until they reached the slim, geometrically harmonious machine that was used to saw bones.

The principle of the bone saw is very simple: it is a serrated steel band wound around two spools, almost like a film projector. Part of the band remains exposed for a length of thirty or forty centimetres, and when a bone is pushed against the serrated edge of the band as it rotates at high speed, the bone is neatly severed. It is also used to carve the bones of large Florentine chops, which are then cut further with a little hatchet, or in any situation where a butcher needs to divide a bone into two or three pieces.

'Now we'll see if you're dead.' He put the plug in the socket and moved the thumb of Ulrico Brambilla's right hand closer to the sawing band, which had started moving very quickly. 'If you don't tell me where you put the two hundred sachets of M6 and how you killed Turiddu, you're going to lose this thumb.'

No reply. Ulrico Brambilla had opened his eyes a little, but could not see, could not hear, and gave only an imperceptible start – only his body, not his soul – when his thumb was neatly severed.

'Tell me where you put the M6. You killed Turiddu to get it from him, didn't you? Tell me where it is, because otherwise the second thumb is going.'

No reply. The thermal collapse had taken away all sensitivity, and had left only a small light in the crypt of his personality, a final vestige of memory, wandering amid the wreck that had been made of him, a single memory, as he stood there, worse than dead, supported under the armpits by his pitiless enemy in front of the angrily advancing band, a single memory: Giovanna's coloured nails, Giovanna's hand with the silver nails caressing his chest, Giovanna with nails each a different colour, the highly aphrodisiac smell of nail varnish and nail polish remover in the hotel room, those beautiful hands dancing in front of his eyes and then over his body, Giovanna was a virgin, she was a whore, but she was a virgin, and so to the wreck of his memory was added another wreck, in the last moments of his death agony, not a memory, but an image of the future: what would have been, if it had happened, his wedding night with Giovanna, after flooding Romano Banco with carnations and devouring the monumental cake, taking her virginity, hearing her scream, and her nails still painted each a different colour.

'You think you can make a fool of me, do you? Want to play dead, do you? Well, I'll make you play dead for real.'

He still didn't hear him, but he opened his eyes again, and this time, in a final flash, his pupils saw: he saw the band of the machine that he knew so well coming closer to his forehead, to his nose, to the bloodstained rosette of his mouth, to cut his face in two exact halves. He did not close his eyes, even though he was horrorstruck, but the flash in his pupils was gone.

'Now die for real, let me show you how it's done.'

The band squealed more loudly, more shrilly. It seemed to hesitate, as if refusing, even though it was an inanimate machine without a soul, to carry out that task, but in the end it did carry it out after all. 'That'll teach you.'

9

Duca stood up. 'So, if your friend is in Ca'Tarino, in Ulrico's butcher's shop, I want you to take me to where your friend is, and if your friend does turn out to be there, I'll let you go.'

'He is there, unfortunately.'

'Then you'll be able to go free.'

'With the Opel?'

'Of course, we don't need it. We're not looking for a car.'

She also stood up and drank a little more Sambuca. 'I really want to see if those filthy bastards are capable of keeping the truth.' She should have said *keeping their word*, but even in the depths of her vulgarity, the romantic word *truth* had an attraction greater than linguistic accuracy.

He did not pick her up on that vulgar phrase she liked repeating. 'Make sure you don't try and trick us,' he said. 'My friend will follow us in his car and he's armed.'

She had clearly understood. She drank some more Sambuca, shrugged, and passed a hand over the swelling on her cheek, but with everything she had drunk she no longer felt any pain. 'Too late,' she said, obscurely. Was it a threat? Or did it only mean that at this point deception was pointless?

Outside, Duca made her get in behind the wheel of the Opel. 'You drive, I don't like driving.'

She looked at him uncertainly. Was he joking?

Duca signalled to Mascaranti to approach. 'The young

lady is taking us to see a friend of hers,' he said to him. 'Please follow us.'

'Yes, Dr Lamberti,' said the spirit of obedience.

They left. Never had Milan had such a lyrical, d'Annunzian[II] spring as that spring of the year 1966. The wind, a mild but impetuous wind, blew over the flat, industrious metropolis as if over a green, undulating, flower-bedecked Swiss plateau and, unable to bend the tall grass of the meadows at its caress as there wasn't any tall grass, it enveloped and lifted and caressed the skirts of the women, gently ruffled the sparse hair of the half-bald workers and the long hair of the youngsters, stirred the long tablecloths on the café terraces, obliged the various Rossis and Ghezzis and Ghiringhellis and Bernasconis who were wearing hats to hold them down firmly on their heads with their left hands, and all that was missing were the butterflies, big white and yellow butterflies, but butterflies are not suited to Milan, he thought, they are too frivolous, maybe in the Via Montenapoleone, but not even there, they would be a bit art nouveau, and art nouveau was out of fashion. 'Go slower,' he said to the woman at the wheel of the Opel: according to her passport her name was Margherita, but it was jarring to call a woman like that Margherita, 'I don't like going too fast.'

Obediently, she slowed down.

'What's your friend's name?' he asked, nonchalantly, as if just trying to make conversation.

'Claudino,' she said.

'The surname,' he said. He didn't like diminutives, he wanted to know the real name, not the pet name women called him.

'Claudino Valtraga,' she replied conscientiously: she had understood which side her bread was buttered. She smiled as she drove skilfully around the Piazza Cinque Giornate. 'But they call him Claudino because he's very tall and well-built, he always goes around in a car because when he's on foot people turn to look at him. Everybody calls him Claudino.'

So Claudio Valtraga was tall and well-built: good. 'Where is he from?'

She smiled again, extracting herself from the tangle of cars that were trying to get out of the Piazza Cinque Giornate. 'I don't remember, he took me to his village once, it's not far from Brescia, somewhere up in the mountains, but I can't remember the name, it was such a small village it only had one bar, his grandfather still lived there, as tall and well-built as he is, but his father and mother were dead, it was so cold that day.'

'How old is he?'

'Thirty-three,' she said, then: 'Can we stop at a bar? I need a pick-me-up.'

The lioness seemed to have grown weaker. 'If you like,' he said: he wasn't in any hurry, it was only two minutes past eleven on a gorgeous May day, and when you came down to it he needed a pick-me-up too. 'But don't try anything, or it'll be all over for you.'

In the Viale Sabotino she managed to find a cheap drinking hole, more of a tavern than a bar. Their entrance, and especially her entrance, in black and white, with those cowboy-style trousers that clung to her thighs like gloves to fingers, was greeted with a salvo of glances: even the two drunks sitting just under the television set, clearly regulars, seemed to wake from their stupor and stared with watery eyes at the brown lioness, her thighs, her eye-catching mandolin-shaped bottom, and even the young woman behind the counter stared at her, if not with envy, with nostalgia, as if there was a vague desire in her to wear those black trousers, that white jacket with the big button in the middle dividing her breasts, and those white boots. There was nothing drinkable, apart from anisette for her, and for him some kind of white wine poured from a little fountain with four spouts, and, partly because of the anisette and partly because of those itchy male eyes which swept over her like the wind and which she probably liked, she became a lioness again. 'Even if you arrest me and Claudino, we'll be out again in a few months, we have friends.'

He didn't doubt that, but he was starting to track them down, these friends of friends.

'I'd like another anisette,' she said.

'Another anisette,' Duca said to the woman behind the bar.

'Toothache?' the woman asked her.

'No, a punch,' she said, touching her swollen cheek, 'a punch from a son of a bitch.'

Ah, so they were getting back to vulgarity. 'Drink your anisette and then let's go,' Duca said.

The woman behind the bar didn't like that vulgar expression: common people are sensitive to words, they prefer posh words so that they don't appear too common. Offended, she went to the end of the counter where the coffee machine was.

'I want another anisette,' Margherita said.

Now he realised what her plan was: to get so drunk that she collapsed, then she wouldn't be able to take them to Ca' Tarino, they'd waste a lot of time on the way there with a drunk woman on their hands, and her friend, starting to be suspicious because of the delay, would probably make good his escape. He tried to explain to her how things were, in a low voice, but clearly: 'You're not drinking any more. You're taking me to your friend right now. If you try anything,

I promise you I'll smash your face in, the punch you got before will be a caress in comparison, and when your face has been smashed in' – and he really would smash it in – 'your powerful friends may get you out of prison, but you won't get your face back the way it was.' His tone was less one of threat than that of a teacher explaining the theorem of parallels.

This talk of disfiguring faces was the kind of language she understood, she could see it in his eyes that he was absolutely determined to disfigure her as he said he would. 'Let's go,' she said, even with a certain politeness because of the fear.

'And drive slowly,' he said in the car: she might even fake an accident, knock down a passer-by, just so as not to take them to her friend.

She drove slowly, and well: he had overestimated her, he had thought she was capable of defending her friend to the end, but these weren't the kind of people who defended their friends.

'As far as your powerful friends are concerned, we've arrested more than half of them at the Binaschina.' He told her the names of four people who had fallen into the trap laid at the Binaschina. 'The ship is sinking fast, don't rely on those people too much, stay with us.'

Those names had an effect on her, they seemed to sober her up, and the lioness turned into a lamb, disgustingly servile. 'Of course I'm with you. Be careful, because he's very big and very well-built, and he's armed, you won't be able to take him on if there are only two of you, he even held three men at bay once and ended up knocking them all out.'

All the better, Duca thought, all the better, he had no intention of keeping him at bay: if the man attacked them, if he fired at them, they had to defend themselves, Mascaranti had a gun, he wouldn't let himself be killed without reacting, and the headline would read something like this: *Gunman Fires at Police*, and beneath, in smaller letters: *He is killed in brief conflict with law enforcement officers*, because however modestly, and even somewhat illegally, the two of them were still some kind of law enforcement officers.

Here was the Naviglio, and as they continued towards Corsico they every now and again came across a stretch of the canal that was like a picture postcard image of old Milan, made even more dreamlike by the wind ruffling the waters. He even saw two women washing on the bank, on special stones: they didn't like washing machines.

'Who told you I had that case?' he asked, not looking at her but at the Naviglio, the wind, the spring that was still managing to display itself even in that bare suburban landscape. 'And why did it take you so long to come and pick it up?'

'Claudino only knew that Silvano had the case,' she said, scared and servile, 'and that Silvano had got it from Ulrico, so we went to Ulrico's and he wasn't there, he'd run away, that was when Claudino realised he'd kept the case, and we started looking for him, we went everywhere, then Claudino thought he must be hiding in one of his shops, a closed butcher's shop is a place where nobody would think of looking for someone, but Claudino knows him and he went to Ca' Tarino, he knocked down the door with his shoulder and Ulrico was inside, so he asked him for the case, he told him he'd given it to Giovanna and that was the last he'd heard of it, then he said Giovanna might have left it in the perfume shop in the Via Plinio, as she'd done before, so Claudino sent me straight to the perfume shop and the woman in the perfume shop told me, yes, Giovanna had left the case there, but then she'd come back to pick it up and told her she was going to a doctor in the Piazza Leonardo da Vinci and so I went to the Piazza Leonardo da Vinci.'

What idiots! So that was how they had bagged them. In the rearview mirror he looked at Mascaranti's Simca keeping pace with him, then looked again at the wind-ruffled waters of the Naviglio, they were in Corsico, but seemed to be in an enchanted landscape of lagoons, and the servility of this false lioness made him nauseous, compared with the luminous clarity of the day.

'So now he's waiting for you to come back with the case?'

At the flashing traffic light just before the bridge over the Naviglio Grande, she turned left into the main street of Corsico. 'Yes,' she said, having executed the manoeuvre.

'Right, now listen carefully to what I'm about to say.'

'Yes,' she said, servile, then said, 'I'm scared.'

'Listen carefully to what I'm about to say and don't be scared.'

'Yes,' she said, ever more servile, 'but I am scared. He'll shoot, he shoots everybody, I know what you want me to do' – she did not realise her voice was quivering with fear – 'but as soon as he realises I've grassed on him, he'll shoot me first. Even with Silvano there was no need to shoot him, he just had to block the road, but he was angry, I told him no, no, no, but he fired and you know what he told me? "With this storm, no one will hear a thing."'

'Just listen and keep calm,' Duca said. 'Stop the car and I'll get in the back and hide between the seats, do you understand?'

'Yes, yes,' she nodded, the fear had even drained the olive colour from her vulgar face. She stopped by the last houses on the Via Dante where it met the Via Milano.

'When we get there,' Duca said, 'park in front of the butcher's shop, I'll be hidden in the back. Stop, get out, and make him open up for you. Is there a signal you've agreed on?'

'No, he just has to hear my voice.'

'Good, get him to open up and don't try any tricks. If you do as I say, in ten minutes you can drive away in this car.' Duca got out, smiled at Mascaranti, who was watching him from the Simca, which had also stopped, and got in the back. 'Go slowly and don't think of pulling any stunts.' Slowly, he slid between the seats: Signor Claudio Valtraga might be watching and seeing his woman arrive with a man would arouse his suspicions, that was why he hid.

In that bright midday giddy with wind, the beautiful white Opel reached Romano Banco, drove through it, entered an area that was partly built-up and partly countryside, veered slightly towards Pontirolo, and finally came to an old Roman square, a complex of four former farmhouses known as Ca' Tarino. Her face grey with fear, she stopped the car near one of the four corners of the rectangle, where the butcher's shop was. The snow-white marble sign said *Butcher: Best Meats*, and beneath it in smaller lettering were the words *Proprietor Ulrico Brambilla*. 'Talk to him, but don't stand in front of the door,' Duca said, 'stand to the side, so that he can't see you when he opens the door and has to come outside.'

'Yes,' she said, grey and servile, and got out.

At this hour, almost lunchtime, Ca' Tarino was deserted, but there, just next to the butcher's shop, two little girls, maybe four or five years old, were sitting on a mound of rubbish, the way children do, because they can, holding on to a large turkey which was keeping obediently still, moving only its neck to peck at the rubbish. On the balcony of one of the four houses, a woman was beating an eye-catching yellow blanket, it was the only sound in that incredible silence that precedes mealtimes.

The entrance to the butcher's shop was on one side, with the shutter down, and on the other side there was a back door.

She headed for the back door, but as she passed the two little girls, virtually immersed in the rubbish – hygiene is a form of superstition – and in the hard feathers of the turkey that was picking at it, a quite unforeseen impulse of female kindness, actually quite disturbing in a creature as loutish as her, led her to say in a low voice, 'Get out of here, girls,' and seeing that swollen, fear-ridden face, the two little girls obeyed immediately, even forgetting about the turkey, which stayed where it was, impassively searching in the rubbish.

She knocked twice at the door, which was slightly off its hinges, and said, 'Claudino, it's me,' she had to raise her voice, because the woman who was beating the carpet on the rail of the balcony must have lost her temper and the *thwack-thwack* of the carpet beater echoed around the rectangle of Ca' Tarino. 'It's me, Claudino, I have the case.'

At that moment Duca opened the car door, slipped out of the car and ran to take up his position next to the back door of the building. A moment later, he was joined by Mascaranti.

PART THREE

He was even wearing a nice sweater knitted by her, he had watched her knit it, had seen it growing day by day in her hands, with a kind of eyelet in the bottom edge in which to hide the two cyanide capsules he could use to kill himself instantaneously.

1

Claudio Valtraga was very elegant. He had taken off the white butcher's jacket and the long apron, had taken what remained of Ulrico Brambilla into the cold room, and had carefully washed himself in the huge sink in that cold room. Unfortunately there were a few little spots of blood – Ulrico Brambilla's blood – on the collar of his shirt, and one quite big one on the right hand cuff, but the cow would be arriving soon, that was what he – mentally, but also verbally – called his companion Margherita, and they would go home and he would change his shirt. He had also combed his hair with the little comb he had in the inside pocket of his jacket, and had even admired himself in the long mirror behind the counter, which bore the words *Ulrico Brambilla – Butcher – Top Quality Meats*, and then had started to smoke, sitting on the marble cash desk, waiting.

He had had time to smoke two cigarettes before he heard the sound of a car, he had a refined ear and could tell it was his Opel, and then he heard her voice, 'Claudino, it's me,' and then again, over the *thwack-thwack* of the woman beating her blanket, 'It's me, Claudino, I have the case.' He jumped down from the cash desk: this was good news. The back door was a bit shaky since he had shoved it in with his shoulder, but the iron transom was still in place, he pulled the transom and opened the door, he didn't see anybody and instinctively stepped outside, all he could see was the turkey, by the time he saw Duca and put his hand inside his jacket to take out his gun it was too late. With a good stone in his hand, which must have weighed a couple of kilos, Duca landed the fiercest punch of his life on the right jaw, aiming just under the jaw, and when the punch arrived, Claudio Valtraga went out instantaneously like a light being switched off and collapsed to the ground, inside the shop. At that very moment, a young man on a motor scooter screeched to a halt, making as much noise as a Jaguar pulling up abruptly at a red light. 'What's going on?' he asked. He had seen Duca land the punch, but he had also seen the woman, in black and white, with all that flesh bulging out from beneath her clothes.

'Police,' Mascaranti said. 'Go home and mind your own business.' In braking, the motor scooter had sent the turkey running, but the two little girls now reappeared and behind them was an old man in dark blue overalls with a bicycle pump in his hand, saying 'Come here, come here,' but without any anxiety.

Mascaranti entered the butcher's shop, and dragged the bison inside and across the carpet of cigarette butts and blood, which was what the floor of the shop had become. Meanwhile, Duca went to the woman, who was standing next to the white Opel and seemed not to have yet understood what had happened, she would never have imagined that her Claudino could end up like that, and so abruptly.

'Get in the car and go,' he said. 'I'll give you three hours to leave the country, in three hours all the border posts will be informed. Go!' he screamed. He had become a wicked person, because the woman would kill herself trying to get to the French border in three hours, and that was precisely what he wanted. 'Go, I said!' And as she jumped in behind the wheel and started the engine, he screamed at the young man on the motor scooter, who was still there, 'Get out of here and leave us alone!' And he went into the butcher's shop, lit in the middle of the day by those six lamps as powerful as small suns, and closed the loose door against the sun and the wind and the bright spring day outside.

'Look, Dr Lamberti,' Mascaranti said in a weak voice, holding open the door to the cold room. There was a contraction, a twisting, in his stomach even though, as a policeman, he had seen a lot of things in his life.

Duca took two steps forward and looked: he was a doctor and had attended the required number of anatomy lessons but the inhuman mess that had been made of that body was greater than his own powers of resistance, and he clenched his jaws and said, 'Close the door.'

Mascaranti closed it, then retched. 'I'm sorry,' he said.

'Go and phone the house, and then the morgue.'

'We'll need a waterproof sheet.'

'Yes, tell the people in the morgue. I'll keep an eye on this fellow.' He leaned over the unconscious Claudio Valtraga, touched him with disgust and immediately found his gun, a small but solid and efficient Beretta. In silence, he handed it to Mascaranti.

'Keep it, Dr Lamberti,' Mascaranti said, 'he'll come round in two minutes and you'll be alone with him while I'm phoning.'

'I don't like guns,' Duca said, 'I don't enjoy using them, I prefer my fists.'

Mascaranti refused to take the gun. 'Dr Lamberti, the two of us couldn't control this guy without a gun.'

'Take the gun and go and phone!' Duca shouted.

Shouting is a more convincing method than speaking. Reluctantly, Mascaranti took the Beretta and went out.

Duca looked at the monumental figure of Claudio

Valtraga on the floor. Not with hate, Dr Duca Lamberti, not with hate, this isn't about revenge, it's about justice, yes, that's understood, a man capable of doing what he had done to a fellow human being, with the help of a saw for cutting bones, arouses ill feeling, but a civilised person has to overcome this ill feeling, he has to understand he is dealing with misfits, with people who would not have reached this point if they had been properly educated.

Never heard such a load of nonsense, he thought as he went behind the work bench, while still keeping an eye on the so-called human being Claudio Valtraga, who would be coming round very soon. Is a wolf a misfit? If it was properly educated would it learn to bow, would it learn to play ring-a-ring-a-roses with children? Had it never occurred to them, he thought as he searched through the various tools of the trade on the counter – three magnificent knives in increasing order of size, a couple of bradawls for making holes in meat, and two types of chopper, a small one, good for veal cutlets, the other so big that a Frank from mediaeval Gaul would have taken it for an axe, obviously used for quarters of beef, to break the spine – had it never occurred to these geniuses that some creatures have only the appearance, the physical aspect of humans, but are in reality, for unknown and so far inscrutable genetic reasons, hyenas, wild animals that no amount of education, except possibly the education of violence, would make less bloodthirsty? Had it never occurred to them? Yes, of course, Dr Lamberti, that was how people thought in the Middle Ages, do you want to go back to the Middle Ages? Well, maybe he did, but for now there was no time to waste.

He took the Franco-Gallic axe from the counter – it was so heavy he needed to hold it in both hands – and turned abruptly: the bison had come to, he had already put his hands on the floor and was trying to get up onto his knees.

Duca took a step forward. 'Stay where you are and lie on the floor with your face down, or I'll cut you in half with this.'

Resting on his hands, Claudio Valtraga slowly lifted his head. His ears, still buzzing a bit, had heard the words, and his mind, still a little dazed, had taken them in, and his eyes, even though a little blurred, had seen the huge axe, which Duca was holding in both hands, the blade facing down, between his legs, ready to raise it and strike. This was his language too, it was the language he understood, so he crouched down, face to the floor, without any further attempt to stand up, convinced by the obvious persuasiveness of the argument, and it didn't even occur to him that a normal man might threaten to strike him with an axe like that but would never go through with it. In fact Duca would only have hit him on the head with the back of the axe, and if the man had been clever, he wouldn't have been afraid of being cut in half and would have leapt to his feet, but a man like that can't be clever, even though he thinks he is, convinced that he's running the risk of being split in two with an axe, so he stayed there on the floor, because if *he'd* had the axe, then he really would have chopped his opponent up.

'Why did you kill Ulrico?' Duca moved in towards him, holding the axe with only one hand now, close to his face.

'Who's Ulrico?' Claudio Valtraga said, his cheek on the floor, crushing a cigarette end. 'I didn't kill anybody.'

What a joker! 'You don't know a thing, right?' Duca was finding it hard to control himself, the man's insolence angered him, why wasn't he allowed to chop his head off? 'So you've never met Ulrico Brambilla, never seen a bone cutter, you were in here by chance, is that it?'

'Yes,' Claudio Valtraga said, thinking all the while, as his strength flowed back, that if he moved quickly enough he'd be able to crush the policeman's head, as he had done when he was a child, with his thumb, to the heads of sparrows and frogs – in a democracy, everyone plays the childhood games he prefers – and in the meantime he was bracing the fingers of his cyclopean hands on the floor and, with imperceptible movements, manoeuvring his feet, which were as big as those of Egyptian sphinxes, into a better position to make the leap he imagined in his zootrophic brain.

'We'll do the interrogation later, when you've changed your mind,' Duca said, watching these imperceptible movements: he had to be alert, or he'd be dead. 'In the meantime, sleep a bit longer.'

The two kicks full in the face did not surprise Claudio Valtraga, partly because he did not even notice them, he did not even have time to see them coming. The first, to his forehead, caused an immediate narcosis, the second, to his nose, sent the blood gushing out: a fine way to cool the man's animal impulses somewhat.

I'm sorry, Duca thought, as if talking to Carrua, or to the goddess of justice, *I didn't have much choice*. If he hadn't done it, in a couple of seconds he would have been pushed against the bone saw or thrown down on the wooden board where the vertebrae of oxen were broken.

He put the big axe down on the work bench, looked for the least dirty, least bloodstained place in the shop, close to the shutter, and stood there waiting, beneath the blazing light of the six lamps.

Mascaranti soon returned from having phoned, and some time later, because he had had to come all the way across the city, Carrua arrived with four officers, by which time Claudio Valtraga had again come to but was sitting quietly on the ground with Mascaranti's gun pointed at him. At last Duca could get away from that laughing stock. A little group of people had gathered outside, even though it was lunchtime, and they were looking avidly at Claudio Valtraga's battered face.

'Go back to your houses,' Carrua shouted, 'go home.'

2

Claudio Valtraga wasn't looking so elegant now, his pale blue jacket was crumpled, it had lost the shape, the fall, that makes for true elegance, his trousers were torn over the knee, and he was no longer as handsome as before: the pieces of sticking plaster on his nose and jaw didn't look good on him. Nor was the office particularly beautiful, it was a clean, respectable office in Milan Police Headquarters in the Via Fatebenefratelli, but it wasn't exactly a model of elegance in furnishings, there was nothing but a table and four chairs and, in a corner, a sorghum broom left there by the cleaning lady.

Claudio Valtraga was sitting halfway along one of the four walls, the one facing the window, with the sun on his face, on the sticking plasters and the feral blue of his beard. Against the wall opposite, next to the window, was a little table and at this table Mascaranti was sitting with his little exercise book and his pink ballpoint pen in his hand. There was also an officer standing next to Claudio Valtraga, a uniformed officer, theoretically armed because he had a gun in his holster, but in practice, even if he had taken it out, Claudio Valtraga would have had time to crush him and Mascaranti. But with all his plasters it didn't look as if he had any more desire to crush anybody, he was sitting quietly on his chair, the fingers of his hands together and his hands crossed on his knees and his eyes a little blurred.

And in a corner, next to Mascaranti's table, was Duca, asking questions. He had just started and Claudio Valtraga was answering well and promptly.

'I want to know about the first two people you threw in the water,' Duca said. 'The girl was Michela Savorelli, she was a prostitute, and the man, Gianpietro Ghislesi, was her pimp. Why did you kill them?'

'Because they were strung out.'

'What do you mean, they were strung out?'

'They were taking M6, they were always strung out, they couldn't work anymore.'

'M6 means mescaline 6?'

'Yes, they were supposed to be circulating it, but they always kept a few packets for themselves, and when they were high they talked, they were a danger to everybody.'

Mescaline 6: this alkaloid, one of the most remarkable hallucinogens known to man, is extracted from a small cactus originating in Mexico, the peyotl. It would have been strange if there hadn't been drugs involved, the business had various branches, the usual predictable and disgusting activities, prostitution, arms smuggling, robberies of course, and, inevitably, drugs. 'What do you mean by circulating the M6?' Duca knew perfectly well, he only wanted Claudio Valtraga to explain it to him so that Mascaranti could write it down.

'Getting it to the customers,' Claudio Valtraga said. 'It isn't easy work, you have to make sure you're given the money first, you have always to watch out for the police, and then there are customers who are in detox and are being watched over by a nurse, and you have to sell the sachet and get the money without the nurses noticing.'

'And why did you decide to kill them?'

'A couple of times, when there were just a few sachets missing, we forgave them and told them not to do it again, but once they did away with a whole load.'

'What do you mean by a load?

'A plastic bag with a hundred sachets in it, it fits snugly in any pocket.'

'So Turiddu Sompani decided to kill them.'

'He didn't, THEY did,' and the way he said *they*, it really was as if the word was in capital letters. Duca already knew who THEY were: Valtraga had given the names and Mascaranti had written them down in his magic exercise book, and they had already been phoned through to Carrua, half the staff of Headquarters was already scattered through Milan, and three telephone operators had lost their voices dictating bulletins to alert the border posts, the stations, the motorways, from the Alps to Sicily. That was why Claudio Valtraga, the bison, had become so docile.

'And they gave Turiddu Sompani the job of killing them?'

'Yes, but they didn't want it to look like murder.'

'And what did Sompani do?'

'He took them to a trattoria near the Conca Fallata, that restaurant that's almost on the Lambro, he said he was their friend and to convince them he gave them a sachet. So, what with the eating and the drinking and the sachet, they were in a high old mood and then Turiddu said to Gianpietro, "Do you think you could cross the Lambro in a car?"'

That was it. When a man has taken a dose of mescaline 6, he feels capable of anything: raping dozens of women, killing dozens of enemies, crossing the Lambro in a car, swimming the Atlantic, M6 gives you power, sexual desire, imagination, lots of imagination, and Attorney Turiddu Sompani had precisely calculated the dose of M6 he had given them. 'So Gianpietro Ghislesi got in the car with his girlfriend Michela and tried to cross the Lambro?'

'Yes,' Claudio Valtraga said, and despite the sticking plasters he seemed on the verge of laughter, even now, at the thought of a man strung out on drugs trying to cross the Lambro in a car.

Unfortunately, Turiddu Sompani had not reckoned with the fact that the waiter who had served them, a short, honest, surly but likeable fellow from Puglia, had followed their conversation and, after the car had plunged into the Lambro, had told the police that he, Turiddu Sompani, had told the two drunk young people – the honest Pugliese thought they were just drunk, he didn't know anything about mescaline – to cross the Lambro by car. At the trial, Turiddu Sompani had firmly denied that he had driven the couple to it, but the surly Pugliese, without any fear, out of simple respect for the truth, insisted on blaming him, and despite all the protection he had, Attorney Sompani was sentenced to two and a half years in San Vittore prison, which was where Duca had met him.

'And why was Turiddu Sompani killed?' He was asking the questions only out of logical curiosity, to see the mental process of these criminals, but by now he'd stopped caring about this whole murky business.

'Nobody wanted to kill him, it was Ulrico.' Claudio Valtraga's eyes, maybe violet, darkened suddenly, gleamed with hate.

'And why did he kill him?'

'Because that evening Turiddu Sompani was supposed to be getting two loads of M6.'

'So according to you, Ulrico Brambilla took the mescaline 6 off Turiddu Sompani and then threw him with his car in the canal?' What extraordinary people!

'Yes,' Claudio Valtraga said.

'But why would Sompani have given him the mescaline 6, and how did he manage to throw them in the Naviglio? Couldn't it have been an accident?'

'No, because the M6 disappeared,' Claudio Valtraga said. 'If it had been an accident the police would have found the M6 on Turiddu.'

There was a logic to all this, but it still didn't quite make sense. 'Let's start again from the beginning, because I really want to get this right,' he said to Claudio Valtraga. 'Who gave Sompani the mescaline 6?'

His eyes lowered in order not to be blinded by the sun that was coming in through the window, as if the sun was functioning as a glaring light in an old-style third-degree interrogation, Claudio Valtraga said, 'Could I have a coffee? I feel really down.'

Duca made a sign to Mascaranti, and Mascaranti in an impulse of criminal rehabilitation said, 'Do you want something strong in it?'

'Oh, yes, thank you, grappa,' the bison moaned.

Mascaranti phoned the switchboard to get a coffee from the bar, and Duca repeated, 'Who gave Sompani the mescaline 6?' Coffee and grappa for people who chopped up men alive with a bone saw: a policeman couldn't get more civilised, more polite than that.

'It was Ulrico who went to get the stuff in Genoa, and then had to bring it to Turiddu.'

So Ulrico Brambilla had been the courier, he didn't only transport the latest model of submachine gun, but also consignments of drugs. 'But then explain to me,' Duca said, slightly irritably – here in Headquarters, surrounded by the representatives of the law, he couldn't kick anyone in the face – 'Ulrico Brambilla goes to Genoa to get the mescaline 6, brings it to Sompani, then takes it back from him and kills Sompani. What kind of story is that?'

'He was supposed to give him the M6, but he didn't, he kept it for himself.'

'And then?'

'Then Ulrico found out that Silvano would be going to get the M6 from Turiddu that evening, to get it circulated, and if Turiddu told Silvano that Ulrico hadn't given him the M6 he'd got in Genoa, Silvano would have known that he still had the M6, so he went to the Binaschina and crashed into Turiddu with his car and pushed him and his lady friend into the Naviglio.'

This too was quite logical: the courier keeps the drugs for himself, instead of passing it to the man who distributes it to the salesmen – it's more advantageous to work for yourself – then kills the distributor to cover up the fact that he didn't hand it over to him. 'And then?' he said to Claudio Valtraga, disgusted.

'And then, as soon as Turiddu died, we waited a couple of days to see if the police had found the M6 on him but it was obvious from the start that you lot hadn't found anything, because he'd never received it, and we went to Ulrico, and he told me he'd handed the M6 over to Turiddu, and I believed him, that's why I can't forgive him.' He'd cut him in half with a saw, but he still couldn't forgive him.

Duca felt his stomach heave up into his throat, a wonderful sensation of moral nausea. 'Go on, toerag,' he said in a muted voice.

He went on. 'It's because if Ulrico had handed the drugs over to Turiddu, then the person who killed Turiddu had to have been Silvano, who'd got the M6 off him and then, to keep it for himself instead of circulating it, threw him, Turiddu, in the Naviglio. That's why I had to deal with Silvano and Giovanna. Because as soon as THEY found out that Ulrico had handed the stuff over to Turiddu, they told me, Deal with it, and I dealt with Silvano, but Ulrico had tricked me.' His anger at having been tricked distorted his face even more than it was already distorted by the sticking plasters and he looked even more repulsive, sitting there with the sun still beating down on him. 'It wasn't Silvano who'd taken the stuff from Turiddu, it was Ulrico who'd kept it for himself.'

Inside himself, Duca started to laugh: Carrua was right, it was a good thing they were killing each other, a good thing they were betraying each other, a good thing they were stealing drugs from each other. Those three falls into the Naviglio and the Lambro made perfect sense now: it was an internal feud among the members of a large concern with wide and varied activities, both national and foreign. There was only one thing that still remained obscure. 'So what happened to the two loads of mescaline 6?'

'Ulrico hid them, but I couldn't get him to tell me where, he kept saying he didn't know anything about it, and then – then I lost patience.'

Of course, a person can lose patience, and that's when he kills. Duca lowered his eyes and looked at the ground, in order not to see that piece of trash, and luckily at that moment an officer came in with the coffee with the grappa and the other officer who was already there served it to the citizen Claudio Valtraga, to give him a bit of a pick-me-up because he was feeling very down, and, until he had had a proper trial, it was forbidden to call him a killer.

'When he's finished his coffee,' Duca said, his eyes still lowered, 'take him back to his cell. I want him out of my sight.'

Yes, Dr Lamberti,' Mascaranti said.

And when the officer had left the room with the citizen Claudio Valtraga, Duca looked up and said to Mascaranti, 'We've finished here, I'm going home,' He lit a cigarette. 'The only thing left is the business of those two bags of mescaline 6. If Ulrico kept the bags for himself, he may have given them to his old friend Rosa Gavoni to hide. These idiots didn't think of looking at her place. Go there and talk to her, for me the whole thing's over.'

'She's in hospital,' Mascaranti said. 'She was taken there in shock after she identified the body of Ulrico Brambilla.'

It was a lot more than shock, he understood her very well. 'Question her as soon as you can, she's bound to talk, to get her revenge on the people who killed her man.'

They left the office with the broom abandoned in a corner and went upstairs, to Carrua's office. Carrua was writing. 'Well?' he said.

'Mascaranti wrote it all down, he'll tell you,' Duca said. 'I've finished and I'm going home.'

'We're getting some big fish here,' Carrua said, 'You wouldn't believe some of the names I've arrested.'

'Be careful they don't break your net, if they're that big.'

'And you're breaking my balls.' He looked daggers at him, a furious Sardinian.

Whereas Duca Lamberti, the furious Emilian, looked at him with a smile. 'That's why I'm going. I've finished. There are some drugs that are missing, it's still a bit unclear what happened to them, but Mascaranti can deal with it. I'm going.'

'Wait a minute. I wanted to tell you you did really well. This was the biggest gang in the North of Italy.'

'It was good of you to trust someone like me,' Duca said. 'You're a talent scout, you recognise genius.'

'Sit down a minute, I have to talk to you, don't be such a smart alec.'

'I won't sit down, thanks, I've been sitting down all this time looking at a toerag.'

'I just wanted to tell you you did very well.'

'You already told me.'

'Let me talk, Duca, otherwise I'll get angry.' He was speaking in a touchingly low voice. 'You did very well and I can see to it that you get put on a salary here.'

'I'd like that, and I like the work. How much will the salary be?' A hundred and forty thousand, maybe, because he was recommended by Carrua, plus travel expenses every now and again, if he was good. If a criminal shot him and blinded him, for example, they would send him at the State's expense to a school for the re-education of blind people, and they would teach him to be a switchboard operator: hadn't there been, up until a few years ago, a switchboard operator in Headquarters who was a blind former police officer?

'Yes, I knew you'd answer that way,' Carrua said, 'but with a hundred and forty thousand lire a month you can't support your sister and niece.'

He'd guessed right, a hundred and forty thousand, he could guess the future, he could even become a psychic. 'Well, then?'

'I think I can have you put back on the medical register,' Carrua said, 'not the same way as that other fellow, what was his name, the one who reminded me of Solvay soda?'

'Silvano Solvere.' He had stopped smiling.

'That's right, Silvano Solvere, he promised you he would get you put back on the register, I can't promise it for certain, but I can tell you that if you write me a letter, just a few lines, you know, within a month you may be able to reopen your clinic and I'll come there for a consultation because –'

'Forget about that, just tell me what kind of letter I need to write.' He was very serious now.

'There's no point in making a face like a rabid dog,' Carrua shouted now, and carried on shouting, 'I have to explain something to you and I'll explain it even if you're rabid.'

'I *am* rabid.'

'And I'll explain it all the same. The letter has to go something like this: I did three years in prison for having, in my capacity as a doctor, killed a patient of mine with an injection of ircodine, for the purpose of euthanasia. I recognise now that, even though driven by idealistic and humanitarian motives, I made a mistake. Euthanasia is an absolutely inadmissible practice, the death of each individual must come only for reasons independent of the will of man and, beyond the duty to help every individual by any means possible, an individual has the right to hope until the last moment of his life. And admitting this mistake I give my word that I will never do it again and I asked to be readmitted to the medical register, etc., etc.'

'Yes,' Duca said.

'What do you mean, yes? If you mean you'll write it, there's the typewriter, write the letter, sign it, give it to me and I'll see to the rest.'

'"Yes" means I'll think about it.'

Carrua was about to start shouting again, but restrained himself. 'It doesn't seem to me there's much to think about, but all right, think about it. But hurry up. The professor who may be able to help me is only in Milan for a few days.'

'All right, I'll hurry up,' he said icily. 'Can I go?'

'Yes, you can go,' Carrua said.

He left the Headquarters building, at the corner with the Via dei Giardini he lit a national-brand cigarette and smoked all of it, to calm down, which was easy enough to do, because Milan at the moment was so beautiful, it didn't even seem like Milan, with that clear air, the light like the Swiss mountains, maybe there had been some meteorological error, and having smoked his cigarette he went on his way, he entered the galleries in the Piazza Cavour, and went to the big bookshop, a kind of gleaming ark containing all the books in existence. He went to this bookshop every now and again, he was friendly with the intelligent-looking young man who worked there, and also the tall young woman who worked there and also looked very intelligent, pleasantly intelligent. They were both there, and they both smiled at him.

'Excuse me,' he said to the young man, 'do you have the edition of the works of Galileo Galilei edited by Sebastiano Timpanaro?'

'The one from 1936? I think so.' Quickly, efficiently, he sent another young woman to look for the edition and after a couple of minutes there they were, the beautiful volumes bound in parchment, with the top edge gilded, the absolutely complete writings of Galileo Galilei. Duca had looked through them once, as a student, at a friend's house.

'I can do you a special discount,' the young man said.

'I don't have any intention of buying them,' Duca said: he would have liked to buy them and read them, read all the volumes, all the pages, but he would satisfy such a desire in another life, not in this one, there wasn't time. He started leafing through the first volume, looking for the index.

The young man smiled. 'If you want to have them to look through for a few days ...'

'That's very kind, I've already found what I was looking for, here it is, in the Galilean Chronology, page 1041 of volume 1: *Recantation*. But maybe I can take advantage of you. Do you have a typewriter I can borrow for a couple of minutes and a sheet of paper?'

'The typewriter's over there, and here's the paper, it's headed, does that matter?'

'No, it doesn't matter, thanks.' There was a kind of little desk, with a little typewriter on it, and a high-backed chair behind it, as if for a university professor, and they gave it up to him with a gentle smile. He sat down, put the paper in the typewriter, in delicate lettering at the top of the paper were the words *Cavour Bookshop*, and under it he wrote: Recantation, copying from page 1041 of the works of Galileo Galilei, volume 1, then he lit another cigarette and continued copying:

I, Galileo, son of the late Vincenzo Galilei, of Florence, aged seventy years, arraigned personally before this tribunal, and kneeling before your Most Eminent and Reverend Lords Cardinals, Inquisitors-General of the entire Christian commonwealth against heretical depravity, having the Holy Gospels before my eyes and touching them with my hands, swear that I have always believed, now believe, and with the help of God will in the future believe, all that is held, preached, and taught by the Holy Catholic and Apostolic Church. But whereas after an injunction had been judicially made against me by this Holy Office, to the effect that I must abandon altogether the false opinion that the sun is the centre of the world and is immovable, and that the earth is not the centre of the world, and moves, and that I must not hold, defend, or teach the said false doctrine in any manner whatsoever, either verbally or in writing, and after it had been signified to me that said doctrine was contrary to Holy Scripture, I wrote and printed a book in which I treat of this same doctrine already condemned, and adduce arguments of great cogency in support of the same, without presenting any solution of these, and for this reason have been judged by the Holy Office to be grievously suspected of heresy, that is, of having held and believed that the Sun is the centre of the world and is immovable, and that the earth is not the centre and moves. Therefore, desiring to remove from the minds of your Eminences, and of all faithful Christians, this grievous suspicion justly entertained towards me, with sincere heart and unfeigned faith I abjure, curse, and detest the said errors and heresies, and generally every other error, heresy, and sect that is contrary to the said Holy Church, and I swear that I will never again in the future say or assert, either verbally or in writing, anything that might give rise to a similar suspicion against me; but that should I know of any heretic, or person suspected of heresy, I will denounce him to this Holy Office, or to the Inquisitor or Ordinary of the place where I may be. Poor man, not only was he recanting but, at the age of seventy, he was undertaking to be a spy and to denounce other heretics like himself. History is the teacher of life, and we learn many fine things. With two fingers, but very quickly, he finished copying Galileo Galilei's recantation: *I, the said Galileo Galilei, have abjured, sworn, promised, and bound myself as above and in witness thereof have with my own hand subscribed the present document of my abjuration,* and recited it word for word, he had even had to recite it, *at Rome, in the Convent of Minerva, this twenty-second day of June, 1633.* And he finished: *I, Galileo Galilei, have abjured as above with my own hand.*

'Thank you,' he said, standing up, to the young man. 'Thank you,' he said to the tall young lady and went out. In the tobacconist's shop, he bought an envelope and an express stamp, wrote on the envelope *Superintendent Carrua, Milan Police Headquarters,* put it in one of the two new postboxes next to the tram stop in the Piazza Cavour, then walked home, stopping in three bars on the way. In each of them he ate a toasted sandwich, without drinking anything, and at home he drank the water from the tap that didn't really taste of a mountain stream – on the contrary – then went to bed and tried in vain to sleep.

3

The telephone. He got up: it was Mascaranti.

'I couldn't question Rosa Gavoni. She died of shock.'

So they might never find out where the two packets of mescaline 6 had ended up. A few hectograms of mescaline 6, you could give a whole neighbourhood of Milan hallucinations with that, Porta Vigentina for example, because it was 6, the most concentrated form: they aren't content with red wine any more, even though that's also a hallucinogen, now they want explosions.

'Rosa Gavoni died of shock, I couldn't question her,' Mascaranti repeated, thinking, because of Duca's silence, that he had not heard.

'Yes, I heard.' It wasn't shock she had died of, the poor woman had had to look at her Ulrico on a marble slab and say, 'Yes, it's him, it's Ulrico Brambilla.' It wasn't shock, it wasn't just dying. 'Search Rosa Gavoni's house, and the butcher's shops, question all the assistants, do whatever you like, but I don't have time to waste on a few hectograms of drugs, I'm not the narcotics squad,' and he hung up, immediately full of remorse because it really wasn't poor Mascaranti's fault. Maybe it'd be better if he took a few tranquillisers, his sister always had some chamomile in the apartment because he didn't want any of those pills made from methane, propane or butane, he was a man, not a diesel engine. Anyway, he'd only have to wait until the next morning, when his sister would be coming back to Milan with his niece and Livia Ussaro, and he might be calmer then. It was only four in the afternoon, he just had to wait until after ten the next morning.

He made himself a chamomile tea, but instead of calming him it irritated him, so he tried to kill time having a bath, then a manicure, then a shampoo, then he went to the cinema and saw a film he thought was stupid but that made the audience laugh a lot, ate two toasted sandwiches in two different bars, and, digging into his reserves, bought a few newspapers and magazines, including two crossword magazines. In a news magazine he saw the headline *Final Revelations on Drugs Ring,* but he didn't read the article because he didn't believe in final revelations, there were two packets of mescaline 6 in circulation and it was foolish to believe there could be any final revelation about drugs, because drugs would never finish.

But at three in the morning he was still awake, he had read almost all the newspapers and magazines, and solved lots of crosswords, even cryptic ones, and had had to look for something else to read. He had found the Italian Touring Club's Guide to Italy, dated 1914, a memento of his father, a loyal member of the club, and had read the anthem of the TCI: *O sacred land, o country dear – o mother always by our side – Your beauty always with us here – Your life will always be our guide – Your love is all we need to know – Away, away, let's go, let's go!* There was also an application form for the club, more than half a century old, which stated that if the application was made by a married woman, she needed her husband's signature – a lot of progress has been made since those dark days, now women go around carrying cases that had submachine guns in them – and he was just reading that the price of a block of sheets containing a 1:250,000 scale map of Italy was twenty-nine lire and one hundred centesimi when the telephone rang, even though it was three in the morning.

Completely devoid of any garment, either nightwear or daywear, he went to the telephone.

'Were you asleep?' It was Carrua.

'No.'

'Good, then I didn't wake you.' How witty! 'Well, *I* was asleep, but they brought me a girl who says she was the one who pushed Turiddu Sompani and his lady friend into the Naviglio. I can barely stay awake, can you come over?'

Of course he could, because he wasn't asleep, and anyway there was a girl who said she was the one who had pushed Turiddu in the canal, which didn't make much sense, but does anything ever make much sense in life?

'I'm sending Mascaranti over in a car to pick you up,' Carrua said.

'Thanks.' He clearly heard Carrua's yawn through the receiver.

And after the yawn, Carrua said, 'She's American.'

Duca said nothing.

'American and stupid,' Carrua said.

That might be the case: America was such a vast, highly populated country, there must be a few stupid people in it, they couldn't all be George Washington. 'I'll be right there,' Duca said.

He went and put on his underpants and his nice pale blue socks with the hole in the big toe of the right foot. He was already downstairs, waiting by the front door, in the deserted Piazza Leonardo da Vinci, when Mascaranti arrived. It was eleven minutes past three in the morning.

4

She had flown from Phoenix, Arizona, to New York, in New York she had taken another plane for Rome, Italy, Fiumicino, in Rome she had got on the Settebello, and had arrived in Milan, Italy, Central Station, at nine minutes past midnight, and there she had got straight into a taxi and said, 'Police Headquarters', she had light brown hair, almost blonde, the driver didn't like to go to Police Headquarters, no Italian citizen likes Police Headquarters, maybe this girl with light brown hair had no money for the fare and he would have to get the police to reimburse him, which meant he could forget about it, but he let her in the taxi because of her nice shoulder-length light brown hair and her sweet face, which touched even him, a loutish Lombard taxi driver on night shift, and he would have liked to ask her what the hell she wanted to go to Police Headquarters for but, contrary to appearances, Lombards are shy and he didn't ask her.

And when they got to Police Headquarters, in the bright, cool May night, she got out, paid her fare, then went in through the vast gateway, and there was nobody there, nor was there anybody in the courtyard, but then a shadowy figure appeared in the dim light, a uniformed officer, and she saw him throw away his cigarette end, so she went up to him, she was fashionably dressed, with her skirt above her knees, and she had long hair, the only unusual thing was that heavy overcoat over her arm, on such a May night.

'What do you want?' the officer asked, rather abruptly,

because every now and again a prostitute came in to seek protection from a pimp who wanted to cut her throat.

'I've come to turn myself in,' she said in her perfect Italian, perfect apart from the way she pronounced the *t*, because a woman from Arizona is almost constitutionally unable to pronounce it the Latin way. 'I killed two people and pushed the car into the Alzaia Naviglio Pavese.'

She could not have been any clearer, but for that very reason the officer did not understand: the rule is that the clearer you are, the less people understand. All he understood was that he had to shut this girl up in a holding room and go and look for somebody, and in fact he did immediately shut her up in a holding room, together with two prostitutes and a perfectly honest woman who worked for Pirelli but had been caught in her car committing an obscene act with her boyfriend. At that hour, however, there was almost nobody in Headquarters, they were all outside, catching thieves and whores and homosexuals and pimps, but then Sergeant Morini arrived at half-past one, with the car full of long-haired men squawking, or at least trying to, because every time they tried to squawk, Morini would slap them, and the officer told Morini that there was a girl there who had come to give herself in, he hadn't really understood why, apparently she had killed two people.

Morini freed himself from the long-haired men, who swore that they were singers or artists, and not male prostitutes, had the nice girl brought to him and listened to what she had to say.

'I've come to turn myself in,' she repeated, in her excellent Italian. 'I killed two people, and pushed their car into the Alzaia Naviglio Pavese.'

Morini looked at her fleetingly: the almost childlike sweetness of that face bothered him a little, it was as if a six-year-old girl had come and told him that she had killed her grandmother. This was Carrua's case, he thought, and he contacted the officer who was on duty outside Carrua's office and found out that Carrua was asleep, because he had not slept since Monday, and at two o'clock on Wednesday morning you can't wake up someone who hasn't slept since Monday. So he was about to send the girl back into the holding room, but that sweet face and light brown hair, the refinement of her demeanour, yes, refinement, made him hesitate. He didn't like the idea of throwing her back in that room with the whores, not this girl, but he didn't have any empty rooms, so he made up his mind and called Carrua on the phone, and perhaps because he was tired, or because he had been thrown by this angelic girl and her unlikely confession, he said, as soon as Carrua replied, 'This is Morini, Superintendent Carrùa,' with the stress on the *u*, instead of the first *a*, which was the correct pronunciation of the name.

'Morini, you idiot, I knew it was you straight away,' Carrua said, sitting up on the camp bed, the pitiful camp bed he slept on every now and again, though very rarely. 'What do you want?'

Morini went red. 'I'm sorry, Superintendent Càrrua,' Morini said, pronouncing his name correctly, 'but there's a girl here who's come to turn herself in.'

'Couldn't you have told me tomorrow morning?' he snarled. He was desperate to sleep, but he put on his shoes because he knew he wouldn't sleep now.

'She says she's the one who pushed that car with Turiddu Sompani and his lady friend into the Naviglio,' Sergeant Morini said, 'and as it's your case I wanted to tell you straight away.'

Carrua gave up tying his shoelaces. He had no idea what was going on, but he said, 'Bring the girl up here.'

'She's American,' Morini said.

'All right, so she's American, just bring her up.'

And now here she was, in Carrua's office, and Carrua was behind the desk, and on the desk was the girl's coat, too heavy for such a warm spring night, and Duca was standing next to her, and after looking at her for a while, not really sure why that sweet face should be making him feel so angry, he said to Carrua, 'The passport.'

5

Susanna Pani: that was the name on the passport that Carrua handed him from among the various documents taken from the girl's handbag. Duca sat down facing her. According to the passport she was one metre seventy-six tall, a remarkable height for a woman, and she was wearing low-heeled shoes, although that wasn't in the passport, in her sitting position her dress had ridden up quite a bit above the knee and Mascaranti who was on the other side of the girl with a new notebook in his hand was trying to make it seem, from the cold expression on his face, that he was not looking at her and even if he was looking at her that it didn't matter. The passport also said that she had light brown hair, that her fingerprints had been catalogued in the National Archives in Washington with the number W-62C Arizona 414 (°4), and that she was born in 1937. She was twenty-nine years old, Duca thought as he put the passport back on the desk, but she looked ten years younger, that angelic quality can make you look younger, but angels don't usually kill two people simultaneously.

'What's the connection between you and Turiddu Sompani?' Duca asked Susanna Pani.

'He had my father arrested,' she said, 'and his friend tortured him and killed him.'

Duca looked at Carrua, his ear echoing with the sweet, childlike sound of that voice.

'I couldn't make head or tail of it either,' Carrua said. 'I mean, I asked a lot of questions, but I'm sleepy.' The whole of that mild May night was a touching invitation to sleep, but with all the thieves and murderers and whores you find in a big city, nobody gets any sleep at Police Headquarters.

Duca tried to find another way in, a Northwest Passage, that would lead him to an understanding of the situation.

'How come you speak such good Italian?'

'My grandfather was Italian,' she said, raising her head proudly. 'He was from the Abruzzi, our real name isn't Pani but Paganica, but the Americans found that a bit difficult, and so my father became Pani when he went to military school.'

'And did they speak Italian in your family?'

'Yes,' she said, her head still raised, sweetly but proudly, 'but I studied it, because my grandfather spoke Abruzzi dialect.' She blushed a little. 'He even swore in dialect. So my father gave me books to study and learn the language properly, and apart from that I had lessons twice a week from a good Italian teacher in San Francisco, because in San Francisco, and Arizona generally, there's a big Italian community.' The subject was clearly one that interested her, and it gave colour to the pearly tone of her childlike voice.

'There's some cold coffee,' Carrua said, 'would you like some?'

'Yes, thanks,' Duca said.

Behind Carrua's desk, Mascaranti got busy with a bottle full of cold coffee and a drawer with glasses in it, then served the coffee to everyone, including the girl, who drank it eagerly.

'Only my mother knows how to make coffee like this in San Francisco.'

'Is your mother also Italian?' Duca said.

'No, she's from Phoenix, but my father taught her, and she can speak a little Italian, too.'

An idyllic American family, of Italian, Abruzzian origin. He drank a little cold coffee, took out a cigarette and offered one to the girl, who accepted and smoked it serenely. It was like a drawing-room conversation: 'Have you seen *Africa Addio*?[12] Did you see Sophia Loren at Cannes?' But there were other questions, of another kind entirely, that he had to ask. 'You said Turiddu Sompani had your father arrested. Why? What had your father done to be arrested? And how could Turiddu Sompani have had him arrested?'

Her reply was quite unexpected. 'Up until a few months ago I didn't know anything about it, even mother didn't know anything, and she died without knowing anything, we received the medal for my father's death in combat, we thought he had died on the Gothic Line,[13] because that's all it said in the citation from Washington. But we didn't really know anything, and luckily my mother died without knowing anything.'

So there it was, nobody knew anything. 'Signorina Pani,' Duca said, 'what exactly is it you didn't know?'

The coffee was probably already stimulating her a bit, and she must have liked the police in Milan, so nice of them to offer cold coffee and cigarettes. 'I work at the state archives in Phoenix,' she said. 'My colleagues say it's boring work, but I like it a lot, I'm in the criminal records division. When I was hired, seven years ago, they'd only got as far as the year 1905, and I managed to classify all the crimes committed in Arizona from then until 1934, it can be tiring work, there were only three of us, but I liked it a lot. We had to divide all the offences into categories, burglaries, homicides, robberies, even the mistreatment of animals, and every offence has its own file and in the file there's a full description of the offence and a photograph of the perpetrator.'

They listened in silence, without asking any questions,

they let her go on as if she was a filly they were taming, maybe she'd eventually get round to explaining what she was doing here in Milan, in Police Headquarters: the police have time.

'Then I got engaged,' Susanna Pani said, 'to a friend from work, he also worked in the state archives, but in the war records division.' As she talked about this friend of hers from work, her voice became, if possible, even more angelic. 'He's Irish, don't ask me his name, please, he mustn't be mixed up in this business, we were supposed to be getting married this month, but I decided to come here and hand myself in, and he didn't want me to, but I told him I had no choice and he was sure to find another woman much better than me, and maybe younger.' With the little finger of her right hand she wiped the tears from the corners of her eyes. 'Don't ask me his name, I beg you, leave him out of this.'

'We're not interested in your fiancé's name,' Duca said, 'we only want to know what happened.'

'Don't call him my fiancé, just say my friend. He works in the state archives in Phoenix, in the war records division, he classifies everything that happened in the war to citizens of the state of Arizona. Every officer, every soldier, every auxiliary, whether he's alive or dead, has a file with everything in it that he did during the war and all the documents that relate to that. These files are in Washington, but a copy is sent to the home state of the soldier or officer, if a soldier was born in Alabama the copy is sent to Montgomery, if he's from West Virginia, they send a copy to Charleston, if he's from Arizona they send a copy to Phoenix.'

For an angel she was very precise, even too much so, but it was better that way. They would know the whole story.

'Of course it takes time,' the angel continued. 'The archives in Washington are a mountain of files, and every document in every file has to be examined by God knows how many offices, so although my father died in 1945 his documents were only sent to Phoenix this year. My friend from work, Charles,' the name came out involuntarily, and she immediately said, 'You mustn't even say his name, I beg you, he mustn't be mixed up in this.'

All three of them, even Mascaranti, agreed that the name of this gentleman to whom she was so devoted would never, ever be uttered, and they agreed in perfect bad faith because the police need to know everything, especially names, just like journalists, who then go and tell everyone everything, all the names.

'And so, as soon as the file arrived, Charles said, "Your father's file has arrived from Washington, I haven't looked at it yet, I'll tell you all about it when I have." I was so happy. The citation about my father's death hadn't said much, only that he sacrificed his life in the service of civilisation, the kind of thing they usually write. He had fallen, they said, on the Italian front, on the Gothic Line, on January 6, 1945. I was happy because I knew that the file contained everything, even his dog tag, and I was only sorry that mother had died without that happiness of knowing all the things father had done during the war.' She lowered her head and the two sides of her hair fell over her face like curtains, then she raised it again abruptly, she had dismissed the memory of her dead mother, and she smiled again a little. 'I waited nearly two weeks, then one evening I couldn't stand it any more and I said to Charles, "Charles, haven't you looked at my father's file yet?" And he said, "Oh, I'm sorry, I've been really busy, I haven't had a chance to have a look at it yet." I thought that was strange, because he knew how much knowing everything about my father meant to me, but I told him it didn't matter, I'd wait. After four months, and after asking him lots of times why he never told me anything about the file, I told him one day that if he didn't show me those documents, I'd leave him, and then put in an official request to the administration of the archives to be allowed to see them, I was the daughter and they couldn't refuse me. So he took me to his office one evening, and we spent the whole night there and I read all the documents. I fainted twice because of the photographs, and when I came round I carried on reading, and by the time I finished I knew why poor Charles didn't want me to read those documents.' She lowered her head again, again hiding her face with her light brown hair, but this time she could not control herself, she began to sob, and said in English, 'I'm glad mother died before finding out something like that, without reading any of those things.'

6

The file was unusually thick for that of an ordinary infantry captain. On the cover it said *Anthony (Paganica) Pani, Cpt. Iftry. (AD, GP, MFR 2961 – b. 1908 d. 1945)* and there really was everything in it, everything about the military career of Anthony Pani. If the file had been about most American officers who had come to fight on the European front, it would have contained a dozen sheets at most. But there was something special about Anthony Pani: he spoke Italian fluently.

The front wasn't moving, and a captain was wasted on the usual patrols, so the Colonel had the idea of sending Captain Pani across the lines to Bologna, where there was a small intelligence unit, and Captain Anthony Pani went to Bologna, practically on foot, guided by two partisans who after a while, because they had asked for cigarettes from a tobacconist who was a friend of theirs, had been picked up by the Fascists, and he had been left on his own, almost in the middle of Bologna, with a radio transmitter in a suitcase, and two pistols in his jacket as big as those carried by cowboys in parades in San Francisco, Arizona.

And yet he managed to save himself. He knew absolutely nothing about being a secret agent, but as his character notes said: *his extremely calm, objective temperament, his resoluteness and his lively intelligence make him suitable for many tasks*, and with extreme calm and resoluteness and objectivity he stopped a woman of about thirty who struck him as suitable for his purposes and said, 'I'm an American officer, I have a radio transmitter and two guns with me. Hide me, not only will you be performing a service for your country, but I'll make sure you're rewarded.' What he didn't tell her was that he also had three million lire on him: he didn't like talking to a woman about money.

The woman looked at him and Anthony Pani knew that he was safe. 'Come with me,' she said. He followed her, keeping a few paces behind her, and she took him to her rented apartment and gave him something to eat, then as he lay on the bed to rest for a while, she began to work on her knitting and in the meantime told him about herself, she told him her name was Adele Terrini, that she wasn't married, that she was only in Bologna for a few weeks, because she had come to keep a friend of hers company, a friend whose husband had been killed by the Germans, but then she had to go to Milan, where she had a cousin who had to hide in order not to be deported to Germany.

All this was completely false, as was explained in great detail in various other documents in Anthony Pani's file. The truth was that Adele Terrini, and the person she called her cousin, that is, Turiddu Sompani, had as their principal activity – but not the only one – the trade in fugitives. They didn't care if the fugitives were Fascists on the run from the partisans, or partisans on the run from the Fascists, or escaped English and American prisoners of war. She would welcome the partisan pursued by Fascists, feed him, dress him, go to bed with him, give him money and tell him the best escape route, he would escape but after a while – as if by coincidence – two Fascists in civilian clothes would stop him, search him, find a revolver on him, take him in, torture him and kill him. Or else it might be a young man who had been drafted into the army on September 8 and was running away in order to avoid being sent to Germany. She would welcome him, hide him, even give him a bath, go to bed with him – they were usually good-looking boys – and then – as if by coincidence – two German soldiers led by a sergeant would arrive and take him away.

Adele Terrini, under the direction of her mentor Turiddu Sompani, was trusted by the Wehrmacht, the Gestapo, the Fascists, and the resistance organisations who received warnings of danger from her – *Run, the Germans are coming* – and everybody knew that they could turn to her and her cousin if they were in danger. Even today there must be a few partisans or Jews who remember her with gratitude, maybe even with emotion, who remember how she hid them in her house, offered them her soft flesh, darned their socks, gave them money to escape. If the partisan was later arrested by the Fascists, or the Jew by the Gestapo, and somehow miraculously survived, what connection could there possibly be with Adele?

In reality, the success of this trade in fugitives was due only to the fact that the mastermind of it all, Attorney Sompani, organised everything in such a way as to wipe out the connection between the fact that the fugitive knew Adele Terrini and the fact that sooner or later this fugitive was slaughtered or spent the most wretched hours of his life. At the time, there were a number of idiots practising the same trade in betraying fugitives, but after a few months the incompetent betrayer would end up lying in a gutter, riddled with bullets like a panettone, and a weary priest would give him a *post mortem* absolution for all his sins. But Adele Terrini and the mastermind, no, they weren't incompetent betrayers, they were born to betray, they betrayed with passion, with genuine warmth, it was a mission for them, and they knew how to betray.

So the reason Adele Terrini was in Bologna was not to

console her friend whose husband had been killed by the
Fascists – such a humane task was alien to her mentality –
she was there because an ex-schoolfriend, with whom, obviously, she had slept, and who was a big Fascist official in
Emilio Romagna, had asked for her help in escaping to
Switzerland, because he didn't feel like being seen in Bologna in his uniform any more, not with so many bullets flying
around, and so she had come running, in her sisterly, even
motherly way, she had talked to the official, the ex-schoolfriend, and had assured him that she would be able to take
him to Switzerland herself. In reality, her intentions were
quite otherwise, and a few metres from the Swiss border the
trusting official would be picked up by a small Fascist squad.
Maybe she sold them by weight.

That day, Tony Pani didn't know any of this. Lying
on the bed, feeling rested, safe – or so he imagined – he
saw something he had never seen in the vulgar, industrial
United States: a woman sitting by the window, calmly knitting. There was something so warm about it, it gave him a
sense of home, of family, it aroused sweet, obscure ancestral
feelings from the Abruzzi, it took him back to his homeland, the homeland of his father, near Mount Paganica,
from which the village took its name, as did they. So, from
that very first day perhaps, she actually personified the hope
that these dark days would soon be over, the hope of a serene world where women like her lived and still knitted,
with ersatz wool right now, but some day soon with real
wool, and her face, and that knitting, inspired him to give
her the nickname Adele la Speranza: Adele Hope. All this
was explained in one sheet in the file, document AD, GP,
MFR2959, which consisted of a letter that Anthony Pani
had written to his wife Monica, but never sent because of
the difficulties of getting mail out.

But on that grey day at the end of September 1944, as Adele Terrini, whom he called Adele la Speranza but who in Ca'Tarino and in Romano Banco was known, obviously, as Adele the whore, knitted and talked about herself – making most of it up – to that stupid American lying on the bed, she was thinking much more pragmatically than he was. Having found, without even looking, an American officer with guns and a radio transmitter, and obviously a lot of money in a belt somewhere on his body – the Americans who parachuted in were millionaires, she knew that – was a big thing, this wasn't merchandise to be sold to just anybody. If she gave him to the Gestapo, all she'd get would be a book of petrol vouchers and not much more: the Germans were stingy that way. The Fascists wouldn't give her anything, because they had nothing and wouldn't even know what to do with such an awkward consignment and would either sell him to the Germans or make friends with him so that they could cross the Gothic Line and escape punishment when the war was over. There was something better she could do: put him to work. Infantry Captain Anthony (Paganica) Pani was an exceptional seam of riches of every kind, material and moral. She had to take him to Milan, where Turiddu would see to everything.

Sweetly, she stopped knitting and went and sat down, sweetly, on the bed where Anthony lay, fully dressed, but she had forgotten two things: that the man was a romantic, and that he had been born and had always lived in a puritan Anglo-Saxon environment, maybe he didn't know the proverb *an opportunity missed is an opportunity lost*, he loved his wife and even if he wanted a woman so much he could scream, he wouldn't go with another woman, and so Anthony Pani was the only man in the world who had been within a radius of ten metres of Adele Terrini and hadn't gone to bed with her. In this connection, there was a note in the file from Adele to Turiddu, a note that a whole team of investigators and historians connected with the Allied army, had found, recorded, and sent to Washington, and the note said – it was only a fragment – *forget about it, Tony's an idiot, he's always talking about his wife and his daughter, oh Susanna, oh Susanna, and even though we sleep in the same room at night I haven't yet managed to* … and there followed a verb that indicated the sexual act in a very explicit way.

7

Adele la Speranza had ably collaborated with Infantry
Captain Anthony (Paganica) Pani, according to document
A.D., GP, MFR3002 of his file: she had kept him hidden in
her apartment in Bologna for a week, and she had provided
him with the means to communicate by radio with Rome,
she had then taken him to Milan, to a small villa in the
Via Monte Rosa where her cousin, Turiddu Sompani, lived.
Even Attorney Turiddu Sompani, the document insisted,
had ably collaborated with Captain Pani, putting him in
contact with the most competent resistance groups in Milan,
providing information that, again according to document
3002, had always turned out to be accurate: a true betrayer
is clever enough to always supply genuine merchandise, so
as to convince the victim of their friendship. The first advantage of this policy of genuineness was that Adele and
Turiddu did not even need to steal the money that Anthony
Pani had on him, as they had thought of doing at the beginning. Until Christmas 1944 they lived well on the information: they passed on all the Germans and Fascist positions
they found out about, they acted as dispatch riders for the
Resistance squads – Captain Pani assumed they were risking their lives, whereas in reality they managed to circulate
in Milan and the surrounding area thanks to the German
and Fascist permits they possessed – and they kept a few
rooms on the second floor of the little villa that could be
used, depending on circumstances, as a night's shelter for

the partisans, or else as a place for Germans to come and spend time with gorgeous female companions of twenty or less, and because of this combination of factors, nobody, neither the Germans nor the patriots, suspected a thing. Every piece of information was well paid for, and Pani assumed they must be working very hard to get that information – which wasn't the case – and, as the proverb says, the greater the effort, the greater the glory.

By just before Christmas the three million that Captain Pani had brought with him had been used up. Following a suggestion from Turiddu Sompani, Adele la Speranza suggested to Anthony that he arrange a drop, and for a few days it looked as though Rome were going to agree to it, a Resistance squad spent three nights in a field near Crema, waiting for a plane to drop cylinders containing arms and money with which to form – as Turiddu had guaranteed he was capable of forming – a new squad of guerillas that would join the other existing squads, thereby covering the whole of Lombardy.

But after those three nights, what came wasn't a drop but a message – document 3042 – *Destroy the radio, put it somewhere safe, BH and BKA double game, take refuge zone four your sector.* The identity of the miraculous guardian angel in Rome who had informed the Allied command that Adele and Turiddu, otherwise known as BH and BKA, were despicable traitors was unknown: not even the war records department in Washington knew his identity.

Receiving this message, Captain Pani felt nothing but rage: it was absolutely inconceivable to him that Adele could have been playing a double game, he was even wearing a nice sweater knitted by her, he had watched her knit it, had seen it growing day by day in her hands, with a kind of eyelet in the bottom edge in which to hide the two cyanide capsules he could use to kill himself instantaneously in case he was tortured. A woman who knitted, hour after hour, during all those months, every time she was there, in the little villa in the Via Monte Rosa, couldn't be a spy for the Germans, but in fact she was a spy for everybody, and he had read very little about psychoanalysis and didn't know that all that calm, feminine knitting was, for a criminal like her, a compulsion, a tic, rather than evidence of an innocence she had never possessed.

And driven by the rage he felt, he contacted Rome and told them that BH and BKA were absolutely trustworthy people and had given him plenty of evidence of this over the past few months. The message that came in reply was: *Ceasing further communication. Dangerous for you. Hope you can reach zone four.* And they kept their word: however hard he tried, he was unable to re-establish contact with Rome.

Then, after his rage had subsided, Captain Pani felt cold, not cold with fear because he didn't believe and would never believe that Adele and Turiddu were traitors, but cold with anger. That was why Americans never had real friends, he thought: because when they found people like Adele and Turiddu, they were suspicious of them and treated them like traitors. Of course, he wasn't so stupid as to say anything to Adele or Turiddu, but the two of them guessed that something had happened and, in order to find out exactly what, Adele made one last attempt to go to bed with him. She did it on Christmas night, hoping to exploit the emotion of the holiday season, she got him to do a lot of talking, first about his wife and little Susanna, who was seven years old that Christmas, she played her part well, she even pretended to stumble and fall so that he would lift her off the floor and hold her in his arms, but all in vain. There were a few things Captain Pani had never told Adele: the four alternative transmission codes, the signal to begin transmission, without which they couldn't send messages from Rome, and the fact that he had almost another half a million hidden.

Then Turiddu Sompani realised that something had changed: Tony had stopped transmitting, he seemed a little tired and didn't speak much, he still liked sitting on the sofa next to Adele, watching her knit, but something had changed, and Turiddu Sompani, the mastermind, guessed what it was; someone in Rome must have aroused his suspicions about them.

If that was the case, the goldmine that Anthony Pani had been for them was completely exhausted. At least, as far as one side went. But he could still be exploited on the other side.

On the morning of 30 December 1944, Turiddu Sompani went to the Via Santa Margherita, in the file there was a photograph of the hotel he entered, whose most important guests were German officers and members of the Gestapo.

8

On the afternoon of 30 December, a German van stopped in front of the little villa in the Via Monte Rosa, there was a photograph of the little villa, even though it had only eight rooms on its two floors it was trying to imitate the Castle of Miramare in Trieste, and this was a very mild winter, at least as far as the temperature went: even in the middle of winter it was sunny and the trees had not yet lost all their leaves, it seemed more like the middle of October than the end of December.

Two soldiers, two men in civilian clothes and a uniformed officer jumped out of the van, burst into the villa – very strangely, the gate was ajar, as was the front door, even though in those days even dogs locked the doors of their kennels – and arrested Adele Terrini, Turiddu Sompani and, obviously, Captain Anthony Pani.

As even the most intelligent traitors are stupid, precisely because they are traitors, something happened – apart from the arrest – which shone a sea of light into the rose-tinted darkness of Captain Pani's illusions: one of the two Germans in civilian clothes, as soon he entered the room where Pani was sitting with Adele, immediately rushed to him and searched the edge of his sweater, the one worked on with such feminine devotion by Adele la Speranza, found the two cyanide capsules hidden in that little eyelet and confiscated them.

Only three people knew that the two capsules were

in the sweater, himself, Adele and Turiddu. True, the thin young man from the Gestapo had pretended to search and to find the capsules as if by chance but, however stupid he might have been, the American had not been fooled by such a coarse piece of playacting.

Then all three of them were taken to the hotel in the Via Santa Margherita, following the script of the comedy dreamed up by Turiddu, the mastermind, and here they were separated. The interrogation of Captain Pani was quite mild, the two men in civilian clothes who interrogated him were intelligent and weary, they probably didn't believe much in secret armies and were more likely thinking more about how to get to a quieter continent, like South America for example, than of how to extract now pointless information from an insignificant infantry captain hurriedly transformed into a secret agent.

At first Captain Pani, who was suffering more from disappointment than from fears for his own fate, pretended to resist – first the flattery, then the punches, then a few kicks to his knees – then, when he realised that these idiots would believe him, he confessed the truth, the whole truth, and nothing but the truth: the four alternative codes, the transmission signal and the whereabouts of the other intelligence units and partisan squads. If he had said it immediately he wouldn't have been believed, and he was able to talk now without feeling any remorse because nobody would be hurt: having informed him of the betrayal, Rome must have informed everybody he knew, and the Germans would not find anybody and would not be able to make any false transmissions with his codes because Rome was no longer dealing with Captain Pani's intelligence unit.

Then Captain Pani was locked up in the cellar of the hotel, where he spent the end of 1944 and New Year's Day

1945, mentally toasting the health and happiness of his wife Monica and his daughter Susanna to whom he had written every now and again, keeping the letters, as spies don't generally use the mail for their family communications. Susanna and Monica were safe and well, that was the most important thing.

On 2 January 1945 two German soldiers came for him and bundled him into a small lorry, Adele and Turiddu were already in the back of the lorry, their faces, like his, bore a few marks, but not very many: it was possible the marks had been applied with charcoal, he would have been curious to find out. After about twenty minutes the lorry stopped, Turiddu winked at Captain Pani, one of the two German soldiers guarding them lifted his arm and motioned them to get out, and Adele took the captain's hand and jumped down from the lorry with him. They were in the Piazza Buonarroti, at the end of the Via Monte Rosa, just five minutes from the little villa that looked like the Castle of Miramare. The lorry left. Turiddu said that with a good bribe you can get anything you want in life, and he was convinced that Captain Pani would believe that he had bribed the Germans, and maybe the captain replied, yes, of course – this wasn't written in any document in the file, but could be deduced.

Then the couple had taken him back to the little villa and the two of them had told him how they had been beaten by the Germans, but then had managed to fool them all the same and to bribe the *Ober*, and Captain Pani had probably replied every now and again, yes, of course. He was watching them, but without a great deal of curiosity, he more or less guessed why they had saved him, and indeed on the morning of 3 January, Turiddu told him his plan: he would arrange for them to go to Rome, that way the captain would be in a safe place and they could help the Allies, if the Allies wanted. They explained the plan humbly, like good, devoted, affectionate servants who are making soft food for their old master ill with bronchial catarrh and are ready to do any service for him. When it came to using fugitives, Turiddu Sompani was a genius on the level of Leonardo, he squeezed them like lemons, from all sides. First he had squeezed money out of Anthony Pani, betraying the Germans and the Fascists to help him, then he had given him to the Germans, and now, in agreement with the Germans, he wanted to take him over the Gothic Line to Rome, where he would simultaneously betray both Germans and Americans. Arriving in Rome with an American officer he had saved was a perfect recommendation: the Americans would embrace him gratefully and he would be able to find out many things that he could transmit to the Germans. At the same time he would inform the Americans of everything he knew about the Germans because the Germans had lost the war and he and Adele were never on the losing side.

This wasn't in any of the documents, but Captain Pani must have laughed inside himself and replied, 'Yes, very good.' Let them take him to Rome, let them 'save' him, the two of them did not know that Rome was already informed about them, and besides, as soon as they crossed the lines, he would find a way to hand them over to the military police, who would put an end to their activities. In the midst of his bitter disappointment, he must have been a little relieved at the thought that they were the ones who were taking him 'to safety' in Rome: all right, take me.

'It's best to leave as early as possible,' Captain Pani said, 'this house isn't very safe any more.' Why had they been so foolish as to try and make him believe, apart from anything else, that in trying to get away from the Gestapo they could go and hide in the very same house in the Via Monte Rosa where they had been arrested? Didn't they have any respect for the intelligence of Americans? No, none at all.

'Tomorrow night,' Turiddu said, 'that way we can celebrate Epiphany in Rome.'

That day Captain Pani discovered three things. The first was that Adele, formerly Adele la Speranza, was ugly, really ugly, because of the abnormal swelling on her face, her herpetic colouring, the whites of her eyes which were no longer white, but dirty grey, all of which made her seem ten years older than she really was, which was thirty. The second thing he realised was that her constant knitting, the fact that she was never seen without her box of knitting needles and balls of ersatz wool, wasn't a sign of feminine passion for domestic chores, but a kind of nervous tic, like people who stamp their feet on the floor or drum their fingers on the table. Because that day, 3 January, it did not arouse any emotion in him, seeing her against the light next to the window, seeing her work on the sweater she had promised she would finish by the next day for him to wear when he went to Rome: all he felt was disgust. And the third thing he realised was that the two of them, Adele and Turiddu, took drugs. Even before this, he had occasionally noticed something odd about their behaviour, but he had thought that perhaps they drank too much. Now he realised that they took narcotics, and he felt even more disgusted.

Even though pretence was not in his nature, Captain Pani pretended he believed them, he drank in everything they told him, all their plans, he treated them as if he was still their trusted friend, just as they had treated him before, and at last, about eleven, he was able to lock himself in his room. He wrote a letter to his wife Monica, *January 3, night, I don't know when I'll be able to send you these letters, but I hope it'll be soon*, and other tender things, because he was a romantic, and he tenderly told her how much he missed her and Susanna, and when he had finished writing the letter he put it together with the others that he had been writing over the past three months, that is, he tipped over the chair, to the underside of which he had nailed a square of material, open on one side like a pocket, and inside this pocket were all his letters, as well as five hundred thousand lire, in those big thousand-lire notes of the time. However fond he had been of Adele la Speranza, and however friendly with Turiddu, as a good infantry captain he had kept some money in reserve: it's always useful to have a reserve, in war or in peace. He checked to see if it was still there – it was – then he put the chair back the right way up, undressed and went to bed. It was just after midnight, he turned out the light and, with great difficulty, fell asleep.

He was woken abruptly by two things: the light being switched on suddenly and a violent punch in the mouth.

9

It was Adele and Turiddu, completely out of their heads on drugs, their eyes fixed and glassy, more fixed than those of a toy dog, stark naked and in a state of sadistic sexual frenzy. Anthony Pani realised it immediately, it was worse than finding himself in a cage with two wild tigers, they were maddened with drugs, and that was an uncontrollable kind of madness.

'You were planning to screw us, you turncoat,' Turiddu said, punching him again, less violently this time, 'we take you to Rome and as soon as you're in Rome you have us arrested, that's what you have in mind, isn't it?'

'But you're my friends, why should I have you arrested?' the captain said, extremely calm and resolute, just as it said he was in his character notes, despite the two punches he had received and his awareness of what might happen.

'You thought we hadn't realised, but we had,' Turiddu said, but without punching him again, 'I was studying you tonight and I saw that you are our enemy and as soon as we cross the lines you'll have us shot,' and he laughed, but it sounded more like a compulsive coughing fit. So they weren't so stupid, they had realised that he had realised. What did they intend to do now?

'I'm cold,' Adele said, 'let's go down in front of the fireplace,' because the little Castle of Miramare had a living room with a ridiculous fireplace, and he knew immediately what they wanted.

'Get up and come downstairs,' Turiddu said.

His mouth edged with blood, Captain Pani immediately stood up, you have to obey mad people promptly.

'Get undressed!' she screamed. 'It's very hot down there.' She was even uglier than her unashamed nakedness, the drugs had altered her gestures and her voice. Captain Pani was wearing nothing but a woollen vest and old-fashioned longjohns. He took them off.

They took him down to the ground floor, wood had been heaped on the wretched fireplace and it was really hot, not only that, but if they continued like this, they'd soon burn the house down.

'Sit down and drink.'

He sat down and drank the half glass of kirsch that she poured for him, her lips cracked in a kind of rictus.

'Drink all of it.'

He drank it all. They stood there in all their foul nakedness, which might have been what disgusted Captain Pani the most, because that nakedness was worse than the most repugnant thing he could imagine, especially hers: her skin was blotchy, perhaps with dirt, her breasts slack and lined, like an old woman's, her blackish red hair lubriciously agitated by convulsive shakes of the head.

'Drink some more.'

He drank some more, it was good genuine German kirsch, probably supplied by the Gestapo, and he was a good drinker: if he had to die anyway, he might as well die drinking excellent kirsch.

'Now you have to tell us where the money is, tell us where the money is and we'll let you go,' Turiddu Sompani said, the Breton Jean Saintpouan, who had surfaced in Europe in the worst years of the war. 'You were going to let us take you to Rome and then betray us. We realise that, but we forgive you. It doesn't matter: we're not going to Rome anymore, but you must tell us where you've hidden the money, we spent a whole night looking for it but couldn't find it, if you tell us where it is, we'll let you go, otherwise, it's going to be bad for you.'

'Let him go like that,' she said, her body burning all over with drugs. 'Don't even give him his clothes.'

'Where's the money?' Sompani, or Saintpouan, said.

'I don't have any more money,' Captain Pani said. 'I used it all up a long time ago.'

Sompani, a big man, already fat, broke the neck of the kirsch bottle and the captain instinctively lowered his head, and then the woman kicked him in the face with her bare foot. A barefoot kick has its own particular efficacy, it may even have more of an effect than a kick with a shoe, and blood ran down Captain Pani's: Adele la Speranza's big toe had hit his right eye, along with a splash of kirsch.

'Don't break the bottle!' she screamed. 'You just have to hit him, otherwise he'll faint, and he mustn't faint.'

Unfortunately Captain Pani was very strong (*unusually robust physique, extreme resistance and muscular agility*, said the notes from his army doctor) and he had not fainted, he was stunned but he had not fainted, and he could see what Adele was doing.

She had jumped, literally jumped, onto the sofa, where her knitting bag was, and now, like some big sex-crazed monkey, she was hopping with joy on the sofa, around the bag, her quivering flesh illuminated by the flames of the fire. Finally, she bent down, her gestures still those of a monkey, searched in the bag and took out a handful of knitting needles, and the captain started to understand.

The monkey jumped down from the sofa. On the little table in front of the fireplace there were slices of bread that were very soft, and she smeared this soft bread on the back end of one of the needles, not on the tip, thus forming a kind of handle, then held out her arm and put the needle into the fire, and as it was heating up she said, 'Now you're going to have to tell us where the money is.'

The Breton looked at her admiringly. 'Where are you going to put it? In his eye?' He laughed, in that hysterical way of his that sounded like coughing.

'No, because then he'll faint, or die.'

'In his ...?' Jean Saintpouan, Turiddu Sompani, coughed again.

'No,' she also coughed, like a crazed animal, showing the captain the red needle. 'In the liver, if you don't tell us where the money is.'

'Why in the liver?' the Breton said, and perhaps he wasn't even Breton.

'Because it'll hurt, but he won't faint, they did it to some German officers in Yugoslavia. Hold him.' And as he held him, she said, bringing the red needle closer, 'Where's the money?'

Of course he could tell them, if he thought it would be any use, but he knew that even if he told them, these people would kill him afterwards anyway and spit on his letters to his family. The only thing that was any use was to show contempt for them and think how angry they'd be when they couldn't get a lira out of him.

'I don't have any money,' he said laconically. He sat there watching the knitting needle start to darken and he saw it disappear into his right side, he no longer even had the strength either to cry out or to move, he only gasped, 'Susanna.'

'Susanna, oh Susanna,' she sang, moving jerkily like a jammed machine. 'With the next needle you'll tell us where the money is.'

'Wonderful,' the Breton said, even more admiringly, still holding firmly to this man who couldn't or wouldn't fight back.

'Where's the money?' she said. With another little bit of soft bread, she made a handle around another needle, and held the needle in the flames.

Captain Pani did not reply. He did not faint, but he could not do anything, just look, with only one eye now, and suffer.

'He won't die, is that right?' Turiddu said: he wouldn't like it if he died.

'No,' she said, 'and he won't even faint, as long as the needle doesn't burst a vein, because then there'll be an internal haemorrhage. If that doesn't happen he won't die, he can hold on for another two or three days.' She aimed the red needle at the captain's right side. 'Where's the money?'

'I don't have any money.' The more the pain increased, the more alert he felt.

She inserted the whole of the needle and coughed, and the Breton held the captain tight as he gave a violent start.

'Where's the money?'

The pain was making him ever more lucid, and ever stronger in a way. 'I don't have any money,' he said, looking at the repulsive monkey who was again fabricating a handle of soft bread around a third needle, and to die more quickly he threatened her: 'If you don't hurry up and get out of this house, it'll be over for the two of you, my friends are looking for me, they could be here at any moment.'

It wasn't a fantasy threat, Rome could well have alerted the other intelligence units and partisan squads to try and save him, and his friends might well come here looking for him.

They did in fact come, but not until the next day: he

was still naked, there in the armchair, in front of the extinguished fireplace, beside the little table on which there still lay the plates with the soft black market bread on it, a bit of German caviar, half a squeezed lemon, a bottle of kirsch still to be uncorked, a syringe stuck in a two-hectogram chunk of cow's-milk cheese and, on another plate, a little bottle of alcohol with some cotton wool.

The squad found the captain still alive because Signorina Adele Terrini from Ca' Tarino had told her friend to leave him like that, and not to kill him: that way he would suffer more.

The squad took him to a safe house where there was a doctor, the doctor took out the three knitting needles, praying that doing so would not cause a haemorrhage. It didn't. He gave him morphine injections and drip-fed him glucose, thanks to which Captain Pani was able to remain alive until Epiphany and while the good children of all the liberated countries were receiving a few little gifts, he was dying, and, knowing he was dying, he mentally said goodbye to his wife Monica and his daughter Susanna.

But before dying he had been able to give a complete and lucid account of his friends Adele and Turiddu Sompani, and a journalist who was part of the unit took many photographs of him, both alive and dead, and of the knitting needles with the handles of soft bread and anything that might be of interest to history, because there is always someone who believes in history. The letters that Captain Pani had written to his wife did the rounds of all the OSS bureaux throughout Europe and in 1947 arrived in the bureau in Washington, and promptly went to sleep for more than a decade, before being examined, together with the other documents.

10

Reading those documents, Susanna Pani had fainted twice. The first time was when she read her father's letters to her mother, but she had immediately recovered and a good long cry in her friend's arms had given her back her energy. The second time she fainted was on seeing the photographs: the unknown Italian journalist who had taken them might not have been a great photographer, the images were far from perfect, but you could see quite well, even too well, the knitting needles stuck in the right side of that naked, dying man who was Susanna Pani's father, or Captain Pani's bandaged face as he lay on a bed in the safe house, only one eye free of the bandages, or the three knitting needles again, photographed lying on a plate, for the use of the historical archives.

The second time she fainted she was unconscious for longer and when she came to she had a fit of nausea that left her quivering and green-faced. She apologised to her friend from work and asked him through her tears what court had sentenced the two torturers, and her friend Charles showed her one of the last papers in the file, one she hadn't yet read, and told her they hadn't been sentenced by any court because, thanks to all that was happening at the end of the war, nobody had denounced these murderers in due time. As the matter concerned an American captain, history had followed the route of the American troops and by the time Washington had asked the Italian government to administer justice, purges had gone out of fashion, the prisons had, in fact, already been emptied of those previously purged, and in the file there was a very polite answer from a department in the Italian Ministry of Justice saying that they were taking note of the denunciation and beginning legal proceedings. But nothing happened. That meant that the couple had not had any trial and therefore had not been sentenced.

And where were they now, she asked Charles, were they still alive? What were they doing? Charles showed her another piece of paper, dated July 1963, in which the war records department in Washington were informed that Adele Terrini and Jean Saintpouan, known as Turiddu Sompani, were still living in Milan – why would they have moved? – at 18 Via Borgospesso, where Jean Saintpouan still had his legal practice.

It did not take long, not even four days, but by the fourth day Susanna Pani had decided to avenge her father. She asked for her summer vacation in advance, withdrew her savings from the bank, and by the sixth day was in Milan, at the Palace Hotel, and was telephoning Attorney Sompani – his number was in the directory: every honest citizen can have a telephone, can't he? – and telling him that she was the daughter of Captain Anthony Pani, and that a friend of her daddy's, who had been in the war with her daddy, had told her about all the things he had done for her daddy, all the help he had given him, and how he had saved him in Bologna, and that she would be so pleased to meet him, Attorney Sompani, and Signora Adele Terrini, she had come to Italy on vacation, she was in Milan for the Fair, could she have the pleasure of meeting him and Signora Adele Terrini personally? They must have so many things to tell her about her daddy.

The Breton couldn't have suspected a thing. If Anthony

Pani's daughter was so keen to meet him, that must mean she knew nothing about the rotten part of his friendship with the captain, only about the good part. He greeted her tenderly, like an elderly uncle, embraced her, and Adele also embraced her. They had grown older and even more repulsive: Adele was nearly fifty-five years old, but drugs and other abuses don't make women any younger, and the man was more than sixty but, apart from the wickedness of his mind, everything in him was fading away.

They took her to the Fair, where she showed an interest in the stalls serving typical Italian wines, as did they, and so she let them talk, and they were happy to talk because all the while Sompani was thinking how he could squeeze this orange that had come out of the blue all the way from America – it was important to have an American friend – and they took her several times to the cinema and to lunch or dinner at the Binaschina. Susanna Pani didn't like the place, that decor that was a mixture of a stable and a luxury restaurant, in fact, she found it repulsive, but she told them she liked it a lot, only she didn't say why: because she had seen the canal, the Alzaia Naviglio Pavese, and it got her thinking.

She had worked for seven years in the criminal records office in Phoenix, she had classified all the crimes committed in Arizona from 1905 to 1934, from the thefts of bottles of milk to matricides, theoretically she was an expert, she knew more than many criminals, so she knew how difficult it was to kill two people simultaneously. In 1929, though, a wife had killed her husband and his mistress by a method she recalled quite vividly. The husband liked taking his mistress to the romantic banks of the Salt River, near Globe, and in the semi-wild setting of the place they committed repeated acts of adultery in his car. Having been informed of this by a detective agency, the wife had simply borrowed a car from a neighbour, gone to Globe, and from there to the Salt River, and there she had spotted her husband's car, in the most deserted and scenic area, right on the banks of the river, all she had to do was creep up behind it and push it, without making the slightest scratch on the bodywork, into the freezing blue waters of the Salt River. She was not caught until three years later, only because she had confided in a man who then began to blackmail her, threatening to inform the police if she didn't pay him off, and when she no longer had any money, he reported her.

This story struck her as very instructive: the Alzaia Naviglio Pavese wasn't the Salt River, but there was enough water to obtain the desired effect, plus there was the favourable circumstance that Attorney Sompani had a car but was nervous about driving and so was happy to let her drive. In the third week of her stay in Milan Susanna Pani studied every detail meticulously, and even went once, by herself, along the Alzaia Naviglio Pavese, beyond the Binaschina, and there she decided that the accident had to happen close to that curious little iron bridge, an astonishing hybrid of the style of a Venetian bridge and the style of the Eiffel Tower, because then she'd be able to go straight to the other side, onto the wider road, State Highway 35, the Strada dei Giovi, where there was a lot of traffic and she'd easily be able to get a lift.

Only once did she hesitate and that was when Attorney Sompani and Signorina Adele Terrini – they had never married, she was still a Signorina – took her to the Charterhouse of Pavia and she saw the statues on the tombs of Beatrice d'Este and Lodovico il Moro. She had never heard of them, even though she had studied a little Italian art history, and suddenly there they were, in all their unbridled beauty and solemn majesty, she would happily have knelt down in front of the man who had sculpted them, she had read that it was Cristoforo Solari, she did not know that critics considered his work contrived and clumsy, and so she would have knelt and kissed his hand in gratitude for the heartrending emotion that the sight of those statues gave her. This was how life should be, beauty, prayer, solemnity, not murder and hate, and she started to think of going straight back to Phoenix, without doing anything, going back to her friend from work, buying lots of books on Italian art and forgetting, forgetting, forgetting, forgetting, but when she at last took her eyes, still moist with emotion, away from Beatrice d'Este and Ludovico il Moro and back to the repulsive faces of Adele Terrini and Turiddu Sompani, who always wore big dark glasses because the drugs made their eyes sensitive to light, the skin of their cheeks grey and flabby, their gestures, however minimal, that were the gestures of old sadists, she realised she would *never* be able to forget.

Two evenings later they had dinner at the Binaschina: this was the zero hour she had fixed for herself. It was very simple, she had calculated everything exactly, you don't work in a criminal records office without learning a few things. At the end of the dinner, while the two of them, half drunk on the chicken with mushrooms, the gorgonzola, the baked apples with zabaglione, were trying to digest it all with a little Sambuca, she stood up, put her coat on and said, 'I'm going outside to smoke.' By now the two of them knew this habit of hers: she couldn't smoke indoors, she loved smoking, but had to be out in the open, even if it was only on a balcony. 'I'll wait for you by the car.' She had done this before, after meals: while they were still chatting a little, she would go outside for a cigarette. Anybody watching would think she had gone out and gone home alone, without them.

And when she had smoked two cigarettes, they arrived in the cosy, solitary parking spot in front of the Binaschina, surrounded by tall slender trees, how sleepy they were, they sat down in the back seat already half asleep, and she got in behind the wheel. From the Binaschina to the place she had already chosen was less than five hundred metres, and when she got to the chosen place, she had said, 'I'm getting out to have a cigarette, I don't like smoking in the car,' after which all she had needed was a little push and the car had fallen in the water of the Alzaia Naviglio Pavese.

11

'Can I go to the window?' she asked. Dawn was coming up, it was already quite bright, she thought she had heard birds singing. They were indeed singing, hidden in the trees in the Via dei Giardini.

'No,' Mascaranti said: it was true that they were only on the second floor, but if she threw herself out in despair, she could still kill herself, it depends on the way you fall, even a half-metre drop can kill you.

'Yes,' Duca said: a moralist like her does not commit suicide.

She hesitated. Carrua said, 'Yes,' he said it paternally, and with a paternal gesture motioned to her to go to the window, and she went to the window, which was pearly white with the light of dawn. 'I won't try to escape,' she said, smiling shyly, then leaned her head out a little and, yes, she heard the birdsong, she heard it because the silence was absolute, the streets completely empty, at the corner of the Via dei Giardini the four traffic lights were flashing yellow into the void, because there was nothing there, it was as if Milan had been totally abandoned by everybody, apart from those few birds singing in the trees swollen with pollen in the Via dei Giardini.

Duca let her listen for a while, then said, 'Are you declaring that you killed Turiddu Sompani and Adele Terrini?

'Yes, she declared it to me too,' Carrua said, sleepily covering his face with his hands.

She nodded and sadly left the window and that improbable spring dawn in Milan and returned to her chair.

'And you came here to Milan, from Arizona, to hand yourself in?' Faced with this young woman, a foreigner to boot – foreigners have their eye on us – he mustn't get angry.

She looked at Duca, hearing that hint of anger in his voice. 'Yes,' she said.

Controlling himself, he said, 'Why?' He already knew why, it was stupid to even ask, but it needed official confirmation.

'Because I realised I'd made a mistake,' she replied in a clear but muted voice, her voice was increasingly muted. 'I shouldn't have killed them.'

Not being able to slap her, not being able to shout, not being able to fire a gun, he said sadistically, 'Why?'

She batted her eyelids, it was an unusual interrogation. 'Because we shouldn't kill, nobody should take the law into their own hands.'

Oh yes, that was what he had wanted to make her say: you shouldn't take the law into your own hands, or we'd end up all killing each other – which might not be a bad idea, he thought. But he wouldn't let go. 'Didn't you know that before you killed them?'

She replied promptly but vaguely, 'Yes, I did, but I was driven by a thirst for revenge.'

Duca got to his feet, went to the door of the office, with his back turned to the girl and Carrua and Mascaranti, lit a cigarette and inhaled a mouthful of smoke, then took a deep breath: maybe he could manage to control himself, he hoped he could, he was in an important office in Milan Police Headquarters, with an important officer like Carrua, he couldn't let himself go, but he found it hard to hold back. 'You couldn't sleep, is that it?' he said, with his back still turned, and his voice was gentle, the anger was only in the question.

She seemed very pleased that someone understood her and when he turned to hear her answer he saw a serene smile of pleasure in her eyes. 'Yes, when you make a mistake, you don't have any peace until you can put it right.' Duca sat down again and looked at her: yes, she had said exactly what was required of a totally honest woman, and even more, she was the essence of clarity and had answered his 'Why?' with complete moral clarity, not even a convent schoolgirl would have answered like that.

He was about to ask her another question when an officer came in with a copy of the *Corriere*, hot off the press and still smelling of ink.

'The Americans did it,' Carrua said. 'They made a soft landing on the moon.

Also in the *Corriere della Sera*, in the local pages, was the trial of the robbers from the Via Montenapoleone: the Burgamelli brothers, accused of the famous robbery, and all the other members of the gang, photographed together in the dock, all claimed they were innocent, they made a scene, they raised their fists at the prosecutor and yelled at him, 'How can this be allowed?' All the defendants talked nonsense, made sarcastic remarks, answered back to the judge, and they might even be acquitted because of insufficient evidence, Duca thought.

This girl in front of him, on the other hand, wouldn't be acquitted because of insufficient evidence, they couldn't give her less than ten years for premeditated double homicide, it was so premeditated that she had come all the way from Phoenix to kill them, and at her trial she wouldn't raise her fists at the prosecutor, she'd say, 'Yes, I killed them, it was premeditated, I worked it all out in advance.' When you have defendants like that, the jury might as well be doing the crossword.

Duca asked the question he had been about to ask her earlier. 'What evidence do we have that you killed those two?' There were lots of crazy people about, people who came into Police Headquarters and said, 'I killed the poet Carducci.' You needed evidence.

Clearly, after seven years working in criminal records, she had anticipated the question. 'It's there, in the pockets of my coat.'

Carrua opened his eyes a little wider. 'Yes,' he said to Duca, 'that's what she told me as soon as she got here,' From the heavy overcoat on his desk he took out two large and rather bulky white envelopes. 'It's the mescaline 6,' he said, holding out the envelopes, and gestured to Mascaranti to give him a cigarette.

Duca opened one of the envelopes: inside it was an opaque plastic bag, one corner was open and peering inside Duca saw that it contained a number of stamp-sized sachets, on which was written, clearly, *Mexcalina 6*. Clarity is what counts, he thought, this was the mescaline that Claudino had spent so much time and effort looking for. 'How did you get this?' he asked Susanna (Paganica) Pani, daughter of Tony, Captain Anthony (Paganica) Pani: he was really curious to know.

It was simple, she explained, it had already happened once before: when she was having dinner with Adele and Turiddu at the Binaschina, a man had arrived and handed over two envelopes like that to Turiddu Sompani.

'What did this man look like?' Duca asked.

'Not very tall, but well-built, very well-built,' Susanna said.

It could only have been Ulrico, Ulrico Brambilla. 'And then?'

'Attorney Sompani took the envelopes and put them

in his pocket, Susanna said, 'but after a while he gave them to me and said, "Please keep them in the pockets of your coat, you have plenty of room, my jacket pockets bulge too much."'

'So that evening this well-built man came,' Duca said, 'he handed over the two envelopes and went away, then Sompani gave the two envelopes to you, to keep until you got home, because otherwise the pockets of his jacket would have bulged: is that what you're saying?'

'Yes, exactly.'

It certainly wasn't because his jacket bulged that Sompani had given her the envelopes, it was one of the rules of the game: especially in a car, some little accident might happen, you might get into an argument with someone, the traffic police might show up and find some of that stuff on you, it's better if they find it on someone else, isn't it? and then you can say, 'I don't know anything about it, I've never that stuff before.' It was because of the same rule that Giovanna, when she had come that evening to have that repair job done on her, had left him the case with the submachine gun: if something went wrong, it was better that they find the sub machine gun in Dr Duca Lamberti's apartment than in Giovanna's car or at the home of Silvano Solvere.

'So you mean that after throwing the car into the Naviglio, the two envelopes were still in the pocket of this overcoat and you forgot you had them?'

'Yes.'

'And when did you realise you had them?'

'When I got to Phoenix.'

'And how did you manage to get them from Phoenix back here to Milan?'

'I didn't do anything, I just left them there, in my coat.'

'But if they'd stopped you and found them, what would you have said?'

'I was coming to Milan to hand myself in anyway, I would have told the truth, it didn't really matter who arrested me, all that matters is the truth.'

Keeping a totally serious face, Duca began to laugh mentally, and nervously: this was really wonderful, the International Narcotics Bureau would be pleased to learn that you can cross the Atlantic twice, there and back, with a few hectograms of mescaline 6 on you, you just have to be crafty enough not to hide it, but put it in the pockets of your overcoat and hold your overcoat over your arm.

And then he laughed even more, while still outwardly impassive, over all that had happened because of that mescaline: the goddess of vengeance had come directly from Phoenix, Arizona, killed the couple and gone back to her country, still unwittingly carrying the mescaline, and for those two envelopes, Claudio Valtraga had killed, first, Silvano, believing that he had kept them for himself, then Ulrico Brambilla, convinced that he had them, and finally he had been arrested and his revelations had made it possible to arrest a number of significant figures. In his encounter with Susanna Pani, the devil had been, as sports people said, soundly beaten.

'I've finished,' Duca said, and went to the window: a tram was passing.

'Take the young lady down,' Carrua said to Mascaranti.

'Goodbye,' Susanna Pani said to Carrua. 'Goodbye,' she said to Duca, raising her voice a little.

'Goodbye,' Duca said and even made a curt little bow: goodbye, goddess of vengeance, goddess of purity of heart and conscience, goddess who came to confess her guilt in order to have – is that what it's called? – the punishment she deserved.

'She could get as much as fifteen years,' Carrua said when she had gone out with Mascaranti.

Duca again looked out of the window: the first lorry was passing.

'Because at the trial,' Carrua went on, 'she'll insist on saying that the crime was premeditated, and no lawyer will ever persuade her to tell a lie or keep quiet about anything, no, she'll tell the whole truth, because she's a complete idiot.'

Duca turned and came back to Carrua's desk. 'Please,' he said in a low voice, 'don't say she's a complete idiot, don't even think it.'

'Why shouldn't I say it?' Carrua said, getting heated. 'She was at home nearly five thousand kilometres from here, nobody knew anything about her, she had nothing to do with that awful bunch, she'd killed some people who deserved to die, why did she have to come back here to get from ten to fifteen years? For whose benefit? When she comes out, she'll be over forty, life will have passed her by, why shouldn't I say she's an idiot? I do say it.'

'No, please, don't say it,' Duca sat down next to him and with extreme patience and with a very low voice, said, 'Don't you like the fact that there are people like her? Or would you prefer everybody to be like Sompani, like Claudio Valtraga?'

'Yes, I do like that fact, but she'll be wasting the best years of her life in prison, and for nothing. That's really stupid.'

'Yes, she'll be wasting the best years of her life in prison,' he said patiently, leaning towards him, 'but that's why you should respect her.'

After a pause, Carrua said, 'I do respect her, but don't bite me.'

'I'm sorry,' Duca said: he was a little tired, and he collapsed on the uncomfortable chair.

Then, glancing irritably at Mascaranti, who had come back in at that moment, Carrua said, 'What was all that? What was that letter you sent me with Galileo's recantation? You know, I'm not that clever, I don't understand, what does it mean?'

Duca turned towards him. 'It means I need fifty thousand lire as an advance on my salary.' The salary for the catcher of thieves and whores: at eleven his sister and niece and Livia were coming from Inverigo and he wanted to take them to lunch and buy them a few little gifts.

'But you haven't even been hired yet,' Carrua said. He stood up, opened the little safe on the wall, fiddled about with something inside. 'Sign,' he said when he had filled out a form.

Duca took the money: it was best for him to buy a shirt immediately, as soon as the shops opened, because if Lorenza saw him with those threadbare cuffs it would sadden her.

Carrua gave him a look almost of hate. 'I suppose that makes you our colleague.'

'Thanks.' Duca put the money in his pocket. 'Can you have Mascaranti go with me?'

'Yes, sir.' Carrua said mockingly to Mascaranti, 'Take our new colleague home.'

Mascaranti stood up. At the door Duca turned and said, almost shyly, 'Can't you do anything for her? Anything at all?'

'Like what?' Carrua roared.

'I thought maybe keep her in a separate room for the time being, not surrounded by whores,' he proposed, shyly.

'And where am I going to find a separate room?' Carrua

said. 'The clientele here is constantly increasing, we'll soon have to keep them in the courtyard.'

'I was also thinking you could have a word with the examining magistrate, explain everything to him,' Duca said, 'and then, as far as her defence goes, you could get her a good lawyer who wouldn't even charge a lira.'

Carrua stood up and snarled, actually snarled mockingly, 'Duca, I serve the law, I couldn't do anything if it was my father or mother. Was I able to do anything for you? Didn't you spend three years in prison even though you were my blue-eyed boy? And now there's nothing I can do for her, nothing at all.' There was real bitterness in the mockery.

It was true, there was nothing they could do, only respect her. He left the room.

TRANSLATOR'S NOTES

1. Giorgio Strehler, distinguished Italian theatre director and founder of the Piccolo Teatro in Milan.
2. A reference to Davide Auseri, a character in the first Duca Lamberti novel, *A Private Venus*
3. Esculapius (Asclepius in Greek): the god of medicine.
4. Livia Ussaro, a major character in *A Private Venus*, whose face was severely disfigured by a gangster while working on a case with Duca. At the end of that novel, she was sent to recover at the villa belonging to the father of Davide Auseri (see above).
5. Occam's razor: a philosophical principle stating that, among several hypotheses, one should always choose the one requiring the fewest assumptions.
6. Plateau Rosa: an area of the Alps popular with skiers.
7. In September 1943, the Italian government, which had just deposed Mussolini's Fascists, signed an armistice with the Allies, to which the Germans responded by invading Italy.
8. A reference to the well-known Italian film comedy *Seduced and Abandoned* (1964).
9. The Alto Adige, or South Tyrol, is a largely German-speaking province of northern Italy. In the 1950s and 1960s, a German-speaking underground organisation in favour of secession from Italy committed a number of terrorist acts.
10. Cesare Beccaria was an eighteenth-century Italian jurist and philosopher, whose most famous work was *On Crimes and Punishments*.
11. A reference to the Italian poet Gabriele d'Annunzio, famous for his sensual style of writing.
12. *Africa Addio*: an Italian documentary film, premiered in 1966.
13. Gothic Line: the last major German line of defence in the Italian campaign at the end of World War II.

A PRIVATE VENUS

*The first book in the classic Italian
noir series, The Milano Quartet*

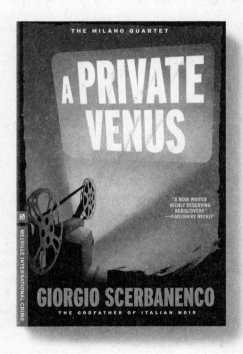

The death of a young woman in a gritty industrial
neighborhood of Milan sparks off a tragic series of events,
which only detective Duca Lamberti is brave enough—
or desperate enough—to follow to their source.

$16.95 U.S./Can.
Paperback: 978-1-61219-335-9
Ebook: 978-1-61219-336-6

Ⅿ MELVILLE INTERNATIONAL CRIME